More Than Enough

DONNA R. MADDEN

MARCUS HENRY PUBLISHING

This is a work of fiction. All the characters, organizations, and events portrayed in this novel are either products of the author's imagination or are used fictitiously.

No part of this book may be reproduced, or stored in a retrieval system, or transmitted in any form or by any means, electronic, mechanical, photocopying, recording, or otherwise, without express written permission of the publisher. v.1

Copyright © 2023 by Donna. R, Madden, all rights reserved.

Printed in the United States of America

Paperback edition ISBN: 979-8-9877343-0-8

eBook Edition ISBN: 979-8-9877343-1-5

Cover Art by: Elijah Toten

This book is dedicated to my husband,
who always reminds me I can do anything I set my mind to,
and my boys who believe in me always.
I love all four of you so much!

Sometimes waiting and wondering is the hardest.
Then an unwanted surprise becomes a turning point.
Needing to become more than we thought possible,
Wanting someone to walk with us,
But not finding what we need,
Until we finally realize,
We need to love ourselves first and that
We are more than enough.

– Donna R. Madden

Contents

1. Chapter 1 — 1
2. Chapter 2 — 5
3. Chapter 3 — 13
4. Chapter 4 — 19
5. Chapter 5 — 41
6. Chapter 6 — 51
7. Chapter 7 — 55
8. Chapter 8 — 63
9. Chapter 9 — 73
10. Chapter 10 — 81
11. Chapter 11 — 89
12. Chapter 12 — 97
13. Chapter 13 — 101

14. Chapter 14   107
15. Chapter 15   113
16. Chapter 16   119
17. Chapter 17   127
18. Chapter 18   131
19. Chapter 19   139
20. Chapter 20   147
21. Chapter 21   151
22. Chapter 22   157
23. Chapter 23   165
24. Chapter 24   171
25. Chapter 25   179
26. Chapter 26   187
27. Chapter 27   195
28. Chapter 28   203
29. Chapter 29   207
30. Chapter 30   211
31. Chapter 31   219
32. Chapter 32   229

33.	Chapter 33	237
34.	Chapter 34	247
35.	Chapter 35	255
36.	Chapter 36	261
37.	Chapter 37	265
38.	Chapter 38	267
39.	Chapter 39	273
40.	Chapter 40	289
41.	Chapter 41	295
42.	Chapter 42	301
43.	Chapter 43	305
44.	Chapter 44	313
45.	Chapter 45	319
46.	Chapter 46	327
47.	Chapter 47	333
48.	Chapter 48	343
49.	Chapter 49	349
50.	Chapter 50	353

Chapter 1

"Girl, hurry up! The party has already started." Trina lit her joint and took a big hit before passing it over to her friend.

"One minute. I'm almost ready." Elizabeth downed the rest of her beer, touched up her lipstick in the bathroom mirror, grabbed the joint and took a hit as they walked out of their dorm room and into the hallway. The girls were trading hits of the joint as they strolled casually across campus arm in arm. It was a beautiful night. The moon was bright, and the stars were shining.

The party was in full swing when they arrived at the fraternity house. They headed straight for the keg and quickly went to the front of the line.

"Well, beautiful, how's it going?" Brady, and one of his fraternity brothers Trent, stood by the keg and filled cups for the girls.

"Going great," Elizabeth beamed at the handsome guy before her. "Is everyone out back?"

"Of course. Let's head that way. Now that you two are here, the party can start." Brady walked to Elizabeth with a gleam in his eye, smiled at her with confidence, put his arm over her shoulder, and led the girls to the back of the house.

Here the music was louder, and smoke filled the sky. The four found their friends standing around under a tree with a bottle of tequila being passed around one way and a joint the other.

After shots of tequila, more beer, and a few hits from the joint, they joined the dancing bodies smashed together on the dance floor, guys and girls gyrating into each other.

Laughter filled the air, along with the pulsating beat of the music. Elizabeth wrapped one arm around Brady's neck while grasping her newly filled beer in her other hand. She moved her hips with his as he ground into her. He leaned over to get a kiss and she gratefully obliged.

Next to them were Trina and Trent. The smile Elizabeth gave Brady reached her eyes, making the corner of them wrinkle. She chugged down the rest of her beer as Trent grabbed her waist; it was time to switch partners.

Elizabeth loved the buzzed and high feeling of her body being light and carefree. Where Brady was hot and just overall amazing to hang with, be seen with, and was great in bed, she moved effortlessly with Trent. Trent was an amazing dancer, and together they moved as one.

Trent grabbed a joint as it was passing by, took a big hit, and leaned into Elizabeth. He touched his lips to hers, exhaling the smoke into her mouth. She held it in for a bit, smiling and looking into his eyes. She blew the smoke out slowly then leaned in to kiss him passionately, hard, and hungrily.

The couple soon found themselves heading toward Trent's bedroom. On their way past Trina and Brady, Elizabeth grabbed Trina's hand and pulled them along. Once inside, Elizabeth was in Trent's arms pressing herself against him. On the other side of the room, Brady held Trina tightly as he kissed her lips.

This was not the first time the girls were together with these guys. Drinking, smoking pot, and having sex with these two was typical. Elizabeth was usually with Brady, though she had been with many. Tonight, though, she wanted Trent, and she made sure he knew it.

Closing the curtains between the beds, she quickly slipped off her top and undid her skirt, letting it fall to the floor. He, seeing her naked body before him, answered her by doing the same. Elizabeth helped him finish the job, pushed him down on the bed, and climbed on top softly, laughing as their bodies found a rhythm. She was soon climbing that mountain and came right before he did.

The curtain between the two beds opened, and Brady and Trina joined them. "I think you have kept my girl long enough, Trent. My turn," Brady exclaimed with a hungry look of intoxication and desire.

She and Trina glanced at each other laughing. "You've taken up the handsomest guy in the room long enough." Trina pulled Elizabeth from Trent and took her place.

Elizabeth was on cloud nine. She loved this feeling of being free and alive!

She watched Brady advancing toward her, his gaze filled with desire. She was transfixed by him; his brown wavy hair, his deep brown eyes you could get lost in, and his hot, fit body. She found herself aching with the need to enter his waiting arms, and soon he was entering her.

Chapter 2

*H*ome... *What is it about coming home that always makes you feel like you are a kid again? How can a box with four walls seem to make everything better? Is it the smell coming from the kitchen, fresh ooey-gooey and warm chocolate chip cookies, a succulent, garlicky roast beef roasting in the oven, coffee percolating in the pot early in the morning, or is it the look of the house which makes you feel secure? Is it a well-manicured lawn with straight lines because Dad is a neat freak, or mom's flower beds overflowing with color, just inviting you to stop a bit on the front porch and swing on the porch swing? I don't know, I can never figure it out, but it doesn't matter. I'm here. I'm home!*

Elizabeth stared at the home where she had lived most of her life as she sat in her car parked in the driveway. She had just completed her fifth and final year at college and was now home, ready to start her adult life and ready to relax and undo all those mistakes she had made during the last couple of years away on her own.

Taking a deep breath and heaving a heavy sigh, she pushed herself from her car, and decided she would come back later to purge the vehicle of all the bags and boxes. Pushing open the front door, she is greeted with the memories which only the sense of smell brings alive. It is the smell of a house filled with family and love. Where the coffee is brewing in the coffee maker, bacon is sizzling on the stove, and fresh hot pancakes are cooking on the griddle.

"Hey, Dad," Elizabeth sang as she sauntered into the kitchen. Seeing her dad at the counter, she wrapped him in a big hug from behind and plopped a kiss on top of his balding head. "I'm seeing a bit more shine on top, Dad," she laughed.

Jackson Parks was still handsome at the age of fifty. Though his hair was starting to thin, he had yet to see any grays, and was still as fit and athletic as he was in his younger years. When Elizabeth looked into her father's large hazel eyes, she saw her eyes staring back. She inherited a lot of who she is from this man sitting on this stool. Being an only child, Elizabeth grew up watching college football and baseball with him, and when she was old enough, excitedly took her mother's seat at all the Saturday home football games.

"Ha, Ha, very funny. So glad you're home, Lilly Billy." Mr. Parks hopped up from his place at the counter and wrapped his only daughter in a tight hug. He was so glad she was finally home for more than a day.

"Dad, you're squishing me!" squealed Elizabeth trying to break free from his python-like squeeze.

"Okay, okay, don't squeeze her to death before I get a hug." Charlotte Parks turned away from the griddle, with fresh pancakes bubbling and browning, to steal a hug from her daughter.

She looked a lot like Elizabeth. She had thick, brown shoulder-length hair, which was naturally highlighted from the sun, and a thin yet sexy five-foot-six frame. She was a young forty-nine and made sure her husband knew it.

Mrs. Parks led Elizabeth toward the kitchen table with her arm around her daughter's waist. "So glad you're home, Lizzy. Take a seat, relax, and let me get you some juice and pancakes."

Mrs. Parks hurried back to the griddle to fill a plate with steaming hot pancakes and slices of bacon, knowing this was her daughter's favorite breakfast. Elizabeth thanked her mom while she poured on the syrup and gulped her orange juice. No matter what restaurants they put on campus, nothing beats homemade pancakes and bacon at your kitchen table and made by the loving hands of Mom.

"I went by the boutique yesterday. Barbara asked me what your plans are this summer and how long you plan on being home. I know it's not your dream job, but she has your old job available, at least for the summer, if you are interested." Mrs. Parks mentioned this while she settled in at the table next to Elizbeth to eat her now lukewarm pancakes.

"I was thinking of finding out if she needed any help again this year. It's not great money, but I already know the ins and outs of working there, and I get an awesome discount, so that's always a plus. It'll give me something to do while I look for real employment. I'll stop by Monday. I'm gonna take the weekend to relax and get organized."

Elizabeth finished her pancakes and juice and placed her dishes in the sink. "Thanks, Mom. Breakfast was delicious. I guess I'll go grab some clothes from the car. I need to take a shower."

"Here, hon, I'll help you." Mr. Parks got up from his seat at the counter and followed his daughter outside.

It was a beautiful early summer day. The sun was shining brightly, there was a light breeze blowing through the trees, birds were chirping, and the neighborhood dogs were barking. As Elizabeth led the way toward her car and opened her door, a pretty, blonde girl about her age yelled from across the driveway and waved.

"Good morning, Mr. Parks. How are you today?"

"Hi, Stacey. I'm doing well. How could I be any different? The day is perfect, and my daughter is home."

Stacey, all smiles, showing a perfect set of white teeth, walked quickly toward Mr. Parks as he talked and extended her hand toward Elizabeth.

"Hi. I'm Stacey. You must be Elizabeth. Your dad talks about you all the time and told me you were coming home this weekend."

Elizabeth extended her hand to the pretty girl, a little insecurely, offered a smile, and shook her hand. "Hi, Stacey. Nice to meet you."

Mr. Parks intervened between the two girls. "Elizabeth, this is our neighbor, Stacey Kempt. Stacey works at the county hospital as a nurse. Stacey, my amazing and beautiful daughter, Elizabeth, or as I affectionately call her, Lilly Billy. Our new college graduate." Mr. Parks said the latter as if he was introducing royalty and placed his arm over his daughter's shoulder pulling her in for an affectionate side hug.

"Dad, don't be so dramatic." Elizabeth giggled while rolling her eyes and shaking her head. Stacey joined in the laughter.

"Your dad is always the dramatic one." Stacey responded with a smile. "Here, let me help you with some of these bags."

Mr. Parks moved boxes and suitcases onto the porch, while the girls carried them upstairs to Elizabeth's room. Stacey took a walk around and admired the pictures in frames, stacks of books on the dresser, and college paraphernalia which adorned the walls. "Cute room you've got here."

"Yeah, thanks. I haven't done much here since I left for college. I think this summer, I'll get organized a little, start packing some things away in storage and throw away the junk. I'll be ready to move out as soon as I get a real job, and my parents won't want to deal with any of this."

Elizabeth dropped the suitcases she was carrying on the floor in the corner and plopped herself down onto her bed. Stacey placed the suitcases she was carrying in the corner, also, then turned to Elizabeth.

"I know you just got home and all, but I am having some friends over tonight to celebrate the beginning of summer. I'd love for you to come. It's not a big deal. Just friends, music, food, and drinks. What do you say?"

Elizabeth took some time to think about it. Stacey seemed like a good person, mature, responsible. Maybe being around a new group of people, not college age, would be a good change for her. "Sure. Why not? Sounds like a good time."

"Great," replied Stacey with a big smile. "I'm glad you'll be there. Everyone's coming over around eight thirty. Come then or feel free to come earlier. You can help me set up. My door is always open!"

Stacey waved as she skipped out of the room and down the steps. Elizabeth heard her say goodbye to her parents as she walked out the door.

"Well, I guess I have time to take a nap. It's been a long day. Then I can go hang with mom and dad before I go out tonight," Elizabeth said to no one, as she laid back down on her bed and closed her eyes.

Chapter 3

Slowly rolling off her bed and onto her wobbly feet, Elizabeth wiped the sleep from her eyes. She stretched to wake up her tired muscles and caught her reflection in her mirror. Seeing her unruly hair, she tried to run her fingers through it, failing miserably as they got caught in a mass of tangles. Giving up, she rubbed her hands over her face trying to rub away what was left of the sleepiness.

Feeling like she had slept forever, she glanced at her phone and noticed the time. It was already three o'clock. She had slept most of the day.

Shocked at her laziness, she quickly unpacked her clothes into the dresser drawers and closet and threw ones that had been stashed away, yet she no longer wanted, onto the floor; she would donate them later.

Remembering the party she planned to go to, Elizabeth jumped in a hot shower and let the water run down her body to wash the road and sleep away.

Clean and slightly refreshed, she grabbed a pair of jeans and threw on a spaghetti strap tank top that bloused at the waist. With a pair of sandals on her feet, she wandered slowly downstairs to see if her mom needed any help in the kitchen.

"Well, hello there, Sleeping Beauty. Glad to see you are still with us." Her mother greeted her as Elizabeth grabbed a can of Diet Coke from the refrigerator and sat at the kitchen counter. "Don't you look nice." Mrs. Parks commented over her shoulder at her daughter.

Stifling a yawn, Elizabeth smiled at her mom, took a big gulp of the cold, fizzy liquid, and hoped the caffeine would give her a jolt. "Thanks. Anyway, what's for dinner? It smells delicious. Is it meatloaf with mashed potatoes and green beans?"

"Of course. It is still your favorite, isn't it?"

"Only when you make it, Mom." Elizabeth smiled at her mother. "Can I help with anything?"

Mrs. Parks walked over to her daughter and wrapped her in a soft, loving hug. "No, honey. For right now, let me enjoy having you here and spoiling you. Tomorrow, I'll be over it and expect you to give me a hand around here."

She patted her daughter's face, gave her a peck on the cheek and a sincere smile, then returned to the job of peeling potatoes and placing them in a pot of water to boil.

Elizabeth and her parents sat down to enjoy supper. No one talked for a while as they were too busy eating and enjoying the peace and quiet.

Mr. Parks finally broke the silence. "So, not to get too focused on the future, but do you have plans for getting a job, Lizzy? We are so proud of you and love having you around. You can stay here as long as you need, but after working so hard to get that piece of paper, you need to put it to use."

Elizabeth started with a small sigh and stared down at her plate. Finally, she looked up. "Dad, Mom, this last semester was difficult, and I had a lot of different things going on. I didn't do as well as I should have, but I got through it. I just hope that I can relax at the boutique for a little bit, while I figure out my future."

Disappointment swam over Elizabeth's expression as she started to mindlessly push her green beans around on her plate. If they only knew how difficult things really became this semester. But she couldn't tell them. Not yet, maybe not ever. Some things are better kept to yourself and dealt with alone.

"Dinner was delicious, Mom. If nothing else, your cooking makes being at home worth it. Keep cooking like that, and maybe I'll never move out!"

Elizabeth sat back, chewed her last bite of meatloaf and potatoes, and finished off her Diet Coke as she tried to avoid the looks of concerned humor on her parents' faces.

"Well, I do what I can to make you happy. I'm glad you are still easy to please, but let's not go that far." Mrs. Parks exclaimed with a smile and light laugh. "I'm sorry you had a hard time this semester, but you got that degree, and you're a smart girl! Get back to the boutique, enjoy your summer, and we will see what your future holds." Mrs. Parks set to work clearing the table and Elizabeth got up to help.

"Thanks for your understanding, Mom and Dad." Elizabeth gave her parents a small smile and received smiles in return from them both.

"Oh, by the way," Elizabeth quickly changed the subject, hoping to catch her parents off guard a little, while their minds were on her troubles last semester. "Stacey, the neighbor, told me she was having a few friends over tonight and asked if I would like to come and meet some people. If it's ok, I think I'd like to go." Elizabeth, not sure about what her parents thought of their young neighbor, asked a little apprehensively. Even though she is an adult, in the world's eyes at least, they still tend to be overprotective of their only daughter and are picky about what she does and who she hangs out with.

"Sure. Go ahead, and have fun," answered Elizabeth's dad. "We were planning on going out tonight anyway but weren't sure if we were still going to go. If you have something to do, we will go out too."

"Thanks, Mom and Dad. I'm going to finish getting ready. Tomorrow will be a family day after church, just like old times." Elizabeth hugged her mom, gave her dad a peck on his cheek, happily skipped out of the kitchen, and up to her room.

She closed the door to her bedroom, let out a big sigh, and leaned her back against it. Shaking her head and trying to clear her mind of her thoughts, she went into her bathroom to finish putting on what little makeup she wore, mainly a little eye shadow, some blush, and of course, a little lipstick.

"Crap, I almost forgot." Elizabeth grabbed her pack of birth control pills from the back of the drawer she threw them in and took her daily pill with a little water. She stopped, stared at the container, and tried to think for a minute. She shook her head because she was not sure of the last time one had been taken, shrugged her shoulders and zipped them back into the small black pouch and placed it at the back of the bathroom drawer where they would stay, away from any wandering eyes. She was not in the mood for questions.

Elizabeth's parents yelled up the stairs that they were leaving. She yelled to them to have a good time. She finished unpacking and organizing her things, adding to the growing pile on the floor of clothes to donate.

"Time for me to get out of here, also. I need to relax and have a good time. New friends, a clean slate, and new adventures. College is finally behind me. Time to get a real life!"

Chapter 4

It was a crisp, beautiful, warm summer night when Elizabeth left her house and started across the yard for Stacey's. The sky was clear, and the first star was already out. Maybe it was Venus; maybe it was Mars; she didn't know, but she was in a positive mood. Something she had not felt in a while.

On the short walk to Stacey's, across the well-manicured yard, Elizabeth couldn't help but think back to the discussion she had with her parents, and how she struggled in school this year. Her priority had not been her classes. She had spent too much time partying and not enough time studying. Elizabeth hoped she could start getting away from the past. Make some positive changes and better decisions. Life is too short. She needs to focus on the future and stop living in the past. She's young and she has a lot of life left to live.

All these thoughts went through her mind as she crossed her yard and entered Stacey's. The backyard was beautifully kept. Stacey did a good job making sure she had flowers in pots and she even had some vegetables already starting to grow.

Elizabeth walked up the steps to the back deck. There were a couple chairs and a lounger with matching pillows to add a touch of color. She immediately felt the hominess of the space. It was somewhere you could relax after a long day and enjoy the outdoors.

Her pulse quickened and her eyes gleamed as she reached her hand toward the door and found herself contemplating the possibilities of the night before her. Elizabeth hoped she would be able to relax and have a good time. These people don't know her or the choices she made in her past. She can start over, wipe the slate clean. Tonight, she can relax and enjoy everything without fear of judgment.

She took a deep breath, pushed back her shoulders, pressed the doorbell, and heard Stacey reply, "Come in, it's open."

Elizabeth stepped cautiously into the house and found that she had entered a comfortable breakfast nook which led into the kitchen. The kitchen was filled with white floor-to-ceiling cabinets and butcher block countertops. It was cozy and usable, with nice modern appliances.

"Hey, Stacey, it's Elizabeth. I got here a little early."

She heard pounding on the wood floor and Stacey peeked her head around the corner. Her eyes were wide, and she was gasping, trying to catch her breath. "Elizabeth, glad you're here. Make yourself comfortable. You'll see some bags with sodas and chips on the kitchen counter. If you don't mind, find some bowls in the cabinet and start setting things out. I'd really appreciate it. I'm finishing getting dressed. I lost track of time while I was cleaning."

"Okay," Elizabeth answered cautiously as Stacey disappeared again and footsteps announced her retreat.

Elizabeth turned in place, looking around the kitchen. Not seeing any chips or drinks on the counter, she started opening closets and cabinets and finally found them in the pantry, then started her search for bowls.

Having a hard time finding what she needed and getting a little frustrated, she wandered into the next room to see if she could find Stacey to ask for some help. Instead of seeing her neighbor, she saw a young man relaxing on the couch reading a magazine. He was leaning back with one ankle resting on his opposite knee.

This stranger was stunning and Elizabeth found herself frozen in place. He had wavy, light brown hair and was wearing a light blue button up Patagonia shirt and khaki shorts with Birkenstocks. She stopped and couldn't help but stare at him.

He looked relaxed, like he belonged there. Stacey didn't say anything about a boyfriend, not that the girls had spent much time together. The man happened to look up from the magazine and caught Elizabeth staring at him. He put the magazine down and stood up smiling in greeting. "Hi, I'm Jacob. You must be Elizabeth. Stacey told me you might be coming by a little early." He reached his hand out to Elizabeth and smiled a wide, confident smile. Elizabeth stepped forward to shake his hand. She couldn't help but notice his eyes were the color of the sky.

"Hi. It's...uh... nice to meet you." Elizabeth returned his handshake a little nervously and found herself tongue-tied. She returned a shy smile and could feel herself blushing a little as they made eye contact.

"I guess maybe you can help me in the kitchen. I can't seem to find where Stacey hides the bowls."

Jacob told her to follow him and led Elizabeth back into the kitchen. He opened a cabinet over the dishwasher and gestured to a shelf of bowls and other kitchen items.

"Oh, thanks. Stacey said to look in the cabinets but wasn't specific about which one."

"Yeah, I heard her. She doesn't do much work in here and isn't great at finding her way around the kitchen. Kitchen duty is usually my job, along with the grocery shopping. She spends most of her time at the hospital and taking naps. My schedule makes it a lot easier. I work normal hours, mostly, so it works out best this way."

As Jacob talked, he started getting bowls, trays, and cups out. Then he started going through the refrigerator and began throwing ingredients together. Elizabeth enjoyed watching him work. She could tell he knew his way around the kitchen, and he looked good doing it, too.

Cooking started to get serious as Jacob began chopping and dicing, while he directed Elizabeth on what she needed to do. In no time at all, the oven was stuffed full of spicy chicken legs and stuffed potato skins. Small crock pots had hot dips simmering and melting while trays were being filled with vegetables, cheese, meats, and fruits.

"Wow. You really do know your way around the kitchen. This is the most cooking I've seen since last Christmas when I was watching my mom cook and bake for holiday gifts and Christmas dinner. This all looks and smells AMAZING!" Elizabeth closed her eyes as she took in a deep whiff of the aromas wafting throughout the kitchen.

"Thanks. Cooking is one of my many talents."

"Cooking better be your main talent. I don't let you live with me because you look good." Stacey interrupted Jacob as she entered the kitchen. She was dressed simply in a gray knee-length pencil skirt, white oversized long-sleeved shirt, and simple flip flops. Her hair was lazily pulled up into a messy ponytail on the top of her head.

"I'm glad you two met, and it looks like you have everything under control here, Jacob. I guess I'm not needed."

Stacey walked over to him and put her arm around his waist, giving him a side squeeze while stealing a carrot off the cutting board and popping it into her mouth. Jacob continued to chop vegetables and arrange trays of food.

"Yeah, and I am sure this is just what you planned, isn't it, Shorty? Always having people over and expecting me to cook the food and fix the trays for you."

Glancing quickly at Elizabeth, he continued, "She has been doing this for years. Since, like birth." He slapped Stacey's hand as she reached for another carrot stick.

Realization washed over Elizabeth. "You're brother and sister?" she asked, with an unexpected feeling of relief. "My parents didn't mention anyone else living here but you Stacey, not that it really came up."

"Your parents are really nice, but I've had such a weird schedule trying to finish up my last semester of school and working; I haven't been home much during the week," explained Jacob.

"Yep, and now that his school years are officially behind him, I planned this party with some of our friends so we can all show him how proud we are of his determination. I invite the people, and he cooks the food. Win-win for everyone." Stacey stood on her tiptoes, planted a kiss on the side of her younger brother's cheek, and went into the pantry to get out some drinks.

"Oh," replied Elizabeth, a little uneasily. "I didn't realize you graduated from college also. I just did, too. I feel like I am intruding now. I really don't need to be here."

"Don't be silly," exclaimed Stacey, rushing over to put her hands on Elizabeth's shoulders. "Someone new is just what we need around here. We've all known each other for a long time. Everyone will love having you here and getting to know you." Stacey squeezed Elizabeth's shoulders with reassurance and flashed her that winning smile Elizabeth remembered from the driveway.

Feeling a little uneasy, and now a bit out of place, Elizabeth smiled her small, shy smile. "Okay. As long as, you're sure."

"We are sure." Stacey finalized the statement by placing some bowls in Elizabeth's hands and started out of the kitchen. "Take these and follow me. We have a dinner party to get ready for."

For the next hour or so the girls put out cups, plates, silverware, and food. Lots of food. They set up a drink table and placed some desserts around to make the setting complete.

Jacob opened a bottle of wine and poured three glasses. They all sipped wine and talked while they finished preparations. Once everything was ready, Stacey and Jacob started cleaning up the kitchen, so Elizabeth refilled her glass with wine and went out to get some fresh air.

"She is really quiet, seems a bit shy," Jacob said to Stacey as he rinsed the dishes, handing them to his sister so she could load the dishwasher.

"Yeah, I talked to her a little today and helped her with some of her bags. She seems quiet, but it could just be she's tired from moving out of the dorms and back home. I say we introduce her around and make her feel at home. You can never have too many friends."

Jacob looked at his sister with a gleam in his eyes and shook his head. "Of course, the social chair of the township thinks that. And I agree, I think it might be good to get to know Elizabeth. I already like the little bit I know."

"Really, Jacob, you're too much." She rolled her eyes at her brother. He laughed at her, rolled a slightly wet dish towel into a rat tail, and started chasing her around the kitchen while cracking it at her rear.

She laughed and squealed, screaming at him to stop.

Suddenly the front door opened; three new people walked in.

"Hey, who's murdering Stacey? You can hear her screaming all the way down the street." Chad, Jacob's best friend, entered the kitchen and yelled over all the commotion he walked in on. He entered the kitchen along with Don and Charity, a newly married couple.

Charity went over to Stacey and wrapped her in a hug, planting a peck on her cheek. "Here's our contribution to the celebration, not that I can drink any."

Stacey took the bottle of wine from her friend's hands laughing at her comment. "Don't you worry about it. I'll gladly drink your glasses. I'm so glad you both could make it!" exclaimed Stacey to Don and Charity. "I don't get to see you often and now with you two married, and expecting, it's like you've become hermits." She gave Don a hug and a punch in the arm to Chad as he tried to steal some food off a tray.

"Is Kristen here yet?" asked Chad with a wince from the punch he took from Stacey. "I need someone to talk to who isn't into abusing the fat guy!"

"Whatever, Chad," chuckled Stacey. "Help me get the rest of this food into the dining room and we can start eating. Kristen will be here late, as usual. We know better than to wait on her."

"Yeah, she's always on Kristen Time." Jacob agreed as he passed out the last few trays to everyone to get into the dining room. "Take these. I'll go find Elizabeth." Jacob handed off trays of food to Chad and left the room.

Elizabeth was leaning on the railing of Jacob and Stacey's deck, sipping her wine, and enjoying the night sky. It was a clear and humid summer night. The sky was still bright, though the sun had set. Elizabeth was lost in thought wondering what some of her friends from college were up to.

Brady was on her mind. They were together on and off for four years but left college with no plans for when or if they would see each other. Realizing that you may not talk with someone again, who was such a large part of your life for so long, was strange.

Jacob paused when he stepped out onto the deck and saw Elizabeth leaning against the railing. He watched her for a moment. Her long brown hair was blowing gently in the almost nonexistent breeze. He noticed how perfect her body was, her curves in all the right places. He walked quietly toward her and joined her at the railing.

"What are you so lost in thought about?" She jumped in surprise when she heard his voice. "Sorry. I didn't mean to startle you." He placed his hand gently on the center of Elizabeth's back in a soothing gesture.

Elizabeth hung her head and took a deep breath to calm her nerves and held up her hand.

"Not a big deal," she answered with a laugh. "You sure can sneak up on a person. I'll have to keep note of that."

"Yeah, don't keep your bedroom door unlocked. You never know." She shook her head at him. "Come on, everyone is here and it's time to eat. I came to get you."

Jacob made a gesture for her to go toward the door. He opened it and placed his hand on her back, guiding her through the kitchen and into the dining room.

Jacob led her to an empty seat. "Everyone, this is Elizabeth, our neighbor's daughter." Elizabeth sat down and he took the seat next to her with Chad on her other side.

"Hey, there. I'm Chad, your knight in shining armor." Chad exclaimed as he stood and took her hand in his, lightly kissing her knuckles. Elizabeth gave him a crooked smile and blushed a little. She didn't quite know what to think of that gesture. Chad was cute. He had short wavy dirty blonde hair and hazel eyes. He was dressed in jeans and a button-up shirt, very relaxed looking.

"Really, Chad?" said Stacey, "Please excuse him. He is the friend you can never get rid of. He's been tagging along behind Jacob for as long as I can remember."

Chad immaturely stuck his tongue out at Stacey and gave a hearty laugh. Everyone followed suit. Introductions were quick, and Elizabeth soon found herself enjoying dinner and conversation. She didn't speak much, but listened attentively, and laughed at the jokes. Dinner was going well, when suddenly, the front door opened loudly and in walked the queen, or at least that is what it seemed like.

The woman who entered the room was dressed perfectly in designer clothes from head to toe. She was wearing black high heels, a tight, black pencil skirt, and a black and white striped blouse. Her blouse had the top few buttons undone, exposing deep cleavage. She had long, flowing blonde hair, and very little makeup; she was a natural beauty.

"Hey! I made it everyone! The party can start now!"

This must be Kristen, Stacey's oldest friend everyone was talking about. Elizabeth watched the beauty with her simple, yet put-together clothing, and the immediate attention she commanded from the guys around the table, and felt her mouth go dry and her chest start to tighten.

This is the kind of girl who always made Elizabeth question everything about herself. She sighed inwardly and put on a smile she hoped looked genuine, as Stacey introduced Kristen to Elizabeth.

Kristen nodded her head at Elizabeth in a half-greeting, brushing her off, then quickly turned all her attention to Jacob, flashing him a pearly white, toothy grin.

"Hi there, Jacob. Haven't seen you in a while. Seems like you're doing well." Kristen came up behind him, squeezed his shoulders, leaning in as close as possible with a chair between them, and took her seat on his other side. Elizabeth noticed that Kristen kept her hand lightly on Jacob's arm as she filled her plate with food and her glass with wine.

Elizabeth flashed a cold smile toward the new arrival and had to bite on the inside of her cheek to keep comments from slipping through her lips. Something about Kristen and the attention she demanded rubbed Elizabeth the wrong way.

Once Kristen was settled, she took control of the conversation. Elizabeth was unable to take part in the discussion and had difficulty keeping up with where it was going. It was like Kristen meant to alienate the new girl as much as possible since Elizabeth had no idea who or what they were talking about. She tried her best to keep up, laughing at what seemed like the right place, putting in a few little "Wow, really?" and "I don't believe it!" determined not to let Kristen get the best of her.

"Alright all, don't hog the wine, fill up everyone's glass, Chad." Kristen held her glass out to make sure she got a refill, grabbed the bottle from across the table and poured some in Jacob's glass before he could object. The bottle continued its journey around the table, until everyone had full glasses and the bottle was emptied. Another bottle was quickly opened and continued the same path. Soon the bottle was back in Chad's hand. He filled his glass, then reached over to top off Elizabeth's.

"Just a little bit more, please." Elizabeth replied politely.

"Oh, what...one glass is all you can handle?" Kristen commented coldly.

"No." Elizabeth looked at Kristen and noticed she was shooting daggers in her direction. What had she done to get this girl to dislike her already? Deciding to ignore Kristen instead of worrying about her, Elizabeth looked at Jacob. "I'll take more of those chicken wings. They are delicious, Jacob."

Jacob reached for the wings and placed a few on Elizabeth's plate. "Thanks. They're my specialty. Some people think they are too spicy. I guess you aren't one of them," Jacob answered, filling his plate also.

"The spicier the better," replied Elizabeth with a flirty smile focused directly on him.

With a last quick glance of disgust at Elizabeth, Kristen took the wine bottle and refilled her glass. "Here, Jacob, let me fill yours."

Kristen reached over to fill Jacob's glass, making a point to place her hand on his arm and flash him her winning smile. Jacob glanced sharply at Kristen and gave her a simple no thank you and turned his attention back to Elizabeth who just stopped eating. She suddenly looked very pale.

"Are you okay?" he asked her as he placed his hand on her back.

"Where's the bathroom?" Elizabeth placed her hand over her mouth. Jacob pointed her in the right direction, and she quickly got up and dashed to the bathroom, just getting the door closed and leaning over the toilet before she got sick.

A few seconds later all the food and wine she had consumed had been expelled from her stomach. She wiped her mouth with toilet paper, flushed the toilet, and stood up.

"How embarrassing!" Elizabeth looked in the mirror as she leaned against the sink steadying herself. She leaned over and rinsed her mouth. Suddenly, there was a knock on the door.

"Hey, it's Stacey. Are you ok?"

"I am now. I'll be out in a minute." Elizabeth rinsed her mouth again, and splashed water on her face, drying herself on a towel hanging by the sink. She opened the door and left the bathroom.

"Dinner was delicious. Thank you for inviting me, but I think I need to go home. I'm not feeling well."

"Man, Jacob, your cooking made her sick. Maybe we all need to stop eating before we find ourselves in the bathroom." Chad joked as he elbowed his friend in the ribs. Jacob threw an irritated glace at Chad and became concerned as he noticed how ill Elizabeth looked.

"No, really. It wasn't the food. I haven't been feeling great the past couple of days. I just think it's exhaustion from getting through the end of the semester. I've been tired. I think I should go. Nice meeting all of you. Thank you again, Stacey." Elizabeth looked at Stacey with sincerity, waved goodbye to everyone, and headed quickly out the door and across the yard toward home.

"Well, that was interesting, and quite a bit disgusting," replied Kristen with contempt. She was standing next to Jacob, as close to him as possible. Stacey came back to the table and passed around the dessert she had sitting on the buffet. Everyone went back to their seats at the table to eat dessert: chocolate cake or cheesecake.

"Well, I feel bad for her. I hope she's okay. Maybe it was your cooking, Jacob." Chad grabbed the cheesecake passed to him and placed a slice on his plate, laughing at his friend.

"Jake, you gave someone food poisoning. I hope we are all okay and don't end up running for the john." Don joined in the joking, trying to lighten the mood in the room.

Jacob shot his friends a look and grabbed a piece of chocolate cake. Kristen sat back down next to him, filled their glasses with wine, grabbed her fork, and helped herself to some of Jacob's cake.

The conversation steered away from Elizabeth. The friends laughed and enjoyed each other's company. Charity and Don soon excused themselves to head home.

Stacey thanked them all for coming and started to take some of the plates and dirty dishes to the kitchen. Chad and Jacob followed suit. Kristen grabbed the wine bottle and her glass. This was her contribution to the cleaning.

"Sis, you look exhausted. Why don't you go relax and get ready for bed? I'll clean this up and put away the food." Jacob preferred less people in the kitchen so he could make sure things got put away correctly.

"Thanks, Jake. I appreciate it. I think I will get ready for bed. I'm exhausted. Would you make some coffee?" Stacey hugged her brother, and he nodded, hugging her back.

"I think I'll wait for coffee in front of the TV and find us something to watch." Chad, always finding a way to get out of work, left the kitchen without waiting for an answer which left Kristen and Jacob alone.

Jacob set to work putting leftover food in Ziplock storage bags. "Kristen, you make a mean pot of coffee. Can you get that going please?"

Always willing to help Jacob whenever possible, Kristen happily obliged and quickly had the pot brewing, filling the kitchen with the aroma of fresh coffee. She emptied her wine glass with one last gulp and noticed that Jacob still had some in his.

Walking over to him, she reached for his glass and picked it up. "Jake, are you going to finish this, or can I?"

"Go for it, Kristen. I think I've had enough." She emptied his glass also and placed it on the counter making sure to brush her hand against his arm as she did. Jacob stopped packing away leftovers and glanced over her way.

Kristen grabbed his arm and slowly turned him toward her. "Dinner was great as usual, Jacob." She rubbed her hands up and down his chest, looking into his eyes. "You know I love your cooking. It is so hot watching a man who knows his way around the kitchen."

Jacob grabbed her hands and pulled them off him, looking down at her. "What are you doing, Kristen? You know what I think about us."

"I know what you say, and I know how you react. They don't equal out. Maybe you should just finally let yourself go. We had fun the time we were together. You know we did. We go well together."

She slowly wrapped one arm around him, stood on her toes, and turned his face toward her with her other hand. She loved his eyes and stared into them. "You know we do." Seductively, she planted a kiss on his lips, knowing he had a hard time refusing her, especially when he had been drinking.

Jacob, though he tried to ignore it, felt his body reacting to her in a way he wished it wouldn't. Yet, she was hot and amazing in bed. And sexy. So sexy. He couldn't refuse her, and though he tried to fight it, he found himself returning her kiss.

Jacob and Kristen's kiss got deeper and more demanding. He pushed her up against the counter, hard, putting his hands up the front of her shirt. He pulled his head back as he kneaded her breast to watch her eyes, closed and euphoric. She opened her eyes a little to see him watching her with lust. Smiling a small, sexy smile, she reached up and pulled his mouth back to meet hers.

"Excuse me for bothering you, but I am out of here." Chad was leaning against the door frame of the kitchen with his arms crossed, laughing, and shaking his head.

Their magic was broken, and the kiss ended. Kristen, frustrated from the interruption, put her forehead against Jacob's chest, willing him not to turn away from her.

Jacob leaned away from Kristen and took a deep breath to regain his composure before turning to face his friend, thankful for the interruption. "Alright, man. I'll see you tomorrow. I'll be over to pick you up in the morning." Jacob tried to walk away, but Kristen held onto a fist-full of his shirt.

Chad raised his hand, interrupting the discussion. "Don't stop what you're doing on my account. I will see myself out. Good night, y'all. Be good, Bro'." Chad turned his back on the two in the kitchen, laughing as he walked away.

Jacob shook his head and turned away from Kristen, pulled out of her grasp and walked toward the coffee pot to fill a mug.

Chad passed Stacey on his way through the living room. "You better watch out. Things are getting a bit hot in the kitchen, and it is not all the cooking going on." He hugged her and thanked her for having them over and let himself out the door.

Stacey heard the voices of her brother and best friend. Kristen's voice was high pitched, tension filled, and she entered the living room soon after.

"I'll see you in your room. I'm going to bed!" Kristen, looking flushed and shaking her head, stormed by.

"Alright, Kris, I'll be there in a bit. You, okay?" Stacey watched her friend walk past. Kristen just raised her hand in a motion of 'don't talk to me' and slammed the bedroom door behind her.

Stacey stood and stared after Kristen for a second, scrunched her forehead in thought, then picked up the last of the food and dishes from the dining room table and headed into the kitchen. Her brother was leaning with both arms on the counter, his head down.

"Hey, little brother, is everything okay?" Stacey placed the dishes next to the sink, filled a mug with hot coffee, and leaned against the counter next to Jacob. He turned toward her, and took a large gulp of his coffee, shaking his head.

"Why do I keep giving in to that girl? Every time, it just makes things worse. I can't persuade her that I'm not interested, when all she needs to do is give me a little alcohol and look at me in that way she does, and I always give in. If Chad hadn't interrupted us, I would have done something I would've regretted later. Again!" He looked up at his sister with questioning in his eyes.

Stacey sighed, placed her mug on the counter, and put her arms around him, and he returned her hug. "I know that you and Kristen have a difficult history and I know she is hard to handle, but at least you know you're alone by choice. She would be yours with a simple statement from you. The positive out of it is that when you hit old age, you don't have to worry about anything. She will always want to be with you. You'll never have to be lonely." Stacey hip-butted Jacob to make him smile. He laughed at her, and they finished cleaning up the kitchen together, locked up the house, then walked toward their rooms.

Stacey hugged him goodnight. "Lock your door, or you might have an unwanted bed mate."

Jacob laughed at her. "Thank you for reminding me." They separated and went into their rooms. Jacob paused, thought of sending a text into the room across the hall, but changed his mind, closed his bedroom door, and turned the lock.

Chapter 5

BZZZZZ, BZZZZZZZ...BZZZZZZ, BZZZZZZ...

The obnoxious alarm of Jacob's cellphone laying on the bedside table woke him early the next morning. Stretching, he rolled over and reached out to turn it off, slapping his hand around. He missed his phone but did manage to knock it and two large books onto the floor with a loud crash.

BZZZZZ. BZZZZZZ...BZZZZZZZ, BZZZZ-ZZZ.

"COME ON! Turn off already!"

Jacob clumsily climbed out of his queen size bed, leaned over to grab his phone from the floor, and quickly turned off the alarm before it went off again. Yawning and stretching wide, he slowly left his room and headed to the kitchen toward the coffee pot.

Once he had a steaming cup of dark, delicious coffee in his hand, he went back to his bathroom and hopped in the shower. A nice hot shower would feel amazing and help to wake him up and wash away that last glass or two of wine from the night before.

Thirty minutes later, he was dressed in slacks, a bright blue button-up shirt, and Dockers. He sat in the kitchen, eating a bagel with peanut butter and drinking his second cup of coffee, when Stacey and Kristen walked in.

Both girls were dressed in tank tops and pajama bottoms. Jacob couldn't help but notice Kristen's tank top did little to hide what she had under it. His thoughts wandered back to last night and their time in the kitchen. Shaking his head, he quickly forced his thoughts back to the present.

"Good morning, ladies. What gets y'all up at this hour?" Jacob asked his drowsy sister and her friend.

Stacey shot him a deadly look as she reached for the coffee and salted caramel creamer, she used to doctor up her drink, while Kristen sat on the bar stool next to Jacob.

"Good morning, Jake." Kristen looked at him with a tired, yet sultry look, grabbed his coffee mug, and took a big swig. Jacob found himself staring at Kristen, again thinking back to their kiss last night and where it could have led.

"Mmm." is all the reply he got from his sister.

"Great coffee," replied Kristen as she flashed him a tired smile. "Did you sleep well, Jacob? I was a little lonely."

Jacob glanced at Kristen, thinking back to the scene in the kitchen last night. "I made it through."

He got up from the counter to put some space between him and a bad idea and to refill his mug. He leaned back on the counter and looked at his sister and Kristen.

"You know, why don't you two get showered and dressed, and head out to church with me?" Jacob asked this to his sister almost every week, hoping that this would be the week she would give in and say okay. "You may find that it's not as bad as you think."

"Yeah, I don't think church is our thing. Thanks for asking, though. You enjoy yourself. I'll be here when you get back. And when I say here, I mean on the couch, in front of the television, still in my cozy clothes," replied Stacey. "But, if you want to get pizza afterward, let us know. We'll meet you there."

"I'd love to, but I need to get out of here soon. I have lots to do today. But meeting for pizza does sound good," answered Kristen.

"All right, whatever. If it gets you dressed and out of the house, meet Chad and me at the pizzeria for lunch. If you're too lazy to show up to eat, I'll be home later." Jacob grabbed his to-go cup of coffee and his keys and headed out the door.

Once in his car, he turned on the radio and was enjoying the beautiful sunny morning as he pulled in front of Chad's house to pick him up. Neither of them has families who go to church, so they tend to hitch rides together, so they don't have to sit alone, even though they know quite a few people who attend on Sunday mornings.

"Good morning," said Chad as he plopped into the front seat." I see you didn't talk your hot sister or her beautiful friend into joining us today. Maybe I need to come and give your sis some of the famous Chad encouragement one morning." Chad raised his eyebrows laughing.

Jacob answered, the same way as usual, with a punch in his friend's arm. "Ouch! Really not necessary!"

"Then stop hitting on my sister and being all disgusting. She's known you for years and you've never had a chance."

"Okay, true. How about you and Kristen? You were being friendly again last night. Anything I need to know about? Did you get lucky?" Chad threw out a string of questions, always entertained by the drama that seemed to follow Kristen and Jacob.

Jacob glanced over at him quickly, then got his eyes back on the road. Shaking his head, he answered with a sigh. "I stopped drinking for this very reason. It always gets the best of me, and Kristen knows what buttons to push. Thankfully, I stopped everything before it went much further than just a kiss."

"Just a kiss? I don't know, that was an awfully long kiss that seemed to be leading to a bit more. Man, that girl has it bad for you. And you, you just keep going right back to what you say you don't want. If I were you, I'd just give in already. Even though she's hot and crazy about you, you two are toxic when you're together. But I would do anything to have that type of woman problem."

Jacob shot a 'shut-the-hell-up' look at his best friend as he reached the church parking lot. He parked, turned the car off, yanked the keys out of the ignition, got out and slammed his door shut.

"Don't tempt me like that. If you were half the friend you are supposed to be, you would have kept that from happening and sure wouldn't be encouraging it. You know she is nothing but trouble. God. What is my problem! Even this morning when they both came into the kitchen, I couldn't help but think about possibly missing church and taking Kristen to bed." Jacob turned his eyes to the heavens when he said this last part and walked with a frustrated gait.

Chad rushed up to his best friend and slapped his hand on Jacob's shoulder. "Dude, it's okay. You could have much worse girls after your hot body."

Jacob stopped walking and turned toward Chad, his eyes blazing with irritation.

Chad, a smile starting to creep up the corner of his mouth, stopped next to his friend. "But seriously. I know.

I should have taken you away from that situation before it went too far. My bad." With this apology, the guys entered the front doors of the church.

Being a little late, as usual, they slipped into a pew at the back just as the pastor walked up to the pulpit. After a prayer, scripture reading, and a few hymns, it was time to stand up and greet each other.

"Hey, isn't that Elizabeth from last night?" Chad elbowed Jacob in the side and gestured across the crowded sanctuary.

Jacob glanced in the direction his friend was pointing, nodded his agreement, and got back to greeting the people around him with smiles, nods, and hugs to the ladies he has gotten to know since he started attending here a few years ago.

As they sat back down, and prepared to listen to Pastor John's sermon, he couldn't help but glance over to where they noticed Elizabeth.

He finally found her, sitting with her parents, directly next to her dad. He glimpsed her smile as she looked at her father. He said something to her, which made her laugh a little. Jacob couldn't help but notice how her face lit up when she smiled. That was something he didn't see last night. She looked so relaxed sitting with her dad beside her. He also noticed how intent she was listening to the sermon. Every now and then she looked down and wrote something. She must have been taking notes.

Suddenly, the congregation started praying, Pastor John made some announcements, the closing hymn was sung, and church was over. Jacob and Chad chatted with friends on their way out. Pastor John greeted them, told them both how glad he was to see them, and said something about the upcoming get together the young adult class was having. Jacob was nodding, but not paying attention. He was scanning the crowd for Elizabeth.

Once they were outside, Chad elbowed him again, "Dude, I think who you're looking for is climbing into a red car over there." Jacob followed Chad's gaze and saw her profile standing by a red Nissan Altima.

"Thanks, Bud. Be right back." Jacob said this over his shoulder as he jogged across the parking lot.

"Elizabeth!" He hollered, trying to get her attention.

"Hey, Elizabeth!" He finally got her attention as she was getting into the front seat of her Altima.

"Wow." Breathed Jacob, catching his breath as he finally reached her car. "Wasn't sure if I would catch you. How are you feeling? You look better than you did last night."

Elizabeth gave him a sharp stare.

"I mean, you don't look sick."

Another very quizzical look.

Jacob took a large breath and laughed at himself. "Here, let me start over. Hi, Elizabeth. It's good to see you at church. You look great and I hope you're feeling better."

Elizabeth laughed and smiled that relaxed smile he saw her give her dad. This close to her he could see how pretty her eyes were. They truly danced when she was amused.

"Hi, Jacob. I'm feeling much better. Thank you. I think I was just exhausted yesterday. I do have to admit, I am a little embarrassed about what happened and that I had to leave early. I'm sorry about that."

"Don't be sorry. It's not like you planned on getting sick. Anyway, to change the subject, Chad and I always go grab something to eat after church, usually at The Pizza Place. Would you like to join us?"

Jacob surprised himself by being this blunt. He sure didn't expect to ask her out to eat, yet he also didn't see himself running across the parking lot to catch up with her, but here he was, doing both.

"You know, I'd like that, but I promised my parents we would spend time together today. I'm on my way to pick us up lunch, so, I'll have to say, no thank you. Maybe we could get pizza another time?"

Just at that moment, Chad pulled up next to Jacob. "Hey there, new girl. Elizabeth, right? Do you mind if I steal my buddy back? I'm about to blow away from starvation here." Chad was making a face like he was sick and dying.

Jacob shook his head at his friend. "I'd say sorry for him, but it wouldn't help. He is always rude and thinks only with his stomach. I guess we should go. I'll catch you later, if you're sure you don't want to join us."

"Thank you, really, but I can't. I appreciate the invitation, though." Elizabeth closed her door, put the key in the ignition, and pulled out of her parking spot. She waved to the guys and flashed a smile as she pulled away.

"Man! You invited her to lunch? Even after she puked in your toilet. You must really like her, yet not enough to stay away from Kristen last night."

Chad hopped out of the car laughing and avoided the punch coming at him. He ran around to the other side and hopped into the passenger seat, letting Jacob drive his own car.

"It's not like that. I was just making sure she was feeling okay. You know, being neighborly and all." Jacob climbed behind the steering wheel and put the car in drive, ignoring the last part of Chad's comment.

"Yeah, right, neighborly. That's also why you couldn't keep your eyes off her in church. Just being neighborly." Chad chuckled a little and reached out to turn the radio up as they headed to their weekly lunch spot.

Chapter 6

Jacob and Chad pulled into the parking lot of The Pizza Place, parked in what seemed to be their spot at the best pizza shop in town, and headed into the restaurant.

Stacey and Kristen showed up and motioned for them as they sat at a booth for four. The two girls sat on opposite sides of the table; Chad quickly slid in next to Stacey, leaving Jacob no choice but to sit with Kristen. They ordered a pitcher of beer and a large pepperoni pizza.

"It took you two long enough. We've been waiting forever." Kristen agreed with what Stacey stated, nodded her head at Jacob, and gave him a flirtatious smile.

"Yeah, what was the hold up?" asked Kristen with fake curiosity. More like being nosey where Jacob was concerned.

Chad put his arm around Stacey's shoulders, making her shake her head and roll her eyes. She reached up, grabbed his arm, and took it down from around her with a look of finality.

Chad shrugged at her. "A guy can try, can't he? You never know, one day you might just surprise me and enjoy my attention."

Turning away from Stacey, he addressed Kristen. "Anyway, to answer your question, Kristen, we happened to see that new girl, Elizabeth, at church today. Lover boy here," he said, pointing across the table at Jacob, "sprinted across the parking lot after church to talk to her."

Seeing the incredulous look on Kristen's face, and questioning look on his sister's, Jacob felt he needed to clear things up. "It wasn't a big deal. I was just seeing how she was feeling. She felt bad last night and left quickly. Checking on her was the right thing to do." He looked at his friends around the table.

Kristen rolled her eyes and took a sip from her soda. "I'd leave pretty quickly, too, if I puked in the toilet at someone's house I hardly knew." Kristen shook her head and scrunched her face up in disgust. "Did she even talk to you? If I were her, I would have hidden my face in embarrassment."

"Yeah, she talked to me," replied Jacob. "She did seem embarrassed, and I assured her it wasn't a big deal. Why do you need to be such a bitch all the time, Kristen? It wouldn't hurt if you showed a caring attitude once in a while. A little respect and caring goes a long way."

Kristen laughed out loud at that statement and leaned over plucking a bit of fuzz off Jacob's dress shirt. "Really?" Incredibly, she added. "Are you implying I don't care? You think I'm an uncaring person? I might be the only person who always cares about your feelings, Jacob. That should mean something." She flashed Jacob a pouty, flirtatious, knowing glance just as the pizza arrived.

She placed her hand on his cheek and slid it down to his chin, rubbed her thumb over his bottom lip, and stared deep into his eyes. She held his gaze for a long second, then turned away from him, focusing on the pizza just placed on the table, throwing her hair over her shoulder, showing off a well-tanned shoulder blade.

As usual, she was as scantily dressed as one could be and still be considered dressed, a tight top with spaghetti straps and lots of cleavage. Jacob glanced at that cleavage, looked away, rolled his eyes at the two across the table, and moved as far over as the small, crowded booth would allow.

Chad served pizza all around and Stacey changed the subject. They started talking about the reality TV show they were all into and what they thought would happen on the newest episode.

Kristen threw in comments based on who she thought looked good, how the girls dressed, and who should end up with who. Jacob was only partly listening as he ate his pizza.

He couldn't seem to keep his mind from wandering back to Elizabeth, her looks, and her smile.

Just thinking about her sent tingles of pleasure throughout his body.

Chapter 7

At church on Sunday, Barbara Stanzel, Elizabeth's old boss, asked her if she could stop by the boutique Monday morning around nine a.m. just before they opened. Elizabeth said she would love to. Getting right to work was exactly what she needed to get her mind off things. Starting summer break with a plan and a job sounded wonderful. She could use the extra cash.

After her encounter with Jacob and Chad, Elizabeth went to the Mainstreet Deli, picked up subs and sodas, then went home and sat on the couch with her parents, eating subs, drinking soda, and watching some of their favorite movies.

It was a great afternoon, and something she really needed. Laughing, relaxing, and eating with her favorite people was a great way to spend a Sunday.

Elizabeth was well rested when she woke up Monday morning.

She woke up early so she could get ready for her first day of work at the boutique. It took her a while to get moving, but a nice hot shower did her a world of good, and a cup of coffee and a cinnamon bagel with cream cheese put her stomach at ease. "I am sure I just feel queasy out of nerves. Starting something new always puts butterflies in my stomach."

Elizabeth pulled into the parking lot of the boutique just after nine. She climbed out of the car, smoothed out her long summer dress, glanced down at her cute sandals, checked her reflection in her side mirror one last time, and headed on in.

The boutique smelled amazing. She really needed to find out what the scent was that Mrs. Stanzel kept in the wax warmers throughout the store. It has always been the same and brought Elizabeth back to happy times working at the boutique on Main Street.

As she walked through the store, she noticed it was filled with the newest styles of dresses, capris, and tops. Jewelry booths filled the entrance of the store, and there were racks of hats and scarves throughout, also.

"Good morning, Elizabeth. Look around. I have added quite a bit of new items since you were last here. I'll be right with you once I count the drawer."

Barbara Stanzel, the owner of the boutique, was a petite woman, about five-feet, three-inches and 120 pounds. She had shoulder-length dark hair, and if you looked close enough, you could see a few strands of gray.

Since Mrs. Stanzel was almost sixty, Elizabeth was always amazed at how young she looked. The big question on everyone's mind was if she colored her hair, but no one was sure.

"Okay, Mrs. Stanzel." Elizabeth continued her stroll around the store. She found herself in a newer section with knick-knacks and home decor. There were those faceless angels she had seen in other stores, the ones with little cards that have bible verses on them, and there were wooden signs scattered around. She also looked at the large selection of scented candles, and wooden wind chimes.

Elizabeth couldn't help but love the look the store had now. She would say it was new, but it could just be new to her.

Mrs. Stanzel found Elizabeth among the knick-knacks and gave her a huge hug. Huge for a small petite woman. "I am so glad you decided to come back to work. I've missed you around here."

Mrs. Stanzel gave Elizabeth a quick tour of the store, all the new items, information about what things are, and then signed her into the computer.

"I never took your information out of the computer, so signing in is the same as it always was. I guess I always knew you'd be back." Barbara flashed her newest employee a happy smile and patted Elizabeth on the arm. "We have some new merchandise we need to get out on the shelves today. We might need to make room and move some things around. I know your gift for organization and color will help us achieve this in no time."

Barbara and Elizabeth went into the storeroom and brought out some boxes of merchandise. Just as Elizabeth opened them and started going through the contents, the door chimed again and in walked a petite and pretty girl with long straight brown hair pulled up in a messy ponytail. She was wearing printed capris with a matching salmon-colored tank top.

"Good morning, Mrs. Stanzel." The girl's voice was sweet and cherub-like. When she noticed Elizabeth, her eyes danced with excitement, and she floated over to where Elizabeth was standing among the boxes. "Hi. You must be Elizabeth. Mrs. Stanzel pointed you out to me at church and told me you were starting back here today."

The girl stuck out her hand in greeting. "My name's Jessica. I was your replacement when you left for school. I'm so glad to meet you."

Elizabeth shook her hand and couldn't help but smile. "Thank you. It's good to meet you, too."

There was something about Jessica she already liked. She brightened up the room just by walking into it and she seemed so genuine.

Both girls went to work placing the new merchandise on the shelf and had no problem making small talk and getting to know each other.

At ten o'clock the store opened. Jessica helped the few customers they had throughout the morning while Elizabeth busied herself with the new merchandise. They sang to the music which floated through the speakers throughout the store while working and were able to break about noon, while Mrs. Stanzel manned the front.

"Wow. I forgot how much I enjoy the relaxing atmosphere of this place," said Elizabeth through bites of her sandwich. "So, Jessica, I know you live around here and that you go to the church, but I don't think we've ever met."

"I live in the next town over, so I went to school there. I needed a job while I was in college and came in here asking. You had just gone back to school, so I stepped right into the job you vacated. Mrs. Stanzel invited me to church one Sunday, so I started attending. I live with my grandmother, and she doesn't attend anymore. It's too much for her to get out, but I like it. Pastor John has good sermons and I'm involved with the young adult group. Hey, you should come one Sunday with me."

"I was thinking about it. I might do that. Where do you attend college?"

"I attend the community college. It's not great, but it's cheap, and I get to stay home and help my grandmother and that saves me even more money. I'm taking General Studies right now. I know a college education is important; I'm just not sure what my purpose is yet. Sometimes I think I might like social work, but I'm not sure. I bet you've had a blast at the university. Independence, no parents, lots of hot guys. I miss that social part. There isn't anything like that at the community college. But congrats on graduating. I cannot wait until I finish."

Elizabeth laughed at the excitement Jessica had when talking about what she thought college was like. Elizabeth stopped eating and noticed she was getting those butterflies again. It must be because of the subject they were talking about.

"Thanks. It was alright. Sometimes it was a bit overwhelming, and you wish you had your own space." Laughing again, she admitted, "Yes, there are a lot of social activities which take up a lot of time. Sometimes, too much time, and the guys are hot, but they also tend to be a little stuck on themselves and not many are interested in anything but one-night stands."

"So, there wasn't one guy that took up your time?"

Elizabeth stopped eating and thought about that question. A head of unruly, long, brown curls came to her mind. A smile played on her lips as she thought of Brady.

Suddenly, Elizabeth felt like her sandwich was not agreeing with her. Placing her hand on her stomach, she excused herself, and took a quick trip to the bathroom, where she found herself, once again, looking into a toilet bowl.

For the second time in two days, Elizabeth was telling someone on the other side of the door that she was fine. She cleaned up, rinsed her mouth, and exited the bathroom.

"Are you sure you're, okay? Should I tell Mrs. S. that you need to go home?" Jessica asked with concern.

"No, no, I'm fine. Just haven't been feeling great the past couple days." Elizabeth smiled what she hoped was a believable smile and drank the rest of her soda.

Since she was not able to stomach eating the rest of her lunch, she headed out to the front to get back to work.

Chapter 8

The afternoon was filled with Elizabeth learning the cash register again, getting to know Jessica, redoing some displays, and putting out merchandise.

"Wow! It's already four o'clock, girls. Today has flown by." Mrs. Stanzel commented as she was breaking down empty boxes and placing them in a pile to recycle. "I'll start closing out the drawer. If you two straighten the shelves, maybe we can get out of here at five on the dot."

She left the front of the store and went into her office.

The door chime caught the attention of Jessica and Elizabeth. The first thing Elizabeth noticed was a head of blonde hair, followed by an overly cheery laugh, which made her stomach clench.

"Hi, Jessica." Elizabeth heard Stacey's voice enter the store following right behind Kristen, the owner of the blonde head of hair and annoying laugh.

"Hey, Stacey. What brings you in?" Jessica replied.

"Oh, just wasting time. I have some extra money to spend, and I need something cute to wear. What better place to go than here?"

Stacey wandered into the store, headed straight for the summer dresses and sandals display which Elizabeth just finished stocking and arranging.

"Elizabeth, I didn't know you worked here." Commented Stacey when she saw Elizabeth organizing a clothes rack.

"Yep. I worked here during high school and quit when I left for college. I saw Mrs. Stanzel in church, and she asked if I'd like to come back to work. So, here I am." Elizabeth finished up with what she was doing and looked at Stacey with a smile.

"Speaking of church, my brother told us he talked to you afterward, yesterday."

"He told you he talked to me?" Elizabeth asked, confused.

"Well, of course," replied Stacey. "He said you were feeling better. I hope you're still feeling okay today."

"Yeah I..."

"She isn't feeling too great, Stacey. She got sick when we were on our lunch break." Jessica interrupted. Elizabeth sighed, a little frustrated and embarrassed.

"Seriously! What is wrong with you? What kind of disease did you bring home from that big fancy college you're attending?" Kristen interrupted the conversation with this remark, rolled her eyes as she stood away from the group, and stared at Elizabeth with a look of disdain on her face.

"I seriously don't know how he could be concerned about you. We have known you for, what? Just a few hours, and you are nothing but a walking germ. Oh well, he can't be too interested. He kissed me Saturday night. Mmm —If Chad hadn't interrupted us, who knows, we could have landed back in his bed."

"Kristen!" yelled Jessica. "You are the rudest person I have ever known. Can't you find better friends, Stacey? I really don't understand it. If Jacob is concerned about Elizabeth, it's because he is a good guy who has a heart of gold. That is something you sure don't understand. If he kissed you, he had too much to drink, again. And I am sure you had something to do with it. Slumming is usually not his style." Jessica directed these statements to Kristen with as much venom and rude demeanor as her sweet personality could possess.

"Yeah, he does have a heart of gold," Kristen said dreamily, looking at her perfectly manicured fingernails. She then glanced over at them and made eye contact with Jessica.

"That's why he cheated on you, Jessica, because of that golden heart of his. You know, maybe if you didn't act like you're too good for everyone, and everything, maybe you could've kept him faithful, and he wouldn't have had to go somewhere else to get what he needed."

Kristen stepped away from the rack of clothes she was looking through to get a better look at Jessica as she said these final words. With her hands on her thin hips, and standing in a model-like pose, she finished with "I'm glad I'm always able to be there when he needs a real woman."

Jessica's eyes widened with outrage and her nostrils flared. You could feel the daggers shoot from her eyes as she stared at Kristen. The smugness on Kristen's face was evident. She always felt that the affections of Jacob were hers to win.

Stacey stepped in between the two women. Her goal was what it always was, to step in before Kristen could really make a mess of things, and to smooth everything over. "Okay, ladies. You know it's closing time. I'm sure these two want to get out of here. Let's go, Kris."

She grabbed her best friend's arm, turned her around, and pulled her out of the store. Kristen looked at her with shock and fury, annoyed that Stacey was siding with the other girl.

"Bye, Jessica. It was good to see you. See you around, Elizabeth." Stacey called to the girls as she left the store. She mouthed "I'm sorry" to them and closed the door to the boutique behind her.

Elizabeth, a little shocked and confused at what just transpired, glanced at Jessica. She noticed the hurt and outrage on Jessica's face.

She approached her and placed a comforting hand on Jessica's shoulder. "Are you okay? I have no idea what the hell that was about, but I guess you know them, and Jacob."

Jessica breathed a deep, loud, frustrated sigh and went back behind the register shaking her head in disgust. "Yeah, I know them. As you can tell, Kristen and I don't get along. Stacey, though, is a good person. Why she hangs out with Kristen, I will never understand. How do you know them?" Jessica asked as she finished straightening some shelves and pointed to the door.

Elizabeth, understanding what her gesture meant, went to the door, turned off the open sign, closed the blinds, and turned the lock. It's 5:00, time to close the store and head home.

"Stacey and Jacob live in the house next to my parents. I met Stacey on Saturday and went to their house for dinner Saturday night. I met some of their friends: Chad, Don and Charity, and Kristen also. I immediately had issues with Kristen. She saw me talking with Jacob and ended up being just as friendly then as she was today." Elizabeth made this last comment with sarcasm oozing from her lips.

Jessica nodded her head in agreement. "One thing about Kristen, if she is not the focus of all the attention, she will say and do just about anything to make sure she becomes it, especially when it comes to getting Jacob's attention."

"Yeah," agreed Elizabeth. "I noticed that."

With concern and curiosity, Elizabeth asked the main question on her mind. "From what Kristen said, I guess you and Jacob dated?"

With another sigh, this one not so deep, just sad, Jessica explained. "Yeah, we dated for about eight months. We broke up around three months ago now, thanks to Kristen. Jacob and I had an argument. It was stupid really. One of those that was about nothing at first, then just spiraled out of control. Suddenly I was yelling at him. Something about him not caring enough. It really made him angry, and he stormed out. Unfortunately for me, Kristen was at his house when he got home. Let's just say they have had many flings over the years, and she knows what to do to get her way with him."

Jessica paused and became thoughtful. "I guess, though, really it was fortunate. I realized I didn't have the feelings for him I thought I did. He wasn't the one for me." She shrugged at this realization. "He and Kristen were just a fling, again. They didn't last long, and he and I have been able to maintain a friendship."

That's all the information Jessica was willing to give, and she was glad Elizabeth didn't ask any more questions.

"I'm sorry to hear that. Jacob seems like he is so much better than Kristen, unless he only goes for the easy, slutty type."

Jessica agreed with Elizabeth and got a good laugh out of it. "Let's get everything finished so we can call it a day."

Elizabeth cleaned up the store area while Jessica balanced the drawer. Once everything was finished, they exited with Mrs. Stanzel.

Even though the day ended on a down note, Elizabeth enjoyed her time at work, and getting to know Jessica, but she was exhausted and starving. She wanted nothing more than to grab some food and sit down. She reached her car, about to open the door when Jessica called across the parking lot.

"Hey, Elizabeth, I'm gonna go grab a sandwich across the street at Main Street Deli. Do you want to go?" Elizabeth's stomach answered for her, so she quickly agreed.

The girls left their cars in the boutique's parking lot. The sandwich shop was just across the street in the downtown square, so they crossed the street and headed to the deli and sandwich shop.

The smell of fresh-baked bread greeted them as they entered. The girls approached the counter to place their orders. Elizabeth, as usual, found herself overwhelmed by all the salad and sandwich choices before her. Everything here at Main Street Deli was amazing. She settled for a grilled chicken Caesar salad with a roll and water to drink.

The girls ate in almost complete silence, occasionally making a small comment about the taste of their food, but mostly lost in the motion of putting food into their mouths.

When they finished their meals, they decided to enjoy the night. They ordered drinks to go and took a walk around the square.

They got to know each other as they walked, and Elizabeth learned a lot about Jessica. She found out Jessica was raised by, and still lives with, her grandmother, loves children, and is the sweetest and most innocent person she has ever met. The entire time they talked, not one swear word left her lips, and Jessica seemed to care so much about everyone and everything.

The girls ended up at the park, just outside of the square. The park is a small green space dedicated to the veterans, past and present of the town. It has walking paths, a dog park, and a gazebo with picnic tables, all situated right on a creek with benches and other places to sit and relax. The girls chose a large rock overlooking the creek and took a seat.

"Here is something I just noticed, and it is pretty surprising also."

"What's that?" asked Jessica.

Elizabeth looked at Jessica with a serious look in her eyes. "I just noticed you have yet to say a swear word. I know it's shallow, but I have never known anyone to talk that clean. Well, except my mom."

Jessica laughed at her new friend. "Yeah, well, get used to it. I am that girl."

"Alright, Jessica, tell me something. Swear words aside, what was up with you and Jacob? How serious were you?"

Jessica looked at her, then turned her head to look over the water with a thoughtful expression.

"Well, if you must know, he is really an amazing guy. We had a lot of fun together. Deep conversations, that kind of thing. There was a time I thought he was the one. Even though we only dated eight months, it was an amazing eight months."

At this, Jessica looked at Elizabeth with a huge grin. "You might think I'm an innocent girl, but trust me when I say, that I am not that innocent. I can tell you all you may ever want to know about that man. And yes, there is a lot to know. If you understand where I am going." Jessica made a sign with her hands. Her hands were together then drew far apart.

"Oh, my God! Jessica!" The two girls fell into each other laughing hysterically. Eventually Jessica caught her breath and continued.

"Seriously though, Jacob and I had a good relationship until that one evening when we had a stupid argument. Kristen tends to be a... well you know, a..."

Elizabeth finished her friend's sentence. "A bitch!"

Jessica grinned and rolled her eyes. "Exactly! I'm glad things happened the way they did. I really am over Jacob. I realized that we get along better as friends than we ever did as a couple." Jessica took a short pause, then looked at Elizabeth and bumped her shoulder. "Why are you asking? Is it that someone might be interested?"

Elizabeth looked at her and raised her eyebrows. "Well, let's just say he's easy to notice and having him as a neighbor isn't a bad thing. Is it okay if I am interested? It wouldn't be awkward, would it?"

Jessica put her arm around her new friend. "No! Of course not. Do me a favor, though, and keep an eye out for Kristen. She can really be... you know... That B word with a capital B!"

"Thanks for the warning. I'll keep it in mind. Come on. I've got to get going."

The girls walked back to the boutique, arm in arm, to get their cars and head home.

Chapter 9

The week flew by as Elizabeth got back into the groove of being home. Most of her days were spent going through the boxes she brought home from her dorm room, purging her room of all the unnecessary memories, and putting mementos she felt was important to keep into one container for storage.

Elizabeth finally made it to the last box, her ongoing chores almost complete. She reached in and pulled out a couple of empty liquor bottles and a corsage from the first formal she and Trina attended.

Elizabeth smiled at the memory of Trina and her getting ready for that formal.

Elizabeth attended with Brady, and Trina with Trent. That was the first official date the girls had with the guys. The liquor bottles were a reminder of how special the girls felt. Hot guys were interested in them; very interested. They drank and danced well into the early morning. Elizabeth ended the night in Brady's bed, and Trina with Trent.

Thinking back now, Elizabeth felt very different. Did Brady ever really like her? Would she consider any of them friends now? She's been home for a couple of weeks and hasn't even thought about any of them much at all.

Thinking back on these memories made her uneasy. God, she acted awful in college. What was she thinking? Elizabeth couldn't help but dislike the person she was just a few short weeks ago. Her behavior upset her. Why couldn't she be more like Jessica, less like herself?

"You're fine, Elizabeth. You're better than all that now. Move on." Elizabeth looked in the box she almost had empty and put the liquor bottles, corsage, and the rest of the contents directly into the trash bag. These were definitely objects to purge from her life.

Work thankfully kept her busy when she wasn't at home, and she and Jessica had become fast friends, like they had known each other forever. There was something about being home and getting into a new schedule that was fun, exhilarating, and exhausting all at the same time. Elizabeth needed this change of routine.

Another fun routine was the fact that whenever Elizabeth went to her car, the mailbox, or came home, she couldn't help but glance next door. She realized, rather quickly, that she wanted to catch a glimpse of Jacob. She hadn't seen him all week and she missed looking at that sexy body and seeing that amazing smile.

It was Saturday night before she saw him again. She and Jessica were working when Jessica noticed him through the window, walking across the parking lot toward the entrance of the boutique. She nudged Elizabeth and nodded in the direction of the door.

Elizabeth looked up as he walked in. Their eyes locked on each other immediately. Elizabeth felt a smile creep over her face, and her insides warm, as he walked toward the girls.

"Hey, y'all." He flashed them that perfect, toothy grin of his, and ran his fingers through his hair.

"Hi, Jacob. I need to get to the back and look up some stock. Umm, see you later." Jessica wiggled her eyebrows at her friend as she walked away.

"Bye, Jessica." Jacob laughed as he watched his ex-girlfriend walk away. "Well, I guess she's busy."

"I guess," Elizabeth answered looking confused yet amused at her friend's retreating back. "So, what brings you in here?"

Jacob placed his arm on the clothing rack next to her. "Not really anything. I was just wondering something." He looked at her directly and Elizabeth again noticed the sky blueness of his eyes. They took her breath away and made her stomach flutter.

"What's that?" Her voice caught in her throat a little bit.

"Well, I haven't seen you all week. I know you're busy, but I was wondering if you would like to grab a pizza and beer Friday night. Bring Jessica. Chad will be there also, and we can hang out a bit. What do you think?"

Elizabeth tried not to sound desperately excited at that invitation and the thought of spending time with him. "Sounds great. I'd really like that. I'm sure Jessica wouldn't mind changing our plans. We were going to a movie. She has her volunteer hours to do, and I will be here until 5:30, but we could meet after."

"Great. I guess we will see you then, if not before." Jacob touched her arm as he said this, smiling at her. Elizabeth's heart skipped a beat.

He said goodbye and turned and left the store. She stared after him and watched him through the window as he left and walked across the parking lot. She could not help but notice how nice his ass looked in those jeans.

Her mom was reading a book on the porch swing where she loved to read, when Elizabeth pulled into the driveway after work. Elizabeth climbed the steps of the porch and joined her mother on the swing.

"Hi, Mom." She plopped carefully on the swing, always concerned with sitting down too hard for fear the swing would dislodge itself from the porch rafters, even though her dad had assured her many times that that would never happen.

"Hey, sweetie! How was your day at the boutique? You must have worked hard. You look exhausted!"

"Wow! Thanks, Mom," Elizabeth said, laughing at her mother's comment.

"I don't mean anything negative, you are always beautiful, but a mom can comment that her favorite daughter looks tired, can't she!"

"You mean your only daughter. And yes, we were busy, but I had a great time. It was good being back there. Now I need to wake up a little, get the blood flowing. I'm going to change and go for a run before dinner." Elizabeth jumped up from the swing, kissed her mom on the cheek, and jogged into the house to change.

A few minutes later she had her wireless earbuds in and was listening to some of her favorite music. She put her running app on, programmed a three-mile run, and took off.

She enjoyed running. It's the one time where she could put all her troubles out of her mind and just relax. Listening to her music and getting lost in the countryside around her kept her from focusing on her problems, questions, and worries.

As song after song played through her ear buds, Elizabeth lost track of time and distance. She was in her happy place. The runner's high people talk about didn't make sense to her at first, but now it did. Even when she only planned to run a few miles, she usually found herself lost in the moment, and before she realized it, she reached her three-mile goal; now she had to run three miles home.

"Oh, well. More time for me." Elizabeth turned around to head for home.

She was lost in her thoughts as she ran. Suddenly, she started to feel lightheaded. Realizing she hadn't planned on completing a six-mile run, she became a little concerned. She needed water. She was probably a little dehydrated.

She thought back to her day at work and remembered not finishing her lunch and having very little breakfast. She also only drank soda at lunch, and with the store being as busy as it was, snacking and drinking were far from her mind.

Now she wished she could turn back the clock and grab a bottle of water from the fridge before heading out for the run.

Focusing on the back-and-forth motion of her legs, and the rhythm of her sneakers hitting the ground, helped to keep her mind off the nauseous feeling starting to seriously hit her stomach.

Just as soon as she thought she could not go another step, she heard a car coming up behind her. Elizabeth stepped off the road, into the soft grass beside her, and that's when her legs became like rubber, and the world turned black as night.

She fell to the ground, as the car pulled up beside her. She thought she could hear someone calling her name and then she felt as if she was floating in the air.

...then a bang ...then a roar ... then nothing.

Chapter 10

Elizabeth had a hard time opening her eyes and was not sure where she was when she did. The room that came into view was white, plain white. She could make out a TV hanging on the wall, a built-in dresser, and a very simple chair pulled up next to the bed. Jacob was sitting in the chair, and then Elizabeth realized she was the one in the bed.

"Hey, you're awake! Let me get your mom." Jacob got up and rushed out of the room. He came back a bit later with Mrs. Parks and Stacey.

Mrs. Parks came quickly to the bed and sat on the edge next to Elizabeth. "How are you feeling, honey?" she asked deeply concerned.

"I... I'm fine...why am I in bed?" Elizabeth tried sitting up. When she did, she started seeing stars, and felt the world start to spin. Suddenly she noticed the tubes in her arm and beeps and noises she hadn't heard before. She realized she was not in the comfortable bed in her room, but she was in a hospital bed instead.

"Wow! Not so fast." Jacob rushed to her bedside and held her shoulders down to keep her from moving too quickly. "You need to rest."

As he encouraged her to lay back down on her pillows and relax, he gently brushed some loose strands of hair away from her face. He stared down at her with genuine concern in his blue eyes.

"You passed out on the side of the road while you were running." Jacob noticed Elizabeth's confused expression in her beautiful eyes and filled her in.

"I had just turned onto the road and saw you. You stepped into the grass and fell. At first, I thought you tripped, until I noticed you were lying in the grass and your eyes were closed. I picked you up and brought you home. Your mom got worried when we couldn't get you to wake up and she called an ambulance."

Elizabeth looked around the room, realization dawning on her face. She had an IV in her arm, and oxygen in her nose, and yes, what she thought were her own clothes was really a hospital gown. Now she was embarrassed and covered herself up with the sad excuse for what they call blankets in a hospital and wondered how her hair and makeup looked.

Even though she was sure she looked rough, she couldn't help but notice the concern which had taken over Jacob's features. She just stared in wonder at him. This guy whom she just met seemed really worried about her.

Finally realizing there were others in the room and coming to an understanding of what Jacob told her, Elizabeth shot a look at her mom. "Mom, you really shouldn't have called an ambulance. I didn't need to be admitted to a hospital. This is ridiculous."

Elizabeth tried her best to sound annoyed, yet she was tired, and didn't really have the strength.

"Lizzy, you haven't been admitted. You're just in the emergency room. They said you were dehydrated, so they started the IV, and when Stacey told us you've been sick the past couple days, the doctor took some blood and is running tests as we speak. How long have you been sick? You really should have told us. I am so worried something is…"

Elizabeth cut her mother off mid-sentence. "Mom! Stop! Please! It's only been a couple of days. I started feeling lightheaded about a week ago, but figured it was just the stress of getting through exams. I only got sick twice. Once at Stacey's and another at work. It's not a big deal. I promise. I'm sure it's just a stomach bug."

Mrs. Parks got visibly upset and annoyed. "Barbara knew you were sick and didn't say anything about it?"

Stacey took this argument as a reason to leave and stepped out of the room.

"She didn't know, Mom. It happened during lunch, and I didn't tell her."

Mrs. Park's phone interrupted their conversation. She looked down at it. "I've gotta take this. I'll be right back." She looked worried about leaving her daughter.

"It's okay, Mom. Go ahead." Mrs. Parks smiled at her and got up and left the room answering her phone as she walked out the door.

Elizabeth quickly realized she was alone with Jacob. She turned and looked at him, covering herself up with the blanket. "Thank you for stopping and checking on me. I went for a three-mile run, but lost track of time and distance, and realized I went much further than I planned. Without water, and a decent lunch, well you know what happened."

"Yeah. It was a good thing I drove by. I don't know, it seems as if you were fine until you met me and ate my food." Jacob sat really close to Elizabeth and smiled.

"I don't think it had anything to do with you or your food. Promise." Elizabeth searched his eyes, as he reached out and grabbed her hand. He held it gently.

"Elizabeth, I…"

At that moment, the doctor entered the room. Jacob didn't get a chance to finish what he started and quickly let go of her hand.

The doctor was an older man with graying hair and a friendly face. "Well, it's good to see you awake, Elizabeth. How are you feeling?"

"Better than I have been, thanks to this." Elizabeth shook the tubes coming out of her and offered the doctor a small smile.

"Hey," interrupted Jacob. "Stacey and I are glad you're feeling better, but I think we will give you some privacy. Let us know when you get home and how you're doing. I'm going to go find my sister and call it a night." Jacob gave her hand a squeeze and left the hospital room just as Elizabeth's mom and dad entered.

Her dad shook Jacob's hand and told him thank you for all he did. Jacob recognized concern and gratitude on the man's face, smiled at him, and returned the handshake.

Once Mr. Parks came in and introduced himself to the doctor, he gave Elizabeth a hug of relief. Elizabeth found herself explaining to her dad and the doctor what she had just told her mom about how she hadn't been feeling well, and when she got sick. The doctor nodded his head with understanding and her father seemed just as concerned as her mom.

The doctor looked at Elizabeth's parents and asked, "Can you two please give us a moment alone? There are some things I need to talk with Elizabeth about and she is old enough that I can do it alone, if that's what she wants."

Elizabeth looked at the doctor and noticed concern on his face. The butterflies returned with a vengeance.

"Mom, Dad, please can I talk with him alone?" Her parents looked at each other, and even though she could tell they were not okay with it, they both nodded, and her father led her mother out of the room.

Elizabeth sat up as far as she could, took a deep breath, and turned toward the doctor. The butterflies were taking over whatever she had left in her stomach. She was glad that there wasn't much in there or she was sure it would be coming up. She took a deep breath, closed her eyes for a second and sent up a quick prayer.

'God, I know you never give us more than we can handle, but what do you do about when we give ourselves things you didn't mean for us to handle? Please give me strength to deal with whatever I am told.'

Elizabeth turned to the doctor. "What's going on, Doctor? Why am I here? Why have I been feeling bad, and why did I pass out?"

The doctor looked at her with a serious expression. "Elizabeth, you are twenty-three years old. When we took your blood, we checked for anemia and mono. Being a college student, we even checked you for vitamin deficiency and sexually transmitted diseases. All these tests came out negative. But we found out something important. Something I was not sure you would want your parents to know until you are ready to tell them yourself. Outside of being rundown, and dehydrated, which is why you are on the IV drip and oxygen, Elizabeth…" He stopped for a moment here and made sure he had her full attention, and eye contact."…You're pregnant."

Chapter 11

Stacey and Jacob slowly left the hospital. It was dark now and a perfectly clear summer evening. As they walked across the crowded parking lot, Stacey noticed how quiet and thoughtful her brother suddenly became. He is only a little over two years younger than she is, yet a lot taller, but she could not help but have a motherly attitude when it came to him. She wrapped her arm around his waist.

"Hey, little brother. Whatcha' thinkin' about? Is everything okay?" she asked him in her concerned momma voice she picked up after their parent's death consumed their lives.

Jacob is the most important person in her life and the only family she has left. Stacey was concerned about him more often than she would like because he took their parents' deaths hard and had a difficult time after their funeral.

He made some bad choices, turned to alcohol, and is now very hard on himself, thinks he can change the world, and fix all the bad things that happen to everyone. He wears his heart on his sleeve and people tend to take advantage of him because of it.

He always has girls chasing after him, one being Kristen. This is a situation Stacey struggles with. Kristen is her best friend, and she loves her dearly, but Kristen is infatuated with Jacob, knows how to get to him sexually, and she takes advantage of it every chance she gets.

He usually handles women smoothly, and though he makes bad choices often where Kristen is concerned, Stacey can't help but notice a slightly different demeanor about him lately when Elizabeth Parks is around or talked about. This event tonight seemed to bring out an overly concerned side in her brother, one usually not seen if someone was truly 'just a friend.'

Jacob looked down at his sister and gave her a small, quiet smile. At five-feet three-inches, she was quite a bit shorter than him and light enough for him to throw over his shoulder like a sack of potatoes, yet he admired and respected her enough to listen to what she had to say. He knew he gave her a hard time after their parents' death and added to her stress levels after that awful accident.

Now his goal is to start being the strong one, the man of the family. He doesn't like it when he worries her, and that is the look he saw in her eyes at this moment.

"Ya' know, Shorty," he nodded his head as if he thought of something he agreed with, "everything is alright. Yeah, it's really good." He showed her a smile of confidence and squeezed her in a side hug as they arrived at their car and climbed in.

Stacey turned her head to get a better look at him sitting behind the steering wheel. "So, I sure am glad that everything will be okay with Elizabeth. It was a little scary how she didn't wake up." She looked at him when she said this to see if any looks of concern came over his face.

He pulled out of the hospital parking lot and onto the road toward home before he answered her.

"Yeah, I agree. Watching her faint was weird. I didn't know what to think, but it all seems okay now. When she gets home, I'll go check on her."

Stacey took a deep breath and turned quickly in her seat. "Jake, what's the deal? Are you starting to have feelings for her?" She stared deep into the sides of his eyes, not backing down from her question. She wanted to know.

Jacob glanced quickly to his side, not wanting to take his eyes off the road for too long and answered her.

"I see her as a friend, and would like to get to know her better, yes. Romantically, I think that is what you really want to know. I haven't known her for very long, so it is too soon for anything romantic."

"And you just got out of a relationship after a nasty breakup. I don't think you need to be getting into another one already," Stacey interjected quickly and without thinking. She usually tried to keep out of her brother's love life, especially when her best friend was the reason for the breakup and all the confusion. It's not a good subject.

"Interesting you should say that. Remember, I was not planning on being out of a relationship. It was your BFF who made that occur. If she would just get the clue that I am not interested in her, maybe she would be able to move on and leave me alone!"

Jacob spat those words out without thinking. That was the wrong thing to say. He knew he should have just let it go, but his feelings were all over the place right now, and he just couldn't keep the words from slipping out. They have both been ignoring the issue for the past few months, and now seemed like the right time to deal with it.

"It's all Kristen's fault. Really?! Is this why you have been a total jerk to her lately, yet falling into her arms whenever alcohol is involved? Yes, she has a thing for you, she always has, but it takes two to tango as they say. She didn't pour alcohol down your throat. She didn't drug you, so you were incoherent. You are an adult; you drank and made a choice which ended your relationship with Jessica. You keep on making this same decision.

Have you ever thought that that happened, and keeps on happening, just like the other night, because you have feelings for Kristen? Maybe you're attracted to her. It is possible. You were once. Don't you remember high school? You cannot blame everything on her."

"Are you finished?" Jacob, furious with his sister, interrupted her in the middle of her rant. "We are not going to fucking argue about this. It is none of your damn business!"

He was fuming and found himself speeding faster than usual. This was one conversation he did not want to have. He doesn't understand why he keeps taking advantage of Kristen's feelings. It was just too easy. He missed the time he spent with Jessica. She is such a sweet person and they had so much in common. Now there is Elizabeth who keeps creeping into his thoughts. Getting home and somewhere where he could be alone and away from his sister, and this conversation, would be a good thing right now.

Stacey was shocked at Jacob's tone with her. He never cursed unless something really got under his skin. She guessed she did. She turned to face the window, watching the dark world rush by. Fine by her. She isn't the one who slept with someone, messed up a relationship and continues making the same bad decisions. She isn't the idiot who can't decide what her feelings are.

They finally pulled into their driveway. Stacey jumped out of the car, told her brother goodnight in the most sarcastic tone she could muster, and ran to the front door and into her room.

Jacob sat in the car a bit before climbing out. He trudged to the back deck and dropped on a seat on the couch. He found himself watching Elizabeth's house and wondering how she was doing. It was a beautiful clear night. He could see so many stars, and the moon was bright and large.

The last time he sat out here on the deck looking at the stars was with Jessica. He started to think back to the time he spent with her. She was fun, yet relaxed. They enjoyed spending time wondering where they would be in the future. Sometimes they even talked about having a future together. They both enjoyed camping, kayaking, and church. That's where they met. They also spent a lot of time out here, sitting on this couch, just talking about God and wondering about their relationship, both their romantic relationship and their personal one with God. They were both new Christians and helped each other through so many questions.

Then there was that night with Kristen. That girl is so hot and sexy. He knows he is attracted to her, but they just aren't good together. Just thinking about that one night, which ruined his future with Jessica, makes him so angry with himself.

He had a crush on Kristen when he was in high school and asked her out once. She saw him as a little brother, or so she said, and just flirted with him. She enjoyed the attention he always gave her. That's Kristen.

After his parents died, he took to alcohol to drown his sorrows. The feelings he had for her came back during this alcohol-induced time of his life and they both acted on them. He and Kristen had a slight history because of the choices they made then. They never had a real relationship but partied together and ended up in bed together often.

He promised himself, when he got sober, that those mistakes would never be revisited. They weren't, until that fateful night when he walked into his house after he left Jessica's.

He and Jessica had an argument. He doesn't even remember what it was about, but he knows he was still angry when he stepped foot inside his house. Stacey had friends over, and Kristen passed him a drink. That's one thing about Kristen. She has known him forever, and she knows him too well. She could tell he was upset, and she knows his weaknesses, and she looks good, damn good! Her confidence and conceit make her more attractive. When he is sober, her ways do nothing for him because he knows what she is truly like, but when he's drinking, it's a totally different story.

One drink led to another, drinks led to flirting, and the fact that her outfit left little to the imagination left him useless. They ended up in his bed. He had to admit, it was always amazing. She knows what he likes and does it well.

A car door slamming closed brought Jacob back to reality. He glanced across the yard. The brightness from the Parks' automatic spotlight gave off enough light that he could make out Elizabeth and her parents getting out of the car.

Elizabeth's dad placed his arm around his daughter's waist for support and Jacob could hear Elizabeth's sweet voice objecting to her father's help.

Jacob's heart filled with relief. She seemed okay. From where he sat on the deck, the reflection of the light made her look like an angel floating across the driveway. There was something about that girl that made him forget about his troubles with Jessica and Kristen.

There was something about Elizabeth that made him want to get to know her better.

Chapter 12

Elizabeth and her parents walked into their house. Her parents were so loving, yet a little overbearing. She could understand, though. Being their only child and having to take her to the hospital, and in an ambulance, was a bit much.

She ended up telling them that she was slightly anemic and extremely dehydrated. Elizabeth could tell they didn't believe her, but they didn't question her any further.

As soon as she got into the house, she excused herself for bed. Both of her parents, though still very concerned, said good night, and watched her ascend the stairs with a slow, laborious step. She was feeling better. The IV fluids really helped her, but she was exhausted.

The doctor told her to take the day off from work, so her mother decided to call Mrs. Stanzel for her. Calling in for a day off so soon after just starting back was not what she had planned on doing. It sure didn't look good.

She complained to her mom, but her mother was not hearing it and got on the phone as soon as they got into the house and called Elizabeth's boss.

Once in her room, Elizabeth brushed her teeth, changed her clothes, and climbed into bed.

She found herself staring at the ceiling, not able to process what the doctor had told her. Shocked is not the word she would use for how she felt. Disbelief. Disgust. Disappointment. Disgrace. Those words were more like it. Her thoughts flowed through her head like water down the side of a mountain. There was so much going on in her mind that she could not make sense of anything.

Pregnant. What am I going to do with a baby? Why me? What will everyone think of me? How will I tell my parents?

As all those thoughts went through Elizabeth's head, she realized the desperation of her situation, and the dam of tears she had been holding back all night exploded. She sobbed into her pillow as hard as she could, yet quiet enough so no one in the house could hear her. Between sobs, she started praying, or better yet desperately pleading to God.

"Lord, I don't know why this happened to me. I know I did wrong in your eyes, but so many people do worse. Please Lord, take this away from me. I don't have time for a baby! I have so much I want to do with my life and a baby will just get in the way. Lord, my parents will be so disappointed in me. What will they say? What will they think? And Lord, what do I say when they ask me who the father is? I. Don't. Even. Know!"

At this, she screamed and cried into her pillow, and had what could only be described as a temper tantrum. Just like a preschool child.

The fear and disappointment she felt overwhelmed her, this was a feeling so intense and deep. One which she had never felt before.

After what seemed like hours, she was exhausted, and had nothing left in her. She fell into a troubled sleep filled with the monsters and demons of her past.

Opening her eyes much later to the sunlight gave her a refreshed feeling. A feeling of relief that the nightmares she had dealt with were over.

That was until she realized the main nightmare, the one that took center stage in her dreams and kept her up most of the night, was not a nightmare at all.

It was her own, new reality.

Chapter 13

Glancing at her phone, Elizabeth realized it was nearly 11:00 a.m. Wow! She really slept a long time, but as the sleep washed away from her, she realized that waking up was not a good idea.

Facing the morning meant facing her problems. She pulled her blanket over her head, took a deep breath, and truly contemplated staying the rest of the day right where she was. In the peaceful tranquility of her soft, warm bed.

Suddenly there was a knock on her door, "Elizabeth. Are you awake?" inquired her mother in a soft, comforting voice.

Upset that she was being forced out of her peaceful tranquility, she answered the knock. "Yeah, Mom, come in."

Mrs. Parks opened the door, entered her daughter's room, and sat on her bed. Looking at Elizabeth with deep concern in her eyes and brushing a few loose strands of hair out of Elizabeth's face, she asked if everything was okay, and if there was anything she needed.

Elizabeth shook her head and tried to erase her mom's concerns. "I feel much better, Mom, than I have in a while. I'm gonna get a shower, and I'll be down soon."

"I am so glad to hear it. Your dad and I were so worried. I'm heading to the store to pick up groceries. Do you need anything special?"

Elizabeth again shook her head no and said thank you anyway.

Her mom leaned down to embrace her daughter, kissed her on top of her head, gave one last look of concern, and reminded her that she was here and ready to listen if Elizabeth needed to talk about anything. She gave her daughter a reassuring squeeze and left the room.

Elizabeth stared at the closed door, wondering if her mother knew more than she let on. Shaking her head, she headed for her bathroom.

After a shower and changing, Elizabeth brushed her teeth, took the iron pills and 'multivitamin' her parents got from the pharmacy, and pulled her hair into a messy bun. She grabbed her phone off her bedside table and headed downstairs.

She noticed a couple texts. One from Stacey and one from Jessica. They were both concerned about her. She ignored Stacey's for now but answered Jessica's. She told

Jessica she was fine. Jessica answered her telling her she was glad and asked if she wanted company later.

Thinking about it, Elizabeth agreed, thinking it might be a good thing to have a friend over, and right now, Jessica was the closest thing she had to a friend.

When she reached the kitchen, Elizabeth made herself a cup of coffee, put some bread in the toaster, grabbed a banana, then spread some peanut butter on her freshly toasted bread.

She took her breakfast to the next room to enjoy the quiet sanctuary. She sat in a comfortable chair in the small sunroom off the kitchen. This is where she liked to sit to relax and think, and that is just how she intended to spend her day.

The sunroom looked out on their back yard and had a perfect view of nature. Colorful trees, grass, her mom's garden, bird feeders, and a bird bath made the yard welcoming. Sitting here in the sunroom, with the floor-to-ceiling windows, brought the outside in.

Her mind quickly wandered to school and the year she had just completed. She and Trina enjoyed partying hard. They were both strong students who focused hard all week, so they decided that they deserved to have fun on the weekends.

Parties were plentiful, alcohol and pot were non-stop, and guys were in and out of their beds. Brady with her, and Trent with Trina, but there were occasionally others.

Elizabeth started thinking about the last few months of school. All those weekends leading up to the end of the school year, or at least the few details she could remember about the weekends. Her mind was a black blur of music, drinking, and Brady.

The more she thought about the past years at college, the more she thought about Brady. They knew each other from the very beginning of freshman year. They met at the freshman round-up held by the student council each year.

He and his roommate, Trent, decided to pledge a fraternity. They invited Trina and her to a party. They partied together ever since.

Placing her hand over her currently flat stomach, she closed her eyes and thought about what the doctor said. She was approximately thirteen weeks pregnant. When she thought backward, she realized she became pregnant in February. Yes, there were a lot parties, but luckily for once, she hadn't slept with many guys that month.

There is a life growing inside her, a life she did not want, and didn't even consider possible. A great despair set over her and she rested her head back on the couch. Even looking outside at the pleasant, sunny day where the beginnings of summer surrounded nature and cardinals flew in excited circles around the bird feeder, Elizabeth could not feel at peace.

Opening her computer, she searched for the only thing she could think of as a solution, the closest Planned Parenthood office. Taking a deep breath, she started to search the Internet. Finally, she found the phone number she was looking for.

Chapter 14

Stacey was in her kitchen enjoying her day off from the hospital. It's days like these that she really enjoyed her nursing job. Everyone else was at work, her house was quiet because her brother was one of those normal people with normal Monday through Friday eight-to-five jobs, so she had the house to herself.

As she sat in the kitchen eating a bowl of cereal and checking her social media and email, her mind kept wandering back to last night and her argument with Jacob.

She hated being mad at him. She should never have pushed the whole Kristen thing. Her thoughts of him and Kristen always get the best of her. They are the two people she loves most in the world.

In a perfect world, getting them together would be awesome. They could all be a family. She also knew that wouldn't work out because Kristen is too self-centered for her brother, Jacob did have feelings for Jessica, and he feels like that relationship was messed up because of Kristen. He made bad choices, but Kristen made sure that it was messed up for good.

Stacey knows her brother and she can tell he is already starting to have feelings for Elizabeth. She can see why. She seems smart and has her head on straight. She has goals and seems to know what she wants out of life, but most important to her brother, she goes to church. That is the number one priority for him. That is where he met Jessica after all.

Stacey finished her bowl of cereal and wandered outside to check their mail. She waved to Mrs. Parks as she backed out of the driveway and yelled across the yard to her.

"Good morning, Mrs. Parks. How is Elizabeth doing this morning?"

"She seems tired, but okay. She just got up. Feel free to go and say hi. I'm sure she would appreciate it." Mrs. Parks continued onto the road, waved, and pulled away.

Stacey walked back into her house and laid the mail, mostly bills and junk, on the counter so her brother could see it as soon as he got home from work.

Checking her phone, she noticed that Elizabeth did not answer her text from earlier this morning but decided she would go say hi anyway.

Elizabeth was in the sitting room off the kitchen, relaxing with her legs over the arm of a plush chair, her eyes closed, and her earbuds in her ears. Music relaxed her, so she was listening and zoned out when Stacey entered her house and found her in the sunroom by the kitchen.

"Hey, Elizabeth. I knocked and knocked. No one answered, but I thought I would come check on you. Your mom told me you were going to be home all day. I hope I didn't bother you." Not getting any reaction, Stacey tapped Elizabeth's foot, and sat down in the empty chair.

Slightly startled, Elizabeth sat up quickly, and snatched her earbuds out of her ears. That small act of moving quickly caused her to be a little lightheaded and dizzy, so she placed her hand on the side of her head and her elbows on her knees. She held her head steady and looked at Stacey with a shocked look on her face.

"Sorry," Stacey said with concern. "I didn't mean to startle you." Putting her hand out to her new friend, she continued, "Are you feeling alright?"

"Yes, really I'm fine. I just moved too quickly and got a little lightheaded." Looking up at Stacey with a smile, Elizabeth tried to reassure the girl across from her. "What brings you over?"

Stacey looked around the room, taking in her surroundings. She couldn't help but notice how tidy and organized everything was in the house. The sun coming in from the large floor-to-ceiling windows gave a very open and airy presence to the room.

"This is a great room," Stacey exclaimed looking around admiring what she saw. "Anyway, I just came to check on you. Jacob and I were worried. What did the doctor say?"

She placed her coffee cup she brought on the coffee table in front of her and slid the laptop off to the side. When she touched the keyboard mouse, the computer woke up, revealing the last website the user searched. She noticed Planned Parenthood on the screen.

"Here let me get this out of your way so you can have more space for your cup." Elizabeth snapped the laptop closed and moved it quickly while avoiding eye contact with Stacey. She was sure the web site popped up before she could close it. Shame and embarrassment shrouded her face.

Noticing Elizabeth's reaction, Stacey picked up her cup, leaned back on the couch and asked, concern filling her voice as recognition dawned. It only took her a few quick seconds to connect all the dots. "Elizabeth, are you pregnant?"

With fear in her eyes, and condemnation in her voice, Elizabeth turned to her neighbor. "It's none of your business. You should leave. I'm feeling tired and need to go lie down."

Elizabeth said this in a dismissive tone, stood up from her chair and headed toward the steps. Stacey could tell she was being dismissed; her stay was over. Standing up, she followed Elizabeth to the door.

"Do your parents know? If you need anything, I can help." Concern was oozing from Stacey's voice.

"It's not what you think, Stacey. And my parents know I am anemic and dehydrated. Thanks for coming over. I'll call you if I need anything." Holding the door open, Stacey knew she had overstayed her welcome, and stepped through the door to the outside, smiling at Elizabeth.

"Okay. Just call me if you need to or need anyone to drive you anywhere." Stacey left and Elizabeth closed the door behind her.

Chapter 15

Mrs. Deloris Green, director of the community supported Crisis Pregnancy Center, smiled a genuine, and loving smile as she said goodbye to the five older ladies and young ladies who made up her weekly devotional she held. This devotion was for the center's customers who were all single moms. Today she had two in their twenties, one in her thirties, and two teenagers, sixteen and eighteen. There were hugs all around as they said their goodbyes and went on their way.

"Mrs. Green, there is a call on the phone you may need to get. It is someone who thought they were calling an abortion clinic. I am scared she might hang up." Mrs. Green's volunteer office assistant interrupted as she was talking with one of the women leaving the devotional.

"Oh my! We can't have that." Mrs. Green quickly excused herself and ran to the phone on her desk, grabbing it from the cradle.

"Hello. This is Deloris Green. Can I help you?" she asked with love and sincerity in her voice.

"I... I ... I am so sorry. I must have made a mistake and dialed the wrong number. I think the person answering the phone said this is the Crisis Pregnancy Center?" asked a very scared and soft voice on the other end of the phone.

"Yes, it is the Crisis Pregnancy Center, but I don't think you made a mistake. Things have a way of happening to ensure we get exactly what we need when we find ourselves faced with a problem. I am glad you called. How can I help you today?"

The mothering and loving tone the lady had on the phone was enough to make the caller feel at ease. The number might have been wrong, but this woman was amazingly easy to speak with.

"I... I don't really know."

With this, the young girl on the other end of the phone started crying. Deloris could hear the sorrow in her voice and the sobs through the phone line.

"Hey, hey, it's alright. We don't judge and we don't criticize here. We want to make you feel at ease and help you with any decisions you need to make. Is there anything I can do for you?"

"I... I just found out I am pregnant. I can't have a baby... my parents ...will be ... so disappointed. I... don't know what to do." The tears and sniffling made the words difficult to understand.

"Honey, do you know where Maple Street is? I have time now, if you want to come see me, we can sit and talk. We can go over your options and find one that you will feel good about. Why don't you tell me your name. Your appointment time will be whenever you can get here."

Deloris's heart was breaking. This girl was the reason she worked here. This girl, and everyone like her. She sounded like she had nothing she could do, no options. Deloris remembered the fear and loneliness she felt when she was seventeen, found herself facing the same dilemma, and felt that she had no one to go to for help. She made what she thought was the only choice she could, and now lives with the guilt every day.

Years ago, she pleaded with God to forgive her, until she heard a message at church, and realized that she was already forgiven. It took her a long time, but she finally forgave herself, and promised God she would help others in the same situation and let them see there are other alternatives.

That became her life mission and is what led her here to the center, and today to this phone call.

"Well, I don't know." The caller became quiet, and nervous.

Deloris was concerned that the girl would hang up, so she did the only thing she knew to do in these situations.

She prayed quietly to herself before she uttered another word.

Lord, help me say the right thing to get this young girl in here. She needs what we can offer. Taking a deep breath Deloris continued.

"I understand how scared you are. Just come in and talk. You will be under no obligation. We can help you with whatever you decide whether it's to keep the baby, have an abortion, or even put the baby up for adoption. We are here to help, and to pray with you. What do you think?"

The girl on the other end felt a sense of peace come over her. "Okay. I'll come in. I can leave now. It might take me about fifteen minutes or so to get there."

"Great." Deloris answered with love and relief. "Let me get your name so we can be looking for you."

"My name is Elizabeth. I'll see you soon."

Elizabeth hung up the phone and Deloris wrote the name down, closed her eyes, and took a deep breath. "Thank you, Lord!'

She got up from her desk chair and gave the note to Jessica, the office assistant.

"Jessica, this is the name of the girl who I was just talking to. Thank you for getting me on the phone quickly. She was very nervous, and very scared, but she is coming in. She will be here in about fifteen minutes. Let's make sure to welcome her and make her feel comfortable."

"That is such good news! You truly have a gift for talking to people." Jessica smiled at her boss.

She loved how happy and joyous Mrs. Green always was. She was the reason Jessica was considering getting into social work one day. She enjoyed working here and learning from this amazing lady.

Jessica headed toward the reception desk to write the new appointment in the books and get some paperwork ready.

She glanced down at the piece of paper when she opened the computer's calendar. The name of their new appointment was Elizabeth. Jessica turned to her computer and wrote down the name Elizabeth, on Monday, 4:00 p.m.

Chapter 16

It was just 3:45 p.m. when Elizabeth pulled into a parking spot at the Crisis Pregnancy Center. It was a quaint two-story house in a part of town that had old houses all converted into businesses.

The Crisis Pregnancy Center was a red brick house with black shutters. There was a small front porch with wooden rockers beckoning you to come sit a while. The landscaping was simple and neatly kept, with large flower containers filled with the colors of summer. There was one other car in this part of the parking lot. Since the driveway wound around to the rear of the house, Elizabeth decided that the employees probably parked around back.

Turning in her seat, she noticed that the bushes planted in the front of the property created enough privacy that she would not be seen when she walked into the building. This made her feel a little more at ease. The last thing she needed was someone who knew her parents see her walk in when they drove by. *Why wasn't the customer's entrance around back?*

Taking a deep breath and sipping on the Sprite she bought at the gas station to calm the butterflies in her stomach, Elizabeth slowly and trepidatiously stepped out of the car.

These people are here to help. They understand. It's their job. They know the best way to deal with this problem. It's okay. You've got this. Elizabeth tried her best to talk herself out of driving away. There was nothing else she could do and no one else to turn to.

Closing the car door behind her, she walked toward the porch of the center, took a deep breath, climbed the few steps, and opened the bright red front door.

The entrance of the pregnancy center was large, clean, and homey. The receptionist's area consisted of a wooden welcome desk with a couple of plush chairs and a table between them.

Through a door to the right was a large living room area with windowed pocket doors, which were closed at the moment. Through the door to the left was another room with plush chairs and a couch all around the walls. This must have been an overflow waiting room.

Elizabeth walked up to the desk and waited for the lady to get off the phone. She had a sweet air about her and seemed to be about Elizabeth's mother's age. Elizabeth wondered if this was the lady she spoke with on the phone.

"I must let you go; I need to get back to work. I'll talk with you later." The lady hung up the phone and smiled brightly at Elizabeth.

Her smile was gentle, understanding, and welcoming all at the same time. It relaxed Elizabeth just a little, but at this point, a little was better than nothing. It seemed like Elizabeth's butterflies had taken hits of caffeine and had multiplied.

"Welcome to the Crisis Pregnancy Center. I'm Deloris Green, the director. How can I help you today?"

Elizabeth, in a quiet and nervous voice answered, "I..." She stopped and had to clear her throat before she could continue. "I called a little bit ago and was told to come on up. If this is a bad time, I can come back later."

"Elizabeth, right? I am so glad you made it." The sweet lady walked quickly around the desk and put her hand out for Elizabeth to shake. "I'm Deloris. We talked on the phone."

Elizabeth took Deloris' hand and returned the handshake. She instantly felt relaxed and offered up a small smile.

Deloris smiled back. "Please follow me into my office where we can have some privacy." She walked around the desk and led Elizabeth through the windowed pocket doors. Her office was through the sitting room in the back. She closed her office door, settled in front of a chair across from the couch, and motioned for Elizabeth to take a seat.

Elizabeth took the seat she was offered on the couch and took the clipboard which Deloris handed to her. "Please fill these out the best you can. I will give you a minute by yourself and will return in a bit. Would you like me to get you a bottle of water?" Elizabeth nodded her head, and Deloris exited the room from a different door at the back.

Sighing deeply and rolling her neck to get the kinks out, Elizabeth started reading and filling out the forms.

The first page was a basic information form. Name, address, phone number, education, etc. The second page started with some personal questions like what brings you here today. That sort of thing. She did her best to fill out the three pages the best she could, and just finished when Deloris came back into the room with a couple bottles of water.

"Are you finished?" Deloris nodded to the informational forms. Elizabeth nodded back and handed them to her.

Deloris got comfortable on the chair across from Elizabeth. She read through the forms quickly, asking some additional questions as she went, and jotting down answers Elizabeth gave.

She eventually got to the question: *What is the reason for this visit?*

Elizabeth's answer was *I need information about an abortion. I just found out I am pregnant.*

Deloris Green looked directly into Elizabeth's eyes, laying the clipboard on her lap. "Why do you think an abortion is the answer to your pregnancy? A baby is a gift, whether we understand it or not. I'd like to talk to you first, and when we are finished, if you still think you want an abortion, I will lead you in that direction. But I want you to open your mind to other options."

Mrs. Green hesitated at this point. Knowing that this was a hard stance to take, she sometimes loses them right here, but in all her years, this is where she gets the response that gives her hope.

If they stay and are willing to listen, she can usually get these scared women to make a better choice. One that not only benefits them in the long run, but also the baby.

Elizabeth looked back into the kind eyes of the lady seated across from her, and once again felt at peace. The same way she felt when she talked with her on the phone.

Elizabeth answered her as honestly as she could. "Mrs. Green, I'm young, not married, and a new college graduate without a good job. I was not planning on this right now. It was an accident. I do not have time for a baby, but…"

Elizabeth nodded her head in agreement and continued. "Okay," she answered quietly. "I'll listen."

Deloris beamed across at Elizabeth. They started talking. Deloris asked questions and Elizabeth answered. Finally, she got to the hard ones. The questions Elizabeth was dreading.

Did she know when she became pregnant?

"Yes, approximately. I was just told I am about thirteen weeks along. So, it was probably the end of February, maybe March."

Does she know who the father is?

Elizabeth hesitated before she could answer. Tears started streaming down her face and embarrassment threatened to overwhelm her. Deloris placed a box of tissues on the couch next to her and sat down also.

She took Elizabeth's hands in hers. "It's okay. I just need to know these answers. Remember, there is no judgment here, only help."

Elizabeth pulled a couple tissues from the box, dried her eyes, and wiped her nose. Shaking her head, she answered between sniffles and tears. "Well maybe. I'm pretty sure, I know who it is, but I'm not positive."

At this, she broke down into terrible sobs. Her whole body shook with the venom that became her embarrassment and tears.

Deloris leaned toward the girl and wrapped her arms around her and let her cry, patting her and reassuring her. Elizabeth broke away from the hug and apologized.

"I'm sorry. You don't even know me, and I'm acting like this. My parents would be so ashamed if they knew. I can't believe this has happened to me! I was always a good girl. I always did what made my parents happy. I never thought I would turn into this, this thing I don't even know! I hate myself and everything I've become!" Elizabeth was now so mad, she felt like she could break something, or better yet hurt someone.

She stood up and began pacing the floor as she yelled these last things. Mrs. Green watched from the couch and allowed her to get it all out. She then stood up and walked over to Elizabeth. Taking a hold of the girl gently by the shoulders, Deloris Green spoke with her whole heart.

"Elizabeth, first, let's get something straight. You are an amazing creation of God's. We all make mistakes. Mistakes may seem awful at the time, but they are not always bad. Especially when we learn from them. Yes, your parents will be hurt and disappointed when they find out. But they will be more hurt and disappointed if you terminate this pregnancy and never even tell them about their grandchild. One day they will find out. It seems like you have a strong and close relationship with them. Your guilt will get to you and you will come clean, eventually. This center can help you through the pregnancy. We can give you items you may need, we offer classes on parenting, devotional support groups, and other positive options like adoption. We are here for you.

Remember, you aren't just pregnant. You are growing a baby. A beautiful little baby. You may not like how this baby was created, but it was created. It has a beating heart and deserves a chance. Even if another mom raises it. It deserves to be loved. Like you are loved by your parents." Finished with her speech, she rubbed Elizabeth's arms then dropped them, taking a step back.

"Thank you," Elizabeth whispered in a hoarse voice. "You're right. I have a lot to think about and need to tell my parents first."

Deloris smiled and walked to a bookshelf which lined the wall behind her and picked up some pamphlets. "Here are some pamphlets on what classes and supplies we offer pregnant women, and here are some on adoption and abortion. I hope you will look fully at all these options with your parents. If, after you talk with them, you still want to discuss an abortion, we can point you in the right direction. But for right now, let's put that on hold."

Elizabeth nodded her head in agreement, took the pamphlets from Mrs. Green and thanked her. Elizabeth followed her toward the front door, gave the woman a hug, and walked to her car.

She felt good and knew that she had to somehow get up the nerve to talk to her mom and dad about everything. The thought filled her with anxiety.

Chapter 17

Jacob and Chad entered The Pizza Place to meet Stacey and Kristen for a quick dinner. They ordered a supreme pizza and a pitcher of beer. The boys poured themselves a glass as they waited for the girls to arrive.

"Hey, Jacob. Hi, Chad" Jessica noticed the boys when she entered the restaurant to pick up her dinner and walked over to talk to them while she waited.

"Hey, Jessica. You want to take a seat, at least until your order is ready?"

Since they had dated for so long, Jacob knew that Jessica always took pizza and spaghetti home to her grandmother on Monday nights. There were many Monday nights that he would join them, eating pizza, and playing Dominoes—Mexican Train.

Jessica nodded her head. "Sure, if I'm not bothering you. Long time no see, Chad. How's it going?" Chad got up and gave the petite girl a hug.

"Can't complain. Still got a job and my health. Of course, I haven't gone to the doctor lately, so I could be dying." Chad answered in his always joking way.

Jessica and Jacob laughed at him, and Jessica slid in next to Jacob; he offered her a garlic breadstick which she gladly accepted. She tore it in half, placed the other half on Jacob's plate, grabbed his glass and took a sip of his beer, just like she always used to do. Catching herself, she looked up at him and smiled.

"Whoops, sorry. Your beer always tasted better than mine."

He smiled down at her. "Help yourself. You always did."

They smiled knowingly at each other. Jacob changed the subject before things got awkward. "How's Granny doing? I didn't see her at church on Sunday."

"She was getting over a cold Sunday, so she thought it best to stay home. She is feeling much better and wanted her weekly stand-by, so here I am. She has a movie she wants us to watch tonight, one of her old favorites."

"You know, Jacob and I were planning on grabbing pizza Friday night and going bowling. Why don't you and Elizabeth show up and join us?" Chad commented smiling at Jessica.

Jacob interrupted, "Just so you know, I happened to ask Elizabeth already when I stopped in and saw her at the boutique Saturday. She said she would, and she was going to ask you, Jessica, but that was before she was in the hospital."

Jacob and Chad shared a quick glance.

"How is she doing? Has anyone talked to her?" Asked Chad.

Jacob answered with a little bit of a nervous and uncomfortable edge to his voice. "I haven't seen her at all, and she hasn't answered my phone calls."

Jessica answered. "I stopped by and saw her for a little bit today. She is getting better, and insists it was just dehydration from all the excitement of leaving school, graduating, and coming home. But anyway, she and I will be there, and yes, she mentioned to me that you asked her already. So, we will both be meeting you here."

They planned a time and Jessica, Chad, and Jacob continued with their small talk while eating breadsticks and drinking beer.

The conversation was easy and fun, as it always was. The three of them were laughing and joking at something ridiculous Chad said when Chad's face got suddenly serious.

He reached over and grabbed his beer mug while looking away quickly. Jessica and Jacob just gave each other a questioning glance as Jessica took another drink of Jacob's beer.

"Well, look who it is. Nice to see you, Jessica." Kristen slid in the booth on the other side of Jacob, placing her arm around his shoulders and taking the extra beer glass sitting on the table as Stacey slid in next to Chad.

"Thank you for ordering a beer for me, Jake. Have you two already ordered our dinner? Mmmm. This beer is good. I so appreciate you thinking of me." As she said this, Kristen leaned over and planted a light kiss on Jacob's cheek and ran her fingers through his hair.

"Why are we blessed with your presence tonight?" Kristen took her eyes off Jacob and threw an icy glare at Jessica as she said this.

"Just waiting for my dinner then I will be getting out of here. It was great seeing you two. I'll see you both Friday." Jessica directed this at Jacob and Chad and slid out of the booth as her name was called to pick up her to-go order.

"Stacey, I wish we could have talked more." The only reply to Kristen was a smirk and eye roll. "Bye, Chad. Bye, Jacob." She smiled at them both as she turned to walk toward the front and picked up her food.

Chapter 18

Elizabeth's alarm went off early Tuesday morning. She rolled over to turn it off, realized she did not have to go to work this morning, groaned loudly, and put her pillow over her face trying to block out the sun.

She heard a car driving and honking as it drove slowly down the road, a neighbor's dog was barking, and someone was mowing their yard. It should be against the law to mow your grass before noon, Elizabeth thought. She tried her hardest to block out all the noise and go back to sleep, but it was no use. It was morning and time was moving on even though she really would like it to stop so she could think and fully evaluate her situation. But no, it's time to wake up and face the music. She needed to talk to her mom about her pregnancy.

Elizabeth spent most of the night looking up her options. She knew what her only choice could be. She had plans for her life, and not being positive about who the father was just proved that being a mom was not a good idea right now.

Thinking about an abortion, though, made her feel extremely guilty. She was not raised to have an abortion. She considered doing it without her parents' knowledge because she didn't know how to face them. They would be so disappointed in her. In the end, though, she realized she had to let them know. She needed their support. She had to talk to her mom.

Elizabeth pulled herself out of bed, went into the bathroom to throw water on her face, grabbed the pamphlets she received from the pregnancy center from her side table, put them in the pocket of her pajama bottoms, and slowly trudged into the kitchen where she found her mom drinking coffee and reading a book.

"Well, good morning, beautiful." Her mother looked at her, put her book down, and pulled her daughter into a hug. "How are you feeling this morning?"

"Good morning, Mom. I feel better today." Elizabeth went to the coffee pot, filled a mug with steaming, hot coffee, added half and half and sugar, and leaned against the counter. She stared across the room, enjoying the heat from her mug, and the aroma of the coffee in the air.

"Do you want me to fix you anything to eat?" asked her mom. "Eggs and bacon or would you prefer a bagel and banana?"

"Is the bagel from the bakery? Cinnamon and raisin?" Elizabeth asked with hope.

"Yes, it is. I know you love them."

"Well then, absolutely. A bagel with cream cheese and a banana sounds like heaven," replied Elizabeth.

"Take a seat in the sunroom, relax with your coffee, and I will get that for you and bring it in."

"Mom, I can do it."

"I know you can but let me serve you. You still look tired. Go get comfortable and I will bring it to you. Please, don't upset me. Let me take care of you."

Elizabeth knew when she would not be able to win an argument, so she went into the sunroom, sat on the couch, and put her feet under her.

Through the window, she could see two cardinals at the bird feeder in the backyard. She watched them and drank her coffee while she waited for her mom to bring her breakfast. She did notice that she was not feeling sick this morning. That was a good sign, wasn't it? Maybe it was more dehydration and having low iron than actual morning sickness.

A little while later, Mrs. Parks entered the sunroom with a bagel loaded with cream cheese and banana on a plate. She placed it on the table in front of Elizabeth, sat on the other end of the couch and watched as her only child pick at her bagel.

Mrs. Parks became concerned, and worry clouded her eyes as she watched her daughter eat, or rather, pick at her food.

"I know there is something going on, Elizabeth," started Mrs. Parks getting right to the point. "You're sick and fainting. A mother knows when there is something wrong with their child. Your dad and I have been talking and want to know something." She paused here waiting for Elizabeth to look up.

Once she had Elizabeth's eyes on her own, she continued. "Honey, are you pregnant?"

Elizabeth stopped chewing and froze. She moved her eyes back to her plate as they filled with tears. Finally, when they could no longer hold the moisture building up, the dam was released, and tears overflowed down her cheeks.

Elizabeth, not being able to hold in her sobs any longer, put down her bagel, laid her hands on her face and let it all out.

"Mom, I am so sorry!"

"Oh, honey." Mrs. Parks closed the gap between her and her daughter. She wrapped Elizabeth in a strong, reassuring hug and rested her head on top of her daughters.

"Shh, Shh. It is alright. I've got you." Mrs. Parks rocked her daughter back and forth as she held her in her arms.

Elizabeth continued apologizing between sobs. After what seemed like forever, her tears started to dry up. She broke away from her mother and reached for her napkin so she could mop up her tears and wipe her nose.

Mrs. Parks gave her daughter time to compose herself, then reaching over, she gently placed her hands on either side of Elizabeth's head and looked her daughter square in the eye.

"So, now that that is finished, I want you to know that your father and I are disappointed, yes, but we love you most of all and want you to know we are here for you, and we want to help you."

Mrs. Parks rubbed her thumbs under Elizabeth's eyes, mopping up the stray tears that fell as she talked.

Elizabeth raised her hand and grasped her mom's. "I know, Mom. I have been giving it a lot of thought."

She passed the pamphlets that she had tucked in her pockets quickly to her mom before she lost her nerve. "This is the route I need to take. I went to the Crisis Pregnancy Center in town and talked to the lady there. Her name is Deloris Green. Mrs. Green tried to talk me into choosing a different path, but I am so young and just don't think that will be possible. I am sorry. I know you and Dad don't support abortions, but I am just not ready to be a mother."

Her mother turned the pamphlets over in her hand, reading the front and back. Mrs. Parks closed her eyes briefly, took a deep breath, and looked up at her daughter.

She saw fear, confusion, and doubt in those hazel eyes she loved so much.

"How about this? Let's go to the Crisis Pregnancy Center together and talk with Mrs. Green; she seems like she is a good lady and is very willing to help. We can figure this out together. What do you think?"

Seeing that her daughter did not look ready to respond, Mrs. Parks added, "Please. We can talk and really look at the other options, keeping the baby, or even adoption."

Seeing the look of doubt and fear still in her daughter's eyes, she added. "Let's first look at what all is available. Like I said, your dad and I want to help you and support you. You aren't on your own. But if you are still against going through with your pregnancy, we will support your decision to have an abortion."

Elizabeth appreciated the fact that her mom was willing to see her side, so she knew it was the responsible and mature thing to see this through.

"Okay. I love you guys. I'll do this for you. I will really look at other options." Elizabeth agreed with her mom, and leaned in to give her a big, thankful hug.

"If you want, I can call her and see if she is available today." Elizabeth's mom smiled and nodded, so Elizabeth grabbed her phone and called the pregnancy center. After a brief discussion with Mrs. Green, they decided on a time. Elizabeth thanked her, said she would see her at one o'clock, and hung up the phone.

"Thank you, Sweetheart!" Elizabeth's mom said as she brushed her hand across her daughter's face. "Finish eating and take a shower. I have some housework to finish then we will leave around 12:30." She smiled and got up from the couch to let Elizabeth finish her breakfast and get cleaned up.

Elizabeth watched her mother leave, took a deep, shaky breath, and looked down at her bagel. She leaned back and finished eating while deep in thought.

Outside the sun was shining and those cardinals were still flying around and hanging out at the feeder. It was a male and female. The male was bright red, and the female was brown with red undertones, and a red beak. Remembering a bird documentary she watched one day, she thought about the facts she learned from the documentary. One fact stuck in her mind. Cardinals mate for life.

How awesome it would be to know you would be with someone forever, thought Elizabeth. *If those cardinals only knew how lucky they were.*

Elizabeth finished eating and went upstairs to take her shower and get ready for her appointment at the Crisis Pregnancy Center.

Chapter 19

Mrs. Green was behind the desk typing at the computer and looked up when she heard the door open. Seeing Elizabeth, she stood, walked around the desk, and held out her hand in greeting. "Hi, Elizabeth. It is so good to see you again."

She turned to Mrs. Parks and shook her hand also. "Mrs. Parks. Thank you for coming. Let's go ahead and go into my office so we can talk."

She led them through the double glass doors and into her office. Mrs. Parks and Elizabeth sat down on the couch. Deloris Green handed the ladies bottles of water and took a seat in the chair across from them.

"So, Elizabeth, I guess you told your mother about your pregnancy?"

Elizabeth looked at the kind lady and nodded her head.

"I am so glad to hear that. When you left here last time, you were pretty set on having an abortion. Is that where you still stand?"

Mrs. Parks moved to the edge of the couch, grabbed her daughter's hand, and looked at Deloris. "I know it is not really my place, but Elizabeth's father and I have talked about this. You see, we had a feeling this was what was going on."

Mrs. Parks then turned to face her daughter and with a firm, yet delicate look she continued. "Elizabeth, we want you to keep the baby. We will help you out. You can stay at home for as long as you need to. We will support you with finding a job. We know your new career is important to you. It is to us, also. You won't be alone. You and the baby can live with us. You know we have plenty of room. We really wish you would consider it."

Pausing just long enough to make sure her daughter was really listening to what she was saying, Mrs. Parks made sure not to lose eye contact with Elizabeth. She saw fear in those eyes. This encouraged her to continue.

"It's okay, honey. There is nothing you can say to make your dad or me mad at you. Honestly, yes, we are disappointed. But there are more things now to consider than just you. Please be honest. It will make it easier. You know we have always preferred the truth over lies."

Elizabeth broke her mother's eye contact, looked down at their interlocked hands, and squeezed. "I know. I am so lucky to have you and Dad. You are both so supportive of me, but I am so scared. This is not the plan I had. It was just a stupid choice and a huge mistake! Mom," Elizabeth paused, scared to be completely honest with her mother, but knew there was no other way. "Mom, I need to tell you something. It won't make you proud, but I need to tell you the truth."

Elizabeth took a deep shaky breath; her face was creased with sadness. "Mom, I think I'm about thirteen weeks pregnant. That means I got pregnant at the end of February, or early March. Here is the problem."

Elizabeth started to cry. She could not stop the tears from streaming down her face. "There was this guy in college. Brady. We spent four years being together off and on. February was one month that we tried to be exclusive. It worked, mostly. Until it didn't. Mom, I don't think I can be sure who the father is! It is probably Brady, but I don't know. I am so, so sorry. I embarrassed you and Dad. You didn't raise me to act like this."

At this, she lost all control. Again, she found herself crying like a baby in Deloris Green's office. Mrs. Parks reached over and grabbed her daughter up in a huge bear hug.

"Oh, my goodness. My sweet, sweet baby." Tears ran slowly down Mrs. Parks face. She could not bear to see her daughter in this much pain.

"It is okay, I promise. Dad and I are not embarrassed. We could never be embarrassed by you. We will get through this. I promise. We love you so, so much." She just continued hugging and rocking her daughter, the pain evident in both of their tears.

"Mom, I made choices I wanted to make, but I know they weren't the best ones. I drank too much, and we had so much fun. Everything just started spiraling out of control. The worse choices I made, the more I felt you would not want to hear about it. I wanted to talk to you, but I felt like you would get so angry, so I kept everything to myself and just kept on with what I was doing. At the time it was fun, but I also felt so alone."

"Well, I am not angry, and you aren't alone anymore. Mrs. Green, is there a way we can get an ultrasound done here, today? I want Elizabeth to see the baby and we need to see how far along she really is. That might make a difference."

Deloris Green looked at the two women across from her. "Yes, there is. We have an ultrasound machine here. We can get you set up in a little bit. We have a nurse practitioner, who is also a volunteer, here today. Let me give you two sometime, and I will go get things set up."

A little while later, the two women were led into a sterile looking exam room. There was a lady in there dressed in black pants and a white blouse.

"Hi. I'm Grace, the nurse practitioner." She leaned over and shook Mrs. Parks and Elizabeth's hands.

"Elizabeth, if you will lie down on the bed and get comfortable, I will get the machine ready." The nurse quickly adjusted the bed back to a reclined, seated position. Elizabeth looked at her mom and went to take her place with her mom by her side.

The nurse pulled a machine over. There was a small TV screen and what looked like a microphone attached to it. The nurse pulled the top of Elizabeth's shorts down below her belly button.

"Okay, Elizabeth. I am going to put some gel on your stomach; it will be cold. I will then take this microphone looking thing and rub it on your stomach. The ultrasound waves will put a picture on the screen of your baby. We should be able to see the baby, figure out exactly how far along you are, and maybe, if we are lucky, hear the heartbeat. Do you have any questions?"

Elizabeth looked at the nurse then at her mom. "Mom, why do I need to see this?"

"Because. Let's just see. It won't hurt anything." Mrs. Parks took her daughter's hand and smiled at her. Elizabeth smiled back and gave a sigh and a little nod to the nurse.

"Okay. You're right. Whatever."

The nurse put the gel on Elizabeth's stomach. She wasn't kidding. It was cold.

Light blue lines and blobs came on the screen. Elizabeth stared at the blobs and shapes she saw, but she didn't recognize anything.

Suddenly, her mom let go of her hand in shock and Elizabeth saw it. It was a head and tiny arms. It almost looked alien-like, but there was no mistaking the eyes and nose and even the mouth.

Elizabeth was amazed and shocked at what she saw on the screen. She saw ultrasound pictures before but seeing this on the screen, this creature that was in her was shocking!

She couldn't remove her eyes. Suddenly she noticed that the nurse was pushing buttons and clicking the mouse as she kept moving the microphone all through the gel. Suddenly there was a noise. It sounded a lot like a swishing noise, but there was a rhythm to it.

"Oh, Elizabeth!" Her mother choked back a sob. It then clicked for Elizabeth.

"What is that sound?" Elizabeth asked the nurse, though in her heart she knew what it was.

Elizabeth's mom answered for the nurse. "That is your baby's heartbeat. That little face looking at you has a beating heart. Isn't that amazing!?" She watched the confusion turn to wonder on her daughter's face as the realization dawned within her. The nurse clicked a few more buttons then turned to Elizabeth and her mother.

"Well, everything sounds and looks perfectly normal. The heart sounds healthy. Elizabeth, you are sixteen weeks along, and everything looks great. Would you like a picture?"

Elizabeth, still shocked and amazed at what she had just witnessed, looked over at her mom. "Mom, if you want it, go ahead. I'm really not ready." The nurse printed out the ultrasound pictures and handed them to Mrs. Parks.

"Oh, Elizabeth. This is your baby! And it is healthy and beautiful and perfect!" Mrs. Parks held her daughter by her chin as tears flowed from her eyes. "Baby, I know you are scared, and so unsure. But I want you to know, we can do this together. You, me, and your father. I promise you; you are not alone, and never were. But it is ultimately your decision. I want you to know that if you choose to keep this baby, it will be a lot of work and responsibility, but God never gives us more than we can handle. I know you can handle this challenge. You are a strong and determined woman!"

Elizabeth reached up and hugged her mom. "Thank you for being so amazing! I am so glad I have you and Dad. I just don't know. I'm sorry."

Mrs. Parks hugged her daughter back hard. "Oh, honey. It's okay. You can take a little more time."

Mother and daughter hugged and cried. Finally, they decided it was time to get Elizabeth off the table and cleaned up. They wiped the gel from her stomach, re-situated her clothes, and left the room together with the pictures of the alien-looking life form growing in Elizabeth's stomach.

Chapter 20

The nurse took them back to Mrs. Green's office and asked them to wait. Mrs. Green came in shortly and sat down in her chair across from them again.

Noticing the pictures in Mrs. Park's hand, she motioned toward them. "Can I have a look?"

"Of course." Mrs. Parks handed the pictures over to Mrs. Green who looked down at them and smiled a sweet smile.

"So, Elizabeth? What are you thinking, or do you need more time to decide?"

Elizabeth looked at the lady across from her. She stared at the pictures in the lady's hand, still shocked that that was in her. "It doesn't seem real. When I look at those pictures, I can see all the little parts. I heard the heartbeat. I know it's real, but it seems impossible. My feelings are so mixed right now. But I am so sorry, I really can't answer that yet. I am so confused."

Elizabeth stopped and just stared at the pictures. "If I keep it, I know I will need to face so many questions and judgments. I don't really know if I'm ready for that."

Deloris looked at her and put her hand on the young girl's leg. "Yes, you might be faced with a lot of questions," she answered Elizabeth's scared and confused eyes. "There will be times it won't be easy, but with your parents' support, and what we offer here at the center, you will have lots of people in your corner. We also have a class that would be perfect for you. All the future moms are single, first-time moms. Some are older than you, some your age, and a few younger. I would love to have you join. We meet on Wednesday nights or Saturday mornings. I would love for you to come and visit with us this Saturday. It might help you make your decision." Mrs. Green gave Elizabeth some information about the group and other services the center would be able to offer her.

"One more thing, Elizabeth." Deloris was looking in Elizabeth's file. "It says here in your file that you're sixteen weeks along. That means what you thought was the date of conception is quite a bit earlier in February. Not that you need to answer, but does that make it easier to know who the father is?"

Elizabeth looked at the woman across from her and did some calculations in her head. The new time frame made it clear. She knew who the father was. There was no doubt.

She stood up and her mom did too. Elizabeth shrugged her shoulders. She had to think about all this more, and right now she was just ready to go, so Deloris led them through to the lobby.

"Thank you so much for all the help." Mrs. Parks leaned in and hugged Deloris. "I appreciate everything. You have no idea."

Deloris hugged her back. "You are so welcome. I am only doing my job. Thank you for supporting your daughter like you are. Elizabeth is lucky to have you by her side. Not all girls have someone they can turn to."

Deloris gave one last squeeze. "Please keep in touch. We are here for you, too. You are Elizabeth's family."

Elizabeth and her mom finished saying their goodbyes. Mrs. Parks agreed to get Elizabeth to see a doctor soon, and they left the center and walked across the lot to get in their car. Elizabeth was deep in thought.

Chapter 21

Elizabeth's alarm went off early the next morning. She turned it off and laid in her cozy bed staring up at her ceiling.

Remembering the discussion with her parents last night, she realized how lucky she really was. Her dad was his typical loving and understanding self. She knew he was a little disappointed in the decisions and choices she made over the past couple years, but his love trumped everything.

She had no clue what the future was going to hold, but she knew she was lucky to have her parents' support and knowing who the father of her baby is made her choices easier to make.

It was time to start her day and get to work, so she pushed herself out of bed, into the shower, and got dressed.

Elizabeth was soon in the kitchen, where she shoved a cinnamon bagel into the toaster, filled a mug with coffee, and grabbed an orange out of the fruit bowl on the counter.

The strong, sweet, and citrusy aroma of the orange filled her senses as she peeled it. She popped one small, juicy wedge into her mouth, enjoying the sweetness, when her mother walked in the kitchen, stealing a wedge for herself, and surrounded Elizabeth in a tight hug.

"How are things with you this morning?"

Elizabeth gave her mom a relaxed smile. "I feel good, Mom. Like a huge weight has been lifted off my shoulders. Thank you for listening last night and being so understanding."

"Elizabeth, you know we love you."

After spreading a huge slab of cream cheese on her bagel, she promised her mom she would be home for dinner, gave her another quick hug, grabbed her breakfast, and left for work.

Main Street Boutique was the best atmosphere to uplift a person. Between all the work which kept her busy, such as straightening shelves, filling and designing displays, and helping customers find the perfect gift for a friend, or treat for themselves, Elizabeth got to spend her day with a sweet and understanding boss, and her best friend.

Some days, like today, being so focused on the activity and work around her, it was easy for Elizabeth to forget about the mess she was in and her pregnancy. Life really wasn't that bad.

Jessica didn't come in until later, so it was just Elizabeth and Barbara Stanzel all morning. The steadiness of the store kept them both busy. Seeing people from the community come in and talk to her helped Elizabeth to remember the joy of being in a small town. She enjoyed chatting with the customers while they milled around the shelves, picking things up and trying on clothes.

"Elizabeth! Hey, how's your day going?" Elizabeth turned to see who was talking to her and smiled as she noticed Chad standing there, with his arms filled with scarves, purses, and socks.

Elizabeth chuckled at the scene in front of her. "Hey, Chad. Nice to see you." Elizabeth studied the pile of products in Chad's arms. "I'm having a great day and can tell you're enjoying shopping. Look, I would love to make the sale, but I don't think those socks are your color."

"Very funny! It is my mother's birthday. I always come in here to find something for her. I am not much of a shopper, though. What do you think she might like?" He held up the purse and scarf.

"Does she like scarves? If so, that is a nice one. It is light and a neutral color. She could wear it anytime and with any color. But that purse is so cute! Small enough not to be a burden, yet it still holds necessities. I personally think the purse is more practical, though, this time of year."

"That's what I was thinking. I also need to grab some earrings. She loves the ones Mrs. Stanzel carries here."

Elizabeth took the items from him that he was no longer interested in purchasing, put them back in their respective places on the shelf, and led him to checkout. He placed the purse on the counter and chose some earrings.

"Chad, I was going to run across the street and grab a sandwich for lunch. Would you like to go with me? Without Jessica here, I'd have to eat alone. Company would be great." Elizabeth asked as she rang up his purchases and placed them in a bag.

"That sounds good. I was planning on grabbing a bite anyway."

"Great. Let me go tell Mrs. Stanzel I am taking lunch and we can go."

Elizabeth let her boss know she was running across the street to grab a sandwich, grabbed her purse, and headed to the door with Chad. They walked the short distance across the street and into the deli. The smell of fresh-baked bread and sandwich meat accosted their senses as soon as they entered.

"It always smells so good in here!" Elizabeth inhaled the aroma as she approached the counter to place her order. She ordered a roast beef sandwich with coleslaw, chips, and water, paid at the register, and sat down at a corner table.

Chad took the seat across from her, placing her water on the table. She thanked him and took a big swig of the cool drink.

They made small talk while they waited for their sandwiches. Church, growing up around the area, and family were the topics of discussion. Finally, their food was placed in front of them, and all talking ceased while they started eating.

Chad finished his sandwich, wiped his mouth, took a drink of his coke, and looked at Elizabeth over his cup. "So, I know a lot about you now, but not if you have a boyfriend."

Elizabeth choked on her bite of coleslaw she just placed in her mouth. "Excuse me, that is rather random!"

"No, I mean, you are a pretty girl, my best friend seems interested, and I am just making sure he is not getting in the way of something and wasting his time."

"Your best friend seems interested? Interested in what and who?" Elizabeth stopped eating and looked at Chad directly into his eyes.

"Now, look, he hasn't said anything, but I haven't seen Jacob act the way he's been acting around you in quite a while. Just sayin' and making an observation."

"Oh, well in that case, no, there is no boyfriend. I am not sure, though, that Jacob is interested. We just talk. He's nice, and…"

"Nice? That's all you think he is, is nice? You don't think he is interesting, funny, outrageously handsome?"

"What!? None of that is any of your business!" Elizabeth turned away from him, feeling her cheeks turning hot.

"Do you really think he is interested? How interested?"

"Well, he doesn't usually run after girls in the church parking lot, so I would say pretty interested."

"Hmmm." was all Elizabeth replied and she felt a smile escape her lips. She looked at Chad and seeing the goofy questioning look on his face, busted out laughing.

Eventually she gained her composure, took a drink, and a bite of chips before answering him. "Chad, I need to get back to work. I will see you both at the bowling alley Saturday. Thanks for the lunch date."

"Date? Well then, I will make sure Jacob knows I went on a date with you. We will see how jealous he gets when he hears about this." Chad wiggled his eyebrows, grabbed their plates and trash, got up and walked to the trash can. Elizabeth, laughing, picked up her water, hung her purse over her arm, and followed Chad out the door. They said their goodbyes and Elizabeth walked across the street back to work.

Chapter 22

Elizabeth didn't have to work Thursday but stayed busy all morning running errands for her mother. When she finally got home later in the afternoon, she dressed in running shorts, a sports bra, and tied on her running shoes. She needed to go on a long run and get her mind focused and clear.

As she was making the last turn toward home, she noticed her handsome neighbor heading to the mailbox. Running shoes and shorts were his only attire. Man, did he look good shirtless! He must have been doing some yard work because there was grass on his shoes, and his chest was glistening with sweat. She hoped she wasn't staring at him, but at the same time, couldn't help herself, and truly didn't really care.

"Hey, Elizabeth. Looks like you made it home this time."

She stopped running and quickly monitored herself to make sure she didn't stink. "Hi, Jacob. You're funny.

Yeah, I guess I did, but I just went for a short run this time. Nothing to be concerned about." She answered back and walked across the yard to see him. "Looks like you've been working hard."

"Yeah, well not as hard as you. I hear you had a lunch date with Chad today. He said you had a thing for his sense of humor." Jacob smiled at her and Elizabeth didn't miss the fact that he was checking her out.

Laughing, Elizabeth shook her head "Yeah, well we had a date. We went and had sandwiches. I enjoyed talking with him. He's good company."

"I agree. He really is." Jacob wiped his hand across his face, smearing dirt across his forehead as he did.

"Umm, you made a mess." Elizabeth reached up and wiped the dirt from his forehead, then wiped her hand on her shorts, laughing at him.

"Yeah, I am sure I look a mess, and that didn't help. I need to grab a glass of water and clean up a bit. Want to come in and get a drink?"

Elizabeth agreed and followed him across the lawn, up the deck steps, and into the door to the kitchen.

"Grab some bottles of water from the fridge, will you?" Jacob crossed to the sink and washed his hands, threw water onto his face, and washed off the sweat and dirt.

Elizabeth went to the refrigerator, took out two water bottles and placed one on the counter next to her. She uncapped the other and took a drink.

She didn't realize how thirsty she was. The cold water was refreshing. Meanwhile, Jacob dried his hands off, walked to the counter, and grabbed his water. He downed the entire bottle of water in one gulp.

"I guess I needed that." He wiped the last drops of water from his chin and turned to face Elizabeth. He reached over and gently brushed some of her hair off her forehead and tucked it behind her ear.

"How are you feeling? I haven't seen you since I left you with your parents in the hospital."

Elizabeth couldn't help but notice how he looked at her. His gaze was so intense. His eyes were so blue, she felt as if she could get lost and drown looking into those eyes.

"I'm good." That was all she answered. There was nothing else to say.

"Good. You scared me, you know. I saw you, then you fell on the ground. I wasn't sure what happened." He moved closer to her and placed his empty water bottle on the counter next to him.

Not wanting to go further into this discussion, Elizabeth answered him quickly, letting him know it wasn't a big deal. "Thank you for being concerned, but you don't need to be. Really, everything is fine."

"Good to hear."

Holding her gaze, he again raised his hand to her face and brushed away the same stubborn lock of hair which couldn't seem to ever stay in place behind her ear.

He leaned in closer to her, and slowly, but gently brushed his lips against hers.

Her lips were cool and wet from the water. He liked the feel of them and the gentleness. He noticed she didn't resist, so he touched their lips together again. His lips were a little more demanding this time. Elizabeth eagerly answered back. Their lips both wanted what the other gave.

She moved in front of him, and put her hands on his hard, shirtless chest. He wrapped her in his arms, one hand on the small of her back, and the other cupping the back of her head. She moved her arms around his neck. Their mouths opened slightly, and their tongues touched. Elizabeth's senses soared.

He was demanding, yet gentle. Warm, yet hot at the same time. This kiss was nothing like she had ever experienced before. There was something to this, something she wasn't used to. It was full of desire, and wanting, yet something more. Caring.

She could feel that he cared about her and was truly concerned about what happened to her. As that realization filled her up, she broke the kiss, pulled away, and searched his face for answers.

He opened his eyes, and seeing her watching him, brushed his hand along the side of her face and touched their foreheads together. They were both catching their breath. He leaned in and placed another soft and gentle kiss on her lips.

"Wow! That was nice. Thank you." Jacob said as he looked at her.

Elizabeth moved her forehead off his, "Thank you for what?"

"For letting me kiss you." Elizabeth, taking in the sight of him, answered him by leaning back in and giving him another kiss. Their lips again opened so their tongues could take part.

"Let's go to the couch and find a show to watch." Jacob took her by the hand and didn't wait for her to respond. She didn't argue or pull away and she let him lead her into the living room and to the couch.

He sat down by the arm, and she sat down next to him. She leaned into his side as he placed his arm around her shoulder and clicked the remote. The TV turned on. He found the local news, turned her face to him, and placed his lips right back where they wanted to be.

The heat between them intensified as they got more and more into the kiss. His right hand found its way over her bra and rubbed her breast. Jacob leaned back to look at her. "Is this okay?" He asked, hoping he knew her answer.

Elizabeth nodded and pulled his face back to hers, while his hand found its way under her sports bra, to her breast. He rubbed her nipple, sending waves of heat and desire rushing from Elizabeth's groin up through her spine.

She groaned and repositioned herself to expose more of her breast to his large hand. He leaned her gently back onto the couch and lifted her sports bra to reveal what was underneath. Leaning down he took her breast into his mouth and sucked, then licked her now hard and erect nipple.

"Oh, Jacob," Elizabeth whispered while arching her back toward him. Realizing what was going on, Elizabeth suddenly lifted his head off her breast. He looked at her and seeing the ecstasy in her eyes, he crawled back up so their lips could meet.

The kiss, the couch, him, it was all amazing. But she knew it wasn't right. Placing her hands on the sides of his head, she gently pushed him away from her lips, breaking their connection.

Breathing hard, she breathlessly told him they had to stop.

"I have to go." Seeing him slowly close his eyes, she lifted her head slightly off the couch. "I'm sorry." She lifted herself up to place a kiss on his lips. "We need to slow down a little anyway. Trust me, I don't want to, but it is the right thing."

Jacob sat up and helped her to a seated position. With his hands on his knees and head down, he slowly regained his composure. "I know you're right, but it doesn't mean I have to like it."

He stood and offered her his hand. She pulled herself up to stand, smiled at him, and walked to the kitchen door with Jacob right behind.

He leaned around her and opened the door. As he leaned in, he spun her around. "I will let you go now, but know I am far from done with you. You drive me crazy."

Again, he leaned down and kissed her, hard. She eagerly answered his kiss.

Jacob reluctantly broke away and looked at her. "I'll see you tomorrow night, right?"

"I'm looking forward to it," Elizabeth answered with a big smile, she gave him one last kiss, they exchanged phone numbers, and he watched her as she crossed the yard to her house.

Elizabeth entered through the back door into the sunroom off the kitchen and hadn't gone more than a couple steps when reality came crashing down on her in the form of her mother.

"Lizzy, I am glad you're home. We got lucky and I got you an appointment Monday morning with an obstetrician. She can see you at eleven and can get your prenatal appointments started. She is a friend of a friend and had a cancellation. Isn't that great!" Elizabeth's mom greeted her daughter at the door and wrapped her in a huge hug after sharing the news.

Remembering the life inside her, Elizabeth answered her mother. "Yeah, that's great, Mom. I'm going up to take a shower before dinner."

Elizabeth went up the steps to her bathroom. Leaning on the sink with both hands, she stared at the reflection looking at her.

"What are you doing? But, God, he is amazing." She continued staring in shock and slight disappointment at her reflection, then finally shaking her head and sighing, she stripped off her clothes, and hopped in the shower.

Chapter 23

Stacey and Kristen pulled up in the driveway just in time to observe Elizabeth crossing the backyard toward her house. Elizabeth looked like she was on cloud nine and Stacey couldn't help but notice the way the girl touched her lips and had a bounce in her step.

"I wonder why she is looking so happy. Looks like we may have pulled in at a good time." Stacey looked at her friend and giggled when she saw the look of shock and frustration on Kristen's face.

"I don't know why she looked so happy, but I know she is so beneath Jacob, so there are no worries there." Kristen glared at the area Elizabeth disappeared.

Elizabeth was out of the girl's line of vision, "Well, let's go find out. Shall we?" Stacey got out of the car, put Kristen's arm in hers, and directed her to the front door and into the house. They found Jacob on the couch watching TV.

"Well, hello there, little brother." Stacey went to him and gave him a hug. "We just saw something interesting."

Stacey sat down in the chair opposite him with a Cheshire cat grin on her face.

Kristen plopped down next to him with a scowl. "Yeah, I would like to know what we just witnessed, also. We just saw the slut next door leave here with an awfully large grin on her face."

"Excuse me?" Jacob spun around shooting daggers at Kristen. "Who are you calling a slut? Sort of calling the kettle black, isn't it!? Anyway, why does it matter to either of you what Elizabeth was doing over here?" Jacob looked between the two girls with annoyance burning off him.

"Ignore her, Jacob," Stacey answered, shooting her friend a warning look. "Elizabeth looked happy, as she should, and it just seemed like she seemed happy. If you were with her, you would fully have my support. She is a great person."

"If you really need to know, though you don't, she just came in and had a drink. We got to talking, and well, the rest is none of your business." Jacob looked at his sister with a grin.

Stacey started to laugh and punched him in the arm. "You go, little brother."

"Really? Are you serious?" Kristen looked at her friend. "How can you be okay with this?"

"Kristen, stop! You promised you wouldn't." Stacey looked at her friend and spoke in a soft and frustrated tone.

"Yeah, well that was before this." Kristen turned away from Stacey and looked directly at Jacob. "You need to know something that your sister found out. It goes against everything you believe in." Kristen laid her hand on Jacob's leg trying to be comforting.

Jacob looked down at Kristen's perfectly manicured hand resting on his knee, then up into her eyes. "What are you talking about, Kristen? Just stop. This thing you think is between us, isn't. I am going out with Elizabeth Friday night. I like her and want to get to know her better. Leave her alone!"

He said this directly to the girl sitting next to him as he stood up in disgust ready to walk away from them both. Kristen stood up and grabbed his arm.

"Your sister found out…"

Stacey looked at her friend with disbelief. "Kristen, don't!"

Kristen shook her head and glanced at Stacey. "He needs to know the truth!" She then looked back at Jacob and grabbed both his arms in her hands so he would be focused on her. "Elizabeth is pregnant and is going to have an abortion, if she hasn't already had one."

Jacob stopped and searched Kristen's face. It took him a minute to process this news. Shaking and tilting his head in disbelief, he roughly threw Kristen's hands off his arms.

"I know you are a jealous person, Kristen, but why would you say that? Pregnant and an abortion? You are crazy!" Angry, Jacob walked away from the girls. He wanted his space.

Kristen, ignoring the signs, walked toward him, making sure he heard what she had to say. "I am not. Stacey walked into her house and saw Planned Parenthood on her computer, and when she questioned her, she asked Stacey to leave. She didn't want to talk about it."

Jacob looked at his sister. "Is this true?" He asked with hurt, disgust, and confusion in his eyes.

"Yes. Sort of," is all Stacey could say. She then explained to him what she saw that day she walked into Elizabeth's house to check on her. "...and when I asked her about it, she told me it was none of my business and asked me to leave. That is all I know."

"That makes you think she is pregnant and getting an abortion? You two are crazy. And you, Kristen, are just jealous because a sweet and gorgeous girl has moved next door to me. One I happen to be interested in. Get over yourself!"

Jacob stopped, looked at the women standing before him, and sighed. "I'm heading over to Chad's for a bit.

Hopefully, some of you will be gone when I get back." Without looking at his sister or Kristen, Jacob spun around and stomped toward the door, letting it slam behind him.

Chapter 24

Friday night was here before Elizabeth realized. Since she didn't have to work, she decided to spend her day getting ready for her night out bowling. She couldn't believe how excited she was to spend more time with Jacob.

She hadn't seen him since Wednesday and whenever she thought about the kiss, and the couch, her insides got warm and turned to mush. She could not remember the last time a guy made her feel that way. Just thinking about him made her warm inside. It wasn't just his body or looks either. He really seemed to be a caring person. With Chad and Jessica there it wouldn't be a real date, but that was what made this even better. There was no pressure on either of them. It was just four friends hanging out and getting to know each other better.

Deciding to primp on herself more than usual, she decided to get a pedicure, and if they had space, even a manicure. A couple hours later, her feet were soaking in very warm water, and she was relaxing in a chair set to massage her back with fake hands. The massage and the warm water were blissful. She missed pampering herself like this.

Once her bright pink polish was on her toes, her legs massaged, warm towel removed from her legs, and her sandals placed gently on her feet, Elizabeth got up carefully and walked over to the manicure station. She took her place at the manicurist's counter and enjoyed small talk while her nails were done. Soon she felt as beautiful as she looked.

When Elizabeth got home, she made herself a cup of coffee just as Jessica knocked on the door. She entered the house and the kitchen, fixed herself a cup of coffee also, and made herself comfortable at the counter.

"So, when was the last time you bowled?" Jessica sipped her coffee and watched Elizabeth over her steaming cup. Taken slightly aback at the briskness in her friend's voice Elizabeth answered rather timidly.

"Well, hi to you too. It has been a while, more than a while. Probably a few years?" This answer came out as more of a question than a definite answer. The look of intensity radiating from Jessica threw Elizabeth off. "I'm sure I will be a bit rusty."

"Hmmm, well the last time we had this bowling outing, a few months ago, me and my partner, her name was Diana, lost to the guys. It was not pretty, and I have been practicing. I am seeking revenge tonight and hope you can step up to the plate."

"Wow! Okay, just so you know, I will probably disappoint you. Unless of course we can have those kiddy bumpers up."

The shock on Jessica's face was too much and Elizabeth busted out in a laugh. She pushed her friend to get her to smile and relax a little. "Come on. It is only a game, right? Fun, friends, bowling, laughs. Right?"

Jessica put down her coffee and smiled, "Yeah, you're right. The guys were all hooting and hollering and getting their manly egos so big it was annoying. I'm not a good sport when I lose. Even when I stink at something, I still get competitive."

Elizabeth smiled, finishing the rest of her coffee. "Competitive? Well, let me ask you a question then. A serious question." She paused, not sure how to continue. Looking directly at Jessica, she just asked the question that was bothering her. "How competitive are you when it comes to Jacob and other girls?"

"Jacob? Why, what's up?"

"Just wondering if there are any feelings left at all. I know what you say, but I'm just making sure."

Elizabeth and Jessica looked at each other and Jessica had a small smile break across her face. "Are you interested in Jacob? How interested?"

Elizabeth tried to keep eye contact with her friend but started blushing and looked away.

"Well, perhaps we had a little moment, and maybe I can't stop thinking about it and him. But I am concerned about you, and how you will feel about it." Now that she had that confession out, she studied Jessica for a reaction.

Jessica reached across the table, raised her eyebrows, and smirked, her eyes shining. "I think that is amazing. Trust me, I am over all that. I thought we had something, but now, really, I have no more feelings for him and am glad we have kept our friendship. A little moment? Come on, do tell." Jessica pressed her friend further.

"Just one time, he might have kissed me." Jessica pressed Elizabeth to continue. "It was a great kiss, and well, man, he is sexy!" The girls busted out laughing.

"Yeah, that he is." Jessica saluted her with her cup of coffee, then finished it off. She stood up from her stool at the counter. "I am glad he likes you. You are such a better choice than Kristen. Just watch out for her. If she finds out you two are starting a thing, she will have it in for you next."

Elizabeth rolled her eyes. "Thanks for the warning. I'll keep it in mind. Come on, let's get out of here. I have been waiting to see him again."

Jessica laughed. "Oh, I guess this is like your first date then. Can't wait to see how it goes. Let's get going." The girls left the house together. Jessica took the short drive to The Pizza Place just in case she needed to find her own ride home.

Soon the girls found themselves parking, then walked into the restaurant. The smell of garlic and pepperoni hit them as they entered. Being relatively early for a Friday night, it was simple to find a seat in the bar area. The girls ordered drinks, Jessica a coke, Elizabeth a water, and some garlic bread knots with marinara to hold them over until the boys arrived. They waited for their food and were singing to the latest country song which was playing through the speakers throughout the bar.

"Well, look at these beauties." The girls looked up and noticed Chad and Jacob heading toward them. Elizabeth's eyes caught Jacob's and she could not stop the grin that spread across her face.

He looked amazing in a pair of black Nike shorts, a sky-blue T-shirt, and a pair of tennis shoes, casual, yet sexy all the same. When they got to the table, Chad made a move to sit down by Elizabeth, but Jacob caught his arm, pulled him away, and took the seat next to her.

Chad put his hands up in submission "Okay, okay. No need to be rude. I guess I will let you sit next to her. We already had a date. She's sweet, but not my type. My type is petite brunettes." He slid in next to Jessica and put his arm on the back of the booth behind her.

Jessica looked at him, laughing at the crazy guy. "You and Elizabeth had a date? Why did I not hear about this?" she asked, turning to Elizabeth.

Shaking her head, Elizabeth also laughed at the silliness of the situation. "Yeah, we had a date just the other day. Chad came by the boutique when I was on my way to lunch, and he tagged along. Just like a little puppy." The look of shock on Chad's face made them all burst out laughing at his expense.

"Oh, whatever. I'm hurt, but will forgive you this time, since it seems you have your eyes set on my handsome friend. I will step aside to give him a chance."

Chad leaned across the table at his best friend and placed a good-natured smack at his arm. "You got this man."

Jacob placed his arm across Elizabeth's shoulders, looking at her for the first time since he sat down. "Thanks, man. I appreciate you letting me borrow this beauty."

Elizabeth looked him in the eye. "Condescending much? Borrow? I don't think so." She reached up to remove his arm and slid away a little. Taking part in this friendly banter and flirting made her feel good, part of a friend group again, and the fact that Jacob sat down by her and felt comfortable enough to put his arm around her, claiming her, made her bubble with warmth.

"Whoa, whoa, whoa, please don't go so far away." Jacob slid over and grabbed her hand under the table.

"Ignore my friend. He's just jealous that he doesn't get to go out with you a second time. It's my turn." She couldn't help but notice the gleam in his eye when he smiled. Looking at him lit her up and warmed her. She couldn't help that either.

"I think I'll let you go out with me tonight, but I do have to let you know I have already promised my amazing pro-quality bowling skills to Jessica. She and I are a team."

"Pro-quality bowling skills. We will have to see about that." He squeezed her hand, then placed his arm back around her shoulders. Elizabeth could not stop the butterflies from fluttering in her stomach, or the heat from building inside her either. This guy was too much, but she gladly scooted over closer to him in the booth.

The four ordered their pizzas and the guys ordered beer. Soon, they were eating and laughing together. The mood at the table was easy, like they had all been friends forever. The three of them had known each other awhile, Elizabeth was the new one, but she felt like she belonged. Truly belonged.

Chapter 25

When they were finished eating, and the girls both insisted on paying for half of the bill, they left the restaurant and went to the parking lot. The night was a perfect, almost July night in the south. The sun was still up. It was hot and humid but smelled of summer, trees, flowers, fresh-cut grass. Elizabeth was loving life. Jacob even took the chance and grasped her hand in his. She looked up at him and smiled a shy smile. He smiled his large, beautiful smile back at her.

"Jessica, you don't mind swapping co-pilots with me, do you? I would like to spend some time with this one alone." Jacob swung Elizabeth's hand to his lips and gave her knuckles a soft kiss.

"No, that sounds good to me. I guess I can handle Chad instead. If it's good with Elizabeth, that is."

Elizabeth grinned. "Yeah. I think it's good with me." Everyone headed toward their prospective cars.

"Umm, no one asked me what I thought about these arrangements. But driving with a girl over him, I guess I can be good with it too." Chad jumped in the front seat of Jessica's car,

Jessica looked at Elizabeth and laughed. "We'll see you two there. Don't take any detours. We need to get this rematch started."

Jacob opened the passenger door of his Jeep for Elizabeth. She climbed in and waited for him to join her.

Jacob climbed into the front seat, turned on the car, then turned to look at her. Those butterflies were there again, making sure she knew she and Jacob were not alone.

"I have been waiting to do this since I saw you sitting in that booth." Jacob reached over, placed his hand on the side of her face and gently pulled her toward him. Elizabeth did not resist. Instead, she placed her hand behind his neck and pulled him closer to close what little space there was left between them. She wanted, no needed, to feel his lips on hers.

They devoured each other like they hadn't eaten in days. Their lips opened and their tongues touched. The heat outside joined them in the small space of the Jeep.

They couldn't get close enough, or kiss hard enough. Jacob's lips left hers and found her chin. Elizabeth tilted her head back to oblige him. Her breath caught in her throat as he continued his kisses on her chin, then her neck, and he finally traveled down to her chest. He paused with his lips hovering over her skin, catching his breath.

He brushed her cleavage lightly with his lips. Elizabeth's breath was hard, she softly groaned as he started back up her body. She swore her heart would explode. The feel of him hovering just above her skin drove her wild. His soft lips on her skin felt amazing. She grabbed his head and led his lips back to hers. Their kiss, demanding at first, became slower, then more relaxed.

Jacob let out a soft groan and brushed his hand along her bare arm. "I missed you. I thought about this moment all last night and all day today." He looked at her with a look of pure desire.

"You did?" That was all Elizabeth could think of asking, as she got lost in his sea of blue.

"Why should that surprise you? You are amazing and beautiful. I absolutely adore you."

Elizabeth thought her face would crack if she smiled anymore. She placed her hand on the side of his face. "Wow! Thank you. I must admit, I've been waiting for tonight also."

"Good. I was worried it was all one sided." Jacob placed a quick kiss on her lips again and slid back to his place at the steering wheel. "I guess we need to get going. I feel a butt whooping about to happen." With this, he looked at her and wiggled his eyebrows. She laughed and clicked on her seat belt.

Elizabeth quickly remembered why bowling wasn't on her list of top things to do on a Friday night. Her ball seemed to have a magnet inside it which attracted it to the gutter. She had yet to knock down more than three pins in a turn. Luckily, the company made up for her lack of athleticism.

Jacob was up. His approach was something magical to watch, his stance and how he approached the foul line and let the ball fly. It made Elizabeth smile as she watched the muscles under his tight shirt ripple with exertion. Again, there was a loud CRACK as his ball expertly crashed into the sweet spot and all the pins fell on command.

"YEAH! There ya go, Brotha'!" Whooped Chad. Jacob did a quick spin on his toes with his hands in the air and came toward Elizabeth with a slight slide in his step. He wrapped her in a hug and planted a deep kiss on her lips.

"That's for good luck." He smiled and gave her bottom a quick smack as she walked by him.

"Thanks. I sure do need it."

"Good thing is you can only improve!" Chad yelled this from the bench at the side of the alley.

"Hey, be nice. No heckling the other team." Jessica gave his arm a punch and took a drink of her coke.

Elizabeth laughed at all of them, picked up her bowling ball and approached the lane.

Letting the ball go, it made its way toward the pins much slower and without the effect of Jacob's, but it stayed in the center. It lightly hit the main pin, and she watched with excitement, as three pins toppled into others, and those toppled down more. When they were all finished falling, there were just two pins left standing.

Jessica jumped off the bench. "Yeah! That's my teammate!" Elizabeth turned around and did a little laughing jig up the alley.

Jacob was there and high fived her and planted a congratulatory kiss on her lips. "That's my girl!" Elizabeth caught the term of endearment and loved the fact that he claimed her as his own already.

Even though her second turn resulted in zero pins falling, she didn't complain. That was the most pins she knocked down in one turn all night. She was totally enjoying herself with this new group that she happily called her friends and an amazing guy who seemed to have eyes only for her.

As the game ended, the guys returned their shoes and the girls settled at a table near their lane. "I must admit, you and Jacob look good together. He really seems to like you. He never takes his eyes off you, especially when you approach the lane and do that little bend-over-release thing you do. I think he likes your butt." Elizabeth opened her mouth with shock.

"Yeah, I agree with that. She does have an amazing ass, and in those jeans, she is driving me crazy." Elizabeth, not knowing the guys were so close, turned quickly to see them sitting down. Jacob had hotdogs and fries for all of them on a tray, and Chad was carrying a pitcher of beer and four cups.

Jacob took the seat next to Elizabeth and planted a soft kiss on her cheek. "Your ass is amazing, along with the rest of you." He placed the tray on the table and turned his head toward her.

Elizabeth loved how his comments made her feel. With a smile, she couldn't help herself any longer and she pulled his face toward her and planted a kiss on his lips. It was a long, soft kiss which ended too soon. Chad and his comments didn't allow any more public displays of affection. "Thank you." Was all Elizabeth said to Jacob as she looked directly into his eyes and gave a smile only for him.

They passed around the food and poured beer for everyone. Elizabeth picked up her cup and started gulping it. She didn't realize how thirsty she was. She paused quickly, remembering her situation and placed the cup down on the table and decided to sip instead. She didn't want to bring attention to herself and didn't want anyone to think anything. So, she drank enough to not gain suspicion, without really drinking anything at all.

They ate, drank, and talked. Chad was fun to be around sober, but when intoxicated, he became downright hilarious.

Suddenly, Jacob's arm wrapped tightly around her, and he leaned in to whisper in Elizabeth's ear.

"Are you good?" he asked with concern. Elizabeth turned to look at him and nodded her head.

"Why do you think I wouldn't be?" She laid her hand on his leg.

"No reason. Just wondering. Are you ready to go?" The look he pressed into her eyes made her insides flutter.

"Yeah, I think so." She gave him a small, crooked smile and squeezed his thigh. They exited the booth.

"Hey, where are you two going?" Chad slurred his words. "It's not the end of the night yet."

Jessica patted him on the shoulder. "I think they have better things to do than hang out with us. I'll take you home after we play another game."

"You'll take me home, will you? I like how that sounds." Jessica rolled her eyes and got up to give her friends a goodbye hug.

"Y'all have fun!" She said with a smile and a squeeze of Elizabeth's arm.

Chapter 26

Jacob pulled in his driveway, and they got out of his Jeep. They met each other at his walkway, and he put his arms around her to stop her from going anywhere. They turned their faces toward each other.

"You got a little quiet. Are you sure everything's okay?" Jacob asked with concern.

Again, she nodded her head. "Yes, I'm fine."

He stared at her, looking into her eyes. The gaze he sent her made her a little uneasy, like words were unsaid between them and he was searching for something. Then as quickly as it came, it was gone. He leaned down and gave her a quick, but deep kiss. "Do you need to go, or can you come inside for a bit?"

She answered him by returning a kiss to his lips. "I'd love to come in."

They entered his house through the back door into the kitchen. There was a note on the counter from Stacey.

Jacob read it, and smiling, he turned toward Elizabeth. "Looks like we have the house to ourselves. Stacey won't be home till late tomorrow. She's with Kristen then going to work."

Elizabeth took the letter from his hand, read it, then turned to look at him. The look on his face caught her by surprise. Desire was in his eyes. And something else. Hunger?

She placed the letter on the counter and stepped toward him, unable to keep herself away from him any longer. "What should we do about that?" She stared directly into his sexy blue eyes.

He shook his head slowly and closed the rest of the space between them. "All night you have been driving me crazy!" He caught her in his grasp and crushed his lips to hers.

She was quickly caught up in him with yearning and wrapped her arms around his neck with cobra-like strength. The taste of his lips was amazing. Her need for him threw her for a loop. Her insides were on fire. He broke their kiss long enough to lead her into his room.

At his door, she hesitated. Noticing her hesitation, he stopped and dropped her hand, and gave a questioning look. She looked down at his chest and placed both her hands there, over his heart. Her hands felt his heart beating fast and the muscles of his chest rippling under her touch. They made their way around his back and down to his tight, strong ass.

She closed her eyes for a second, trying to decide if she could do the right thing and leave right now before things went too far. It wasn't fair to ask him to deal with her reality. If she continued with this, the decisions she needed to make would become more difficult. Opening her eyes, and looking up into his, she noticed something new there, but wasn't sure what it was.

It didn't matter. Need. Desire. Lust. Those feelings took over her. She quickly closed the gap which had formed between them, squeezed his ass, and clamped her lips on his. She had never wanted anything so much in her life.

Things happened quickly. Not letting go of her lips, or her, Jacob kicked his door closed and dragged them both to his bed. They fell onto the bed with their arms wrapped around each other.

Elizabeth separated herself from him long enough to stand up and do a strip tease in front of him. She pulled her shirt seductively over her head. She stood before him in her sexy black lace bra. His look of desire was evident. He reached toward her, but shaking her head, she took another step back, undid her pants and slowly slid them down past her ass, her thighs, and finally kicked off her sandals and stepped out of her pants. She stood before him in a black lace bra and matching thong.

He moved too quickly for her now and he grabbed her around the waist, throwing her on the bed. She squealed with pleasure, a smile coming to her lips, which he quickly smothered with his mouth. Stopping, he knelt above her, taking her all in. Slowly she reached behind her back, unhooked her bra, and slid the straps down her arms. He grabbed it from her, taking in the sight of her now naked breasts. His eyes traveled down to her scant pair of panties. Slightly raising her hips, she wriggled out of them and tossed them to the floor. Again, he was above her, watching her. His jaw twitched. He passed his hand down her front, over her breast and stopped at her stomach. The feeling of his touch lit a fire deep inside her.

She needed to see him naked also. She pulled at his shirt. He helped her by tugging it over his head, then he got up off the bed, unbuckled his shorts, pulled them down, and jumped back onto the bed beside her.

He lay beside her, staring at her nakedness. He rubbed his hands across her breast, down her chest, and between her legs. She was wet. He could feel how much she wanted him. She groaned despite herself and pulled down his boxers.

He was then lying naked next to her, and she took his hardness in her hand. He returned the groan and grabbed her head bringing it closer to him. They kissed with a need and a yearning that ate through Elizabeth's body.

Jacob's hands pressed her and groped her in all the right places. She returned the favor.

Finally, when she thought she would die from anticipation, she pulled him over her. He understood what she wanted. He paused long enough to open the drawer in the small table by his bed, took out a condom, placed it on his hardness, and entered her waiting, warm, and wet body.

Elizabeth was lying on his chest catching her breath when they were both finished. It was pure bliss what they just did, lying here, and naked in Jacob's bed. She kissed his chest; he rubbed her head. Placing her head on his shoulders, he lifted her mouth toward his.

They lost themselves in a deep, deep kiss. Jacob rolled on top of Elizabeth, smothering her again in him. His kisses trailed slowly down her body driving her wild with ecstasy. Soon she found herself filled with him again. Their bodies rocked together in a rhythm which took them both to the crest together.

Exhausted, exhilarated, and happy, Elizabeth found herself dozing off in Jacob's arms.

She awoke to the sun peeking through the curtain. Even though her eyes were closed, she felt Jacob's arms around her and snuggled back to his embrace. He tightened his hold on her and kissed the side of her head. "MMMM. Good morning"

Elizabeth answered by rolling over and placing a delicate kiss on his lips. "Good morning back." She rested her head on the pillow and opened her eyes to see him watching her. He smiled. She smiled back.

"You are beautiful, even in the morning." He ran his hands through her hair pulling her face back toward him. They started, again, getting into a deep passionate kiss, but Elizabeth pulled away.

"As much as I would love nothing more than to spend the day here, under the covers, naked with you, I really need to go home, take a shower and let my parents know I am still alive."

"I guess you're right. But give me another minute." He started kissing her all over and feeling her body. She found herself, once more, lost in Jacob.

Finally, they were finished again. He kissed her long, and deep, as she giggled and pushed him away.

Looking in her eyes, he smiled at her. "Can I see you later?"

"I would love that." Elizabeth finished her answer with another kiss on his lips. She rolled out of bed and put on her clothes quickly before she was enticed to stay again. She opened his bedroom door and turned back to look at him. She smiled at what she saw. He was lying without blankets in pure, beautiful nakedness.

Looking him up and down, she responded with difficulty. "I really wish I didn't have to go, but I'll see ya later." She smiled, waved, looked directly into his eyes, and blew a kiss in his direction as she exited and closed the door behind her.

Chapter 27

Elizabeth quietly crept into her house, up the stairs, and into the shower. She had to get ready for work and was running a little behind. Soon she was bouncing down the steps and into the kitchen to grab a bagel. She said a quick good morning to her mother and headed out the door. There was a surprise waiting by her car and she broke into a big smile when she saw it.

Jacob, in a pair of shorts and sandals leaned against her door.

"Good morning, beautiful." he said, wrapping his arms around her, as she melted into his embrace.

"Didn't I just leave you?" she asked, wrapping her arms around his neck.

"What, do you not want to see me, or get a kiss before work? If not, I can go." Jacob joked around pretending to leave but didn't get far. She did not let go of him and tugged him back.

"Don't you dare go anywhere." She put her mouth on him in a soft, slow kiss. "Mmm. That was nice and a great way to leave for work."

"I'm glad I could help you start your day in a positive way." He smiled and kissed her again lightly. "I'll see you later. Maybe I will make us a nice dinner."

"I'm looking forward to it." He opened the door for her, she got in, started the car, and pulled out of the driveway.

Soon Elizabeth pulled into the parking lot at the boutique. She parked in what she had come to see as her spot, turned off the car and stared at the scene before her. They had placed some benches under a tree, with a bird bath and a garden table to give guests a place to sit and relax. Elizabeth was awed at the sight in front of her. There, like at home, she watched two cardinals land in the bird bath. A bright red male and a female sporting light brown, red-tipped feathers, and a red beak.

A saying her grandmother used to tell her came to her mind.

Red bird, red bird, fly to the right... I hope to see my honey tonight.

All the time Elizabeth saw the cardinals at her house, she was reminded of the fact that they mate for life, and here was the first time she thought of this saying. Thinking this helped her to feel happier than she has in a while.

She will be seeing her honey tonight. The thought made her smile. She got out of the car and, with a bounce in her step, approached the boutique, plucked some dead flowers from the flowers in the pot by the front door, and entered the store.

"Good morning, Mrs. Stanzel. Good morning, Jessica." Elizabeth went over to her friend and gave her a big hug, clocked in for the day, and got to work arranging and rearranging displays, and dusting shelves.

"Well, someone is in a good mood this morning." Jessica approached her with an amused look.

"I don't know what you mean." Elizabeth didn't make eye contact when she said this, but broke out in a big, goofy grin.

"I am going to guess that someone had a good night last night and that is what's causing this bounce in your step and bubbliness to your personality." Jessica grabbed the dusting spray and cloth from Elizabeth so she would have to stop working and look at her.

"A good night, yes. And a good morning." With this confession, Elizabeth received a smack of shock and amazement from Jessica

"What! Oh, my, gosh! Are you serious?" Jessica was jumping up and down in front of Elizabeth. "Please tell!"

"No. I will not. Some things are secret, amazing secrets, but still secret." Both girls made eye contact and Jessica squealed in delight, Elizabeth found amusement in her friend's reaction, gave her a hug, and let her know they needed to get back to work.

It was a great day. Elizabeth was floating on a cloud of happiness full of memories of last night with Jacob. There was nothing that could deflate her mood or bring her back down to earth.

Except for the customer who came in later that afternoon. Stacey. She approached Elizabeth with a serious look on her face. "Do you have a minute? We need to talk."

Elizabeth put down the stock she was placing on shelves when she saw the serious look painted on Stacey's face. "Uh, sure. Jessica, I'm gonna step outside for a bit."

Jessica was checking out a customer, so she just gave her a thumbs up. Stacey turned and walked toward the door and Elizabeth followed.

The girls did not say a word until they got to the benches and bird bath where Elizabeth saw the mated cardinals earlier in the day. Stacey then turned toward her, crossed her arms across her body and shot daggers at Elizabeth. "What the hell are you doing?"

Elizabeth was taken off guard, and seriously confused with the question.

She put her hands up in a questioning gesture. "I'm sorry, but I don't think I understand."

"You and my brother? He really likes you, but what about being pregnant? Have you had your abortion yet, or are you just gonna string him on and expect him to take in a baby?"

The realization of what Stacey said sent shock waves through Elizabeth. "Please keep your voice down! I haven't told anyone yet."

"Yeah, I'm aware of that!"

"Jesus, Stacey. I'm not stringing your brother on. I happen to like him, and no, I haven't done anything yet. Not that it's any of your business."

"When my brother is involved, it is my business." Stacey was shooting daggers at Elizabeth. "Wait a minute, you're not planning on having an abortion, are you? You changed your mind. I can see it in your eyes."

"Stacey, again it is none of your business what I do, but honestly, yes, I have decided to keep it. I wouldn't ask him to deal with any of this. It is not his problem, so things have gotten a little more difficult."

"Well, my only concern is Jacob, and I can tell you he doesn't need another broken heart. So, stop whatever you're doing with him, and make a decision. Not being honest with him is not fair. I don't want to make a bigger deal about this than necessary, but you should know he already knows you're pregnant."

"What? What do you mean he knows? How does he know? Who told him? When?" Shock and fear were plastered on Elizabeth's face.

"I told Kristen, and she told him. Thursday. Please just deal with this and let him know what you need to tell him, and soon." With this Stacey spun around and stalked off across the parking lot.

Elizabeth turned and plopped herself down on the bench watching the cardinals in the bird bath. "I cannot believe he knew Friday night. That must be why there were times he seemed off. What a mess."

She thought back to the night, and morning, she and Jacob just had together. Realization washed over her. She knew there was no way what they had would be able to become more. She couldn't and wouldn't ask him to stay with her as she got fatter, and then after she became a mother. This baby is not his problem, and she wants to make sure it stays that way. He doesn't need any of this.

Turning, she noticed the cardinals were still in the bird bath. As she watched, the male cardinal looked her way, chirped at his mate, and they flew off together.

Elizabeth walked slowly and thoughtfully back to the boutique. Concern and confusion washed through her. *What am I gonna do? Jacob's gonna hate me or at least be so disappointed.* What started out as an amazing weekend now became a nightmare. She was looking forward to seeing Jacob tonight but not now. She decided to give him a heads up and sent him a text telling him about Stacey's visit.

Your sister just stopped by the boutique and wasn't happy. We need to talk tonight.

Okay. What's going on? Everything alright? – Jacob

We will talk tonight. I'll see you soon.

She added a kissy face emoji to her text to make it seem like it wasn't such a big deal. She waited for an answer from Jacob but didn't receive one. Watching her phone screen, she realized how nervous she became. Tears started falling from her eyes. Wiping her face, she walked in the door of the boutique and got back to work. She might as well take her mind off the discussion she is about to have with a guy she cares about.

Jessica looked at her as she entered the store. She looked concerned and shot a look at Elizabeth. Elizabeth just smiled at her and went to assist some customers. Luckily the boutique was busy enough, so the girls didn't have time to talk. Jessica couldn't ask any questions anyway that Elizabeth wanted to answer.

Chapter 28

When Elizabeth got home from work, she quickly went into her house. She needed a cup of coffee and hopefully some time with her mom. Thankfully, her mother was reading a book in the sunroom when Elizabeth walked in, and the smell of fresh coffee filled the air. She grabbed a cup out of the cabinet and said hi to her mom as she filled her cup and fixed her coffee. Her mother looked up as Elizabeth sat down next to her.

Laying her book down, she turned and faced her daughter. "Haven't seen you much the past couple days. How are you feeling?"

It was a simple question. It required a simple answer, but instead of answering with words, Elizabeth answered her mom with tears. Again, her tears were like a broken damn. She had to put her coffee cup down or she would spill it. All the stress she felt from her talk with Stacey came bubbling to the top. Her mother reached over and wrapped her daughter in a hug, said nothing, and just let her cry. Eventually, Elizabeth's tears dried up and she calmed down. Mrs. Parks patiently waited for her daughter to start talking.

"It's been a hard day, Mom." Elizabeth pulled a tissue from the box on the table and wiped her eyes and blew her nose. Her mother just nodded her head and waited.

Elizabeth knew her mother and knew she was going to wait for Elizabeth to talk. If she wanted to leave and not talk, that would be fine too. It always amazed her how patient her mother was and how easy it was to talk to her. She should have been a psychologist.

"I screwed things up, Mom." She paused, not really wanting to say anything, but knew she had to. "Jacob and I have been talking, and we like each other. We did things, and now I need to stop things. Break things off between us. He will hate me anyway, once I tell him about the baby, but he sure doesn't need to waste his time on me."

Tears started again, but Elizabeth was determined to finish what she wanted to say. "I always make wrong decisions, Mom. Why? Why can't I just be like other girls? Have fun if I want? Have a great guy like me? But no! I get pregnant doing what everyone has done, and when a great guy does end up liking me, I screw that up also! I am such an idiot!" Tears fell again and she reached out for another tissue, wiping violently at her face and nose.

Elizabeth's mom lowered her head, breaking their eye contact and let out a heavy sigh. Looking back into her daughters face she gave her a frustrated shake of her head. "There is nothing I can say except that you need to stop being so hard on yourself. What other girls do, or don't do, doesn't matter anymore. You made your choices. You made mistakes, but you are not an idiot. You made a bad choice, and it sounds like that is continuing. Look, your dad and I weren't born yesterday. We know you did things in college that don't make us happy." With this she gestured toward her daughter's belly. "And we also know you didn't come home last night. With what you just said, I figure you spent the night with Jacob, and he didn't know about your pregnancy. That was wrong. You need to fix it. If he is upset and decides not to see you again, that is his decision. You need to worry about yourself. The drama has got to go." Her eyes held Elizabeth's.

"I know, Mom. He asked me to come for dinner tonight. I'll go over now and tell him everything. You're right. He deserves to know the truth."

Elizabeth stood up and leaned over to hug her mom. "I love you, Mom." She gave her an extra big squeeze, left the kitchen through the back door, and headed toward Jacob's before she lost her nerve.

Chapter 29

Elizabeth paused at the back door but didn't have to wait long before it opened. Jacob stood there in black running shorts and a tight, gray T-shirt which showed off the outline of his chest and abs. Elizabeth looked away, took a breath, then looked back into his sea-blue eyes.

"Hi." She gave him an unsure crooked smile. "Can we talk?" He nodded and took a step back into his kitchen.

"No, I'd rather speak out here." Jacob shrugged and gave her a confused look but followed her.

She stopped at the couch, decided against sitting down and went over to the railing instead. Jacob grabbed her from behind and turned her to face him. He reached out to pull her closer, but she stepped back and put her hand up to keep him from touching her or getting too close.

"Please don't. I need to tell you something, and if you hug me, or kiss me, I'll lose my nerve."

Jacob looked at her. The hurt and confusion were clear in his eyes. "Elizabeth, what's going on? What are you not telling me?"

She took a deep breath, gaining courage. "Your sister came to the boutique today. She told me Kristen said something to you." She watched his face.

Understanding dawned on his handsome features. "Yeah, she did. Is it true?"

Taking another deep breath, Elizabeth turned away from him and leaned on the railing of the deck. "Yes. It's true. I'm sorry. I should have told you." She turned her head to look at him. There was fury in his face, almost to the point of hatred.

"Jacob?" Elizabeth, surprised at the look she saw, stepped closer to him, and placed her hand on his arm.

"Seriously?! Why would you do that? I thought I knew you!" Jacob roughly brushed her hand from his arm and took a step away from her.

"Wait!" Elizabeth tried to figure out what his comments were about. It didn't make sense. "I don't understand. Why would I do what?" She knew she needed to clear things up, but how could this be a reaction to her being pregnant?

"An abortion, Elizabeth! When you're pregnant, sometimes people take the easy way out and get an abortion. I know that is the choice you made."

"Who told you that? Wait, is that what Kristen said?"

Jacob looked at her with his eyes wide and shooting daggers at her.

"Jacob, yes, I am pregnant. But I didn't have an abortion. I thought about it and thought about it."

"Was it that much on your mind?" It was like he was accusing her.

"Yes. It was." Elizabeth breathed hard and placed her hand on her head. She felt a headache coming. She was already tired of all this extra stress.

"Look, honestly, I didn't know what I was going to do. I thought an abortion would be an easy decision, but it wasn't. I also couldn't picture being a mother. Either way, it was gonna suck for me. If I had an abortion, I would live with that forever. My parents would have been disappointed, and I would have lost you."

She paused and touched the side of his face, making him look in her eyes. "But now, I have decided to keep it. I just found you. I like this. I like us." Elizabeth dropped her hand and put more separation between them. "I'm gonna be a mom. It's been a lot for me to take in, but I'm good with it now. But we can't be together. It's not fair to you."

He walked to her and placed his hand on her arm. "Why do you think we can't be together? We can still see where this goes." He looked at her and pulled her to him, kissing her lightly on her lips. It was a sweet, tender kiss. One she wished would never end, but when it did, she put space between their lips.

"I can't and won't do that to you. I'm sorry. We need to stop. I must focus on what I need to do, and I don't need to put you through that also."

She leaned in and brushed her lips against his again. "Thank you for this weekend, Jacob." Her hand lingered on his cheek. Her eyes watched his. She wanted to remember how he felt; she wanted to burn his eyes into her memory, those beautiful sea-blue eyes.

Finally, she let her hand fall to her side, she turned and walked away before he saw the tears fall from her eyes.

Elizabeth sat on the bench outside her kitchen door and put her face in her hands. A low serene chirping made her look up. The cardinals were on her fence singing a song together. "You two are so lucky. You will never have to be alone. You know you're loved and wanted." She continued watching the birds until they flew away together singing their love song.

Looking down, Elizabeth touched, then rubbed her stomach for the first time.

Chapter 30

"You ready, hun?" Mrs. Parks quietly entered Elizabeth's room. Elizabeth looked up from where she was sitting on her bed and gave her mom a small smile.

"Yeah. I am." Her mom came over and sat down beside her, placing her arm around Elizabeth, and pulling her close. Elizabeth rested her head on her mom's shoulder and closed her eyes taking a deep breath. Knowing her mother was there with her helped her to relax.

"You didn't talk to us when you came back in the house last night and I wanted to give you space. How did things go with Jacob?"

Elizabeth shook her head. "I don't want to talk about it." She sighed. "Mom." She sat up and looked at the woman sitting next to her. "I told him about the baby." For the second time she placed her hand on her stomach. "It scares me to death, the thought of becoming a mom, but I have no choice and I can't make this a part of his life, too." She was looking down at the hand still moving in a circle on her stomach then she slowly looked at her mother.

Her mom lifted Elizabeth's chin, gave her a smile, and pushed the hair off her forehead and behind her daughter's ear. "I'm proud of you. I know that was a hard decision, but it will all work out." They gave each other a hug and left for the doctor's office.

Later, in her car on her way to the boutique, Elizabeth could not stop thinking of her morning. The obstetrician wasn't as bad as she feared it would be, though, it was a little uncomfortable. The doctor said she was in perfect health and performed another ultrasound. Everything was perfect. The baby is healthy, and Elizabeth is healthy. She will be a mother around November 23rd. Near Thanksgiving. Elizabeth's mom was thrilled and called the baby the best Thanksgiving gift ever.

When she parked and turned off her car, she laid her head on the steering wheel. "Breathe, Liz. Just breathe. One day at a time!" Talking to herself and taking a few deep breaths seemed to help. She felt calmer and steadier. She was ready to face the next few hours at the boutique. "I am so glad it's a short day."

Lifting her head, she spoke words that didn't feel real until this moment. "I am going to be a mom around Thanksgiving. Oh my God!"

This was real. Elizabeth knew she was pregnant, knew she was going to be a mom, but reality did not really set in until the moment the doctor gave her a due date. She felt as if she were in a dream, but she wasn't. This was real.

The boutique was busier than usual when Elizabeth walked in, so she got straight to work. She helped one man and his boys find the perfect gift for his wife and their mother's birthday. She checked out some teenagers and their clothing finds. The busy and chaotic atmosphere was exactly what she needed to get her mind off things and pass the time.

"Wow, what an afternoon!" Jessica came over to her, placing her arm around Elizabeth's shoulder. "You have been quiet today. I feel like we haven't even said hi to each other since you walked in. How are you doing? I haven't seen you all weekend."

Elizabeth placed her head against her friend's arm. Relaxing for a bit. "I'm fine. I'm just lost in thought and the craziness was a godsend."

"Well, look, would you like to go get a bite to eat when you get off tonight? Or do you have plans with Jacob?"

"No, no plans. Jacob and I aren't seeing each other." Elizabeth didn't really want to talk about this, but here she was.

"What?" Jessica stared at her friend in shock and noticed a look which told her not to pry. "Well, we can talk about that later. I'm leaving here and heading to my volunteer job to get some hours in. I can meet you at The Pizza Place later. What do you say? Maybe go to a late movie after?" Jessica squeezed her friend's shoulder and gave her an encouraging smile.

"That sounds great. Though, maybe not the movie. I feel exhausted. It's been a long day, but I could really use some girl time." Elizabeth smiled at Jessica and gave her a hug. Pulling back, she looked at Jessica with a quizzical gaze. "Your volunteer hours? You really are a saint, aren't you? Where do you volunteer?"

"The Crisis Pregnancy Center here in town." At this Elizabeth's gaze became emotionless, but Jessica didn't seem to notice. "I just do odd jobs for them. Organizing donations, washing clothes, preparing items for pickup. It is fun, and a great organization that helps so many. I really enjoy it."

Noticing her friend's look, Jessica questioned her. "Are you feeling, okay? You look a little sick. Are you feeling ill again?"

Elizabeth smiled what she hoped was a convincing smile. "No, I'm good. But yeah, let's meet at The Pizza Place after work. I'm looking forward to a girl's night."

Jessica agreed with that, clocked out, said goodbye, and left the boutique.

It was 8:15 before Elizabeth left the boutique and met Jessica. The girls ordered a pepperoni and mushroom pizza and drinks. Elizabeth felt she needed to tell Jessica about the baby. A friend to confide in would be helpful, and now that she knew Jessica volunteered at the pregnancy center, she felt that she would understand.

"Hey, Elizabeth. Did you hear anything I just said? You seem like you're on another planet." Jessica waved her hand in front of her friend's face trying to get her attention.

Elizabeth shook her head trying to get herself to focus and looked at her friend sitting across from her. Her eyes started filling with tears. "I am so sorry, Jessica!" Elizabeth grabbed for her napkin as tears quietly rolled down her face. She dabbed at her eyes, rolling them toward the ceiling.

Very concerned, Jessica leaned forward grabbing her hands. "Oh, Elizabeth, what's wrong?"

Breathing in a shaky breath, Elizabeth looked into the sweet, understanding eyes of the girl across the table. "I really hope you don't think anything bad about me after I tell you this."

Elizabeth put her hand up to stop the words of denial that were getting ready to pour from Jessica. She took in a deep cleansing breath and started. "I know you won't. I'm just nervous and need you to listen." Elizabeth noticed Jessica sit back with a serious look. "Jessica, I appreciate you and am thankful I've gotten to know you, and I consider you a friend. My only one, really. It has been a crazy couple of weeks, and I've had some news that surprised me and scared me all at the same time. Even though it shouldn't."

Here she paused and looked down at her hands on the table which were balling up her napkin. Continuing to look down, she stated in a nervous voice "I found out I'm pregnant."

The shock and concern on Jessica's face was evident. Elizabeth rambled on, scared to pause, afraid she might not finish.

"I'm due around Thanksgiving. I have already gone to the pregnancy center. At first, I wanted an abortion and called there to ask about one. I ended up talking with Mrs. Green. She and my mom both made me realize I'm not alone and have support. I was having a hard time deciding what to do and was really considering an abortion. Then I realized I couldn't go through with it. Today, I went to the doctor, which is why I got to work late. He says everything is great. I'm still doubting everything and am scared to death, but well, that's it." She stopped at this point and breathed. She didn't realize she had been holding her breath until she finished and let it out, then she finally looked up across the table.

Jessica was frozen for a minute taking it all in, then jumped up and ran around the table to sit next to Elizabeth. She wrapped her in a big hug, laughing and crying at the same time. Elizabeth couldn't help herself and found herself laughing and crying, too.

"Wow! That's amazing. I guess. I mean, not that you wanted an abortion, or are confused and scared, but about the baby."

Jessica pulled away and looked at her friend at arm's length. "What happened with Jacob? Did you tell him?"

Concern filled Jessica's eyes at the thought of Jacob getting upset about this. Elizabeth told her everything that happened, Kristen told him just part of the story, him filling in the blanks, and then Elizabeth telling him the truth.

"I told him I couldn't deal with a relationship right now and apologized for leading him on when I knew I shouldn't have. That was Saturday. I haven't seen or talked to him since." Jessica embraced Elizabeth again when she saw tears forming in her eyes.

"I'm so sorry!" Jessica reassured her.

Elizabeth took a breath, wiped away the tears, and started to laugh out of frustration. "I am so tired of crying all the time!"

"It's the hormones. They say they are all over the place when you're pregnant. But seriously, are you going to be okay? You're dealing with a lot."

Elizabeth, feeling better, looked at Jessica, smiled, and gave her a thumbs up. "I will be. I know I'm not alone.

There are lots of people on my side to help me figure this nightmare out."

"Nightmare? I know I'm not in your situation, but isn't calling being pregnant a 'nightmare' a bit harsh?" Jessica looked at her friend.

"No, that's not what I mean. What I mean is that I know I have more support than a lot of people and I'm extremely thankful for that; I've realized it might not be as bad as I thought, and at first, like I said, I wasn't excited, and I was very scared and embarrassed. I still am and haven't gotten excited about being pregnant yet, but I'm good with things. It's pretty amazing, really. But wow. Scary!"

Elizabeth smiled and laughed at the realization. "I'm gonna be a mom. That sounds so strange."

Jessica, laughing too, again hugged her friend, then looked at Elizabeth. "Yeah, you are. And don't be embarrassed. Be proud of your decision. I'm sure it's gonna be hard, but I'll be here to help you and be a friend when you need it."

Elizabeth smiled with joy. "Thank you so much. I'm gonna be needing you a lot."

"Good. I like to be needed."

Chapter 31

The next couple of weeks passed quickly and before Elizabeth knew it, it was the end of the summer. Since it was her day off, and a beautiful sunny day at that, Elizabeth chose to spend it out in her mother's garden. Weeding the flowers and vegetables always helped her to relax. She needed to think through the phone conversation she had last night.

Her friend, and college roommate, Trina, called her. It was the first time the two girls talked all summer. It was at that time Elizabeth realized how much her life had changed since she walked into her house back in June. Just a few months ago, she and Trina shared everything, literally. Not just gossip and laughs, but joints, homework, beer, and even guys.

Here they were on the phone, talking about their summers and their next steps. Trina was preparing to move down to Florida to find a marketing job, just like they always talked about in their dorm room late at night.

She wanted to know if Elizabeth was still interested in going. The beach, a job, and each other was a dream of theirs. They took the motto "YOLO" to the next level and always said, 'You only live once, so you might as well live how you wanted, while you can'.

Instead of Elizabeth eagerly agreeing with her friend and packing to go with Trina to look for a place in Florida, she found herself telling Trina about her summer and being pregnant. Trina was shocked, and when she found out how far along Elizabeth was, she wanted to know who the father was and immediately thought of Brady.

Thoughtfully, Elizabeth answered her friend. Because of her due date, and how far along she is, she was positive Brady was the father.

Trina then asked her a question, which Elizabeth never considered until that moment. Was she going to let him know? That was something she had to really think about.

They finally got off the phone with Elizabeth telling Trina to enjoy herself and be careful and she promised she would let her know when the baby arrived. Now pulling weeds and cleaning up the vegetable bed, Elizabeth found herself missing the life she led at college and the life she and Trina planned. The beach would have been amazing to live by, working all day and being able to walk in the waves at night. If she had some extra time after work, she could run on the beach with the waves at her feet. On the weekends, they could have had one long beach party.

"Could 'a, should 'a, would 'a. Can't live life that way." Elizabeth got up from her kneeling position, brushed the dirt from her hands and knees and felt the baby beach ball she had growing. She laughed at the irony. "Well, I may not have a beach ball to play with, with sand under my toes, but I have a beach ball to rub and to watch grow into something more amazing."

She looked down at her stomach which pushed her dress out more and more every day. Sometimes she felt little movements in there, like the little one was doing flips. Surprisingly, Elizabeth found herself smiling at her new reality.

Her summer had been different than what she originally thought it would be. A new group of friends, her church, her work, and the meetings at the pregnancy center kept her occupied and busy. The unexpected, and relatively short-lived relationship with Jacob, was a sore spot in her summer, which she tried her best to avoid thinking about. Between work, church, her group meetings at the pregnancy center, and spending time with Jessica and her parents, Elizabeth didn't have much extra time left to avoid Jacob, which was basically why she kept busy in the first place.

Elizabeth was picking up groceries after work. She was having Jessica over and the girls planned to make a nice dinner for Elizabeth's parents. She was so focused on her list and the music she was listening to on her phone that she wasn't really focusing on her surroundings. She turned the corner to head down the next aisle and ran directly into a person who fell in her cart and grabbed at the sides.

"Whoa! Slow it down!"

Elizabeth, embarrassed and shocked, looked up to see who she had ran into and who the familiar voice belonged to, only to realize she knew him.

"Jacob!" She tried to relax, but those butterflies started flopping around in her belly. She smiled up at him, despite herself. His typical, simple attire of khaki shorts, Birkenstocks, and a t-shirt looked amazing on him, and she couldn't help but stare from head to foot, and back again. Stopping at his eyes, she gave him a flirty smile.

"I'm so sorry. I need to pay better attention." She looked up at him and tried to sound genuine. "I haven't seen you in a while. How ya doing?"

He looked at her and quickly stepped away from her cart. She noticed him glancing down at her belly. His eyes hung out there for a second before he slowly trailed his eyes upward and met her gaze. There was something in his gaze that she couldn't quite understand, regret or maybe longing.

He gave her a very slight smile. "I'm good. Sorry about running into you. I'm in a hurry, but glad you're good. I'll see ya around." He placed his hand on her arm as he passed, gave her a forced grin, and walked away without looking at her again. She turned in confusion to watch him.

"That was weird and a little rude." She told no one as she continued her shopping trip. When she got home, she relayed the meeting to Jessica as they cooked their dinner.

"That doesn't sound like him." Jessica was cutting the vegetables, onions, green peppers, and carrots for the pot roast they were making.

Elizabeth leaned on the counter, drying her hands on the towel. She just finished peeling the potatoes and put them in a pot with cold water. "I know, it was so weird. I felt like he wanted nothing to do with me. I shouldn't be surprised, I guess. I have been ignoring him and avoiding him as much as possible."

Jessica didn't say anything and continued vigorously cutting the vegetables. Elizabeth watched her, amused. "You know, those vegetables did nothing to you. You don't have to kill them!"

Elizabeth carried the roasting pan with the roast over to her friend. "Here, we need to get this in the oven." She sat the pot on the counter, picked the vegetables up off the board and placed them in with the roast, put it into the hot oven, then spun around to face Jessica.

Crossing her arms over her chest, Elizabeth shot her an accusatory tone. "Okay, what's going on?"

Jessica stopped her now crazy cleanup of the counter and faced Elizabeth. She was playing with the towel in her hands until Elizabeth reached over and roughly took it away.

She used the towel to point at Jessica. "Spill the beans. Now! You've been acting weird all night."

Jessica placed her now empty hands in a praying motion in front of her and looked at Elizabeth with worry in her eyes. "It's just something Chad told me."

"Oh, yeah? When did you talk to Chad?" Elizabeth looked with interest at her friend. She had noticed that he kept stopping by the boutique more and more to talk with Jessica. They were both sitting together in church and were finding more time to hang out.

"It's not a big deal. We're just talking. Anyway, it's not that I was talking to Chad, but what we were talking about." Jessica stopped and made eye contact with Elizabeth. Elizabeth had no clue where this was going, but she was interested.

"He told me that Jacob and Kristen are now a thing. He, I mean Jacob, is seeing Kristen." She stopped here, squinted her face, and grabbed Elizabeth's arms before she continued her torrent of words. "I'm so sorry. He told me last week. I didn't know how to tell you. If it makes you feel better, he said he thinks Jacob is just using her for sex again. And he also thinks Jacob is trying to make you jealous." Jessica stopped abruptly, noticing the hurt in her friend's eyes and shut her mouth tight.

Elizabeth looked at Jessica with shock and disgust and turned abruptly around. "No, that doesn't make me feel any better." She crossed her arms over her chest and took deep breaths to keep the tears that were pooling in her eyes from overflowing.

"I've noticed her car in their driveway a lot, but just figured she was there with Stacey." She lifted her hand to wipe angrily at the stray tear that broke free, closed her eyes, and turned toward Jessica.

"I shouldn't be so upset. I broke it off with him." She looked at her friend and lost her cool. "Oh my God! What a jackass!"

Elizabeth threw the towel against the wall, hitting the spice rack, and sending some spices toppling over. "He's not doing it to make me jealous. We're all adults. He's made his choice, and he just chose her even though she's a royal bitch to us. She is pretty, thin, and blonde. That must be his type. Not some brown-haired girl with a fat belly." Elizabeth knew she sounded like a child. It was easier to put herself down than admit how upset the situation made her.

Jessica crossed the kitchen and took Elizabeth in her arms. "Aww, honey, don't let him get to you."

Elizabeth hugged her friend, took a breath, and got herself together. She walked over and tore a paper towel from the roll hanging under the cabinet.

Wiping her face clean of tears, she placed her hands in front of her. "Okay, that will not happen again. I can do better than a man who jumps from woman to woman. Whoever I end up with will have to be good enough for the both of us."

She had her hands on her stomach and looked at Jessica as new tears started flowing. These were more than just new tears. They were also sad and lonely tears.

"I'm tired of being alone, Jessica. You have Chad, Stacey has her new boyfriend, and now even that bitch has taken someone. I feel like I will always be alone. I always have the worst luck with relationships."

Jessica again took her friend in her arms. "You know what, you out of all of us, are the only one truly never alone." She pulled away from Elizabeth, looked her in her eyes and placed her hands on either side of Elizabeth's growing belly. "You always have a little man with you. And this one will love you more genuinely than any other man ever could."

Elizabeth smiled at Jessica, taking in the words she just said, and laughed at this statement shaking her head.

"You kill me. You are determined this is a boy."

"Yes, I am. I can see you with your little guy."

"Well, I hope you aren't disappointed."

Elizabeth hugged her friend hard. "I love you and am so glad we're friends."

"I love you and the little guy, too." The two girls went outside to sit in the late afternoon sun while they waited for the roast to cook.

Chapter 32

"I hate this!" In frustration, Elizabeth tore off her favorite jean shorts and threw them across her bedroom where they encountered bottles of lotions and nail polishes on her dresser. The bottles made an awful noise when they clattered on the counter and some on the floor.

"Oh my God, what happened? What's wrong?" Jessica raced out of Elizabeth's bathroom to see what happened to her friend.

"Nothing! I just couldn't get my favorite cutoffs on. They're too small, and so I threw them." Elizabeth, realizing she was being ridiculous, tried to look irritated, but the silly look on Jessica's face made it difficult.

"Stop looking at me like that, or I will throw you too. You aren't much heavier than my shorts." Elizabeth sat down on her bed pouting like a child.

Starting to dig through her friend's drawers, Jessica found a cute pair of black sweatpants shorts for her to wear with the pink tank top she had on. "Here, you will look amazing in this. Put it on, and I guess we need to go get you some maternity clothes."

Jessica said this while jumping up and down clapping. "It will be so fun! We're going shopping."

Elizabeth took the shorts and put them on, shaking her head while doing so. She looked in the mirror and did a side view. Even though she was starting to get a baby bump, she couldn't help but notice she still looked good, and the bump just added to her cuteness.

Jessica came up next to her and stared into the mirror with her arm around her. "You make one cute pregnant momma, who needs new clothes. Let's go shopping!" Jessica grabbed her friend's hand, dragged her out of the house and into the car.

The mall wasn't very crowded when they got there. It was such a nice day outside; most people were probably either working or enjoying the sun. Jessica took Elizabeth in and out of the maternity sections of a lot of different stores. Being uncomfortable at first, Elizabeth soon relaxed and found some cute clothes that would take her through the next few months, at least, while still looking stylish. It was close to lunch time when they decided to take a break and went into the food court to grab a bite to eat.

The girls entered the food court linked arm in arm. "So, Momma, what are you and the baby hungry for?" Jessica adoringly asked Elizabeth.

"I love the burgers and fries here, and I'm famished and exhausted."

The girls got in line at the burger stand to wait their turn as patiently as possible.

"Hey, look who it is." Elizabeth nudged Jessica to look in the direction she was facing. Chad and Stacey were walking their way.

"Well, hello, ladies. I thought we might see you here." Chad walked up to them with a big smile plastered on his face, with Stacey following closely behind. He wrapped Jessica in a hug, throwing her in a circle and planted a light kiss on her lips. She smiled in response. He then turned to Elizabeth and gave her a gentle hug, "Not gonna throw you around. So, did you two have a good time shopping?"

"Momma here found some adorable clothes she can fit into. Baby boy is growing a bit." Jessica placed her hand on Elizabeth's belly and gave it a gentle tap.

"Baby boy?" Stacey, finally catching up to the small group, jumped into the conversation.

Elizabeth hugged Stacey and quickly cleared things up. "We don't know yet, but Jessica is betting a week's paycheck on the fact I'm having a boy." She shot Jessica a look, rolling her eyes at her friend, making Jessica break into a laugh.

"Well, I can't help it. I just have a feeling. I see you with an adorable little man in your arms." Jessica put Elizabeth in a side hug, and the girls smiled at each other. Elizabeth didn't realize how stressed she felt until that hug and that look from her friend; it really calmed her.

"It's great seeing you two, but Chad, I think we need to get going. You can talk to Jessica later." Stacey grabbed Chad's arm to get his attention. He gave her a quizzical look, but before he could ask her anything, the reasoning for her request made itself known.

"Well, look who y'all found hanging in the mall. What a surprise." The voice that tore through the air grated into their brains.

Elizabeth squeezed Jessica's hand, closed her eyes, and mentally prepared herself for the mental stress that always starts when Kristen is around. Elizabeth felt Jessica give her hand a tight squeeze and looked up at her friend. The sight in front of Elizabeth shook her to her core.

She'd been trying her best to avoid Jacob, and over the past couple weeks she had been doing a good job of it, having just glanced at him and waved a couple times. The grocery store awkwardness was the closest they had been since she turned her back on him and left him in his backyard. But now, all that avoidance came crashing to a halt as she found herself looking at him across the food court.

It wasn't just the sight of him which drew her attention, though he looked amazing like always; it was the fact that his and Kristen's fingers were interlocked together that threw her for a loop. She pulled her eyes away from the scene before her, and slowly looked up at his face. What she saw there did not make her feel any better. He looked happy and relaxed. If this meeting made him as uncomfortable as it made her, she couldn't see any signs of it.

He suddenly made his feelings clear when his hand released Kristen's, and instead went up to her waist, pulling her closer to his side. He leaned in to kiss her cheek. Kristen ate this movement up and snuggled right into his side. Into the side that Elizabeth used to enjoy snuggling up to.

Not wanting to let them see how much this bothered her, Elizabeth looked at Jacob, tilted her head and gave her friend next to her an okay squeeze of her hand to reassure Jessica she was fine.

"Hi, Jacob. Hi, Kristen. Looks like you're both doing well." Elizabeth gave him her sexiest, I-don't-give-a-shit smile.

"Hi, Elizabeth." He gave her a quick once over with his eyes and tightened his grip on Kristen's waist. "You look good."

"Thanks." She noticed Jessica grab a couple bags of burgers from off the counter, and motion to her. "It was good to see you, and all of you, but we're gonna go eat. Baby's hungry." She patted her belly, gave Chad and Stacey hugs, and left them behind with Jessica following.

Elizabeth found a table far enough away with a column in front of them to slightly block their view. She didn't want to see that scene anymore and needed to get it out of her head.

Dropping her bags on an empty chair, she collapsed in a chair next to it, with exasperation coursing throughout her body. She looked up at Jessica who was placing the food on the table.

"You did great, Elizabeth." Jessica ensured her friend as she emptied the tray of food and sat down across the table. "That was an unexpected shock, but you held your own."

Elizabeth looked at Jessica, and picked up a French fry, slowly nibbling on it in thought. "Did I? I felt like I was just ogling at his arm around her like an idiot." She opened a ketchup packet, squeezed it on her hamburger wrapper, and dipped another fry in it before she continued. Elizabeth couldn't find any words to say, shaking her head and putting fries in her mouth. Finally, she glanced up at Jessica who reached over and grabbed her hand.

"Girl, you did amazing. And just so you know, you look amazing. He noticed that. I could tell." Jessica smiled with encouragement at Elizabeth.

"You think I look amazing?" Elizabeth did some posing with her fry in her hands making them both laugh.

"Yeah, I do, and you are." Elizabeth felt better, so thankful she had Jessica. If Jacob wanted Kristen instead of her, let him have her!

Chapter 33

Elizabeth and Jessica were enjoying the last of the summer sun, lying on lounge chairs out in Elizabeth's backyard. It was late summer. They were enjoying the warm afternoon sunshine, and the waning summer days, both working on their tans. They both wore bikinis and although Elizabeth had a small beach ball growing, she still liked how she looked in the bikini.

Jessica was applying more sunblock and was deep in thought. "Hey, Elizabeth?"

"Mmm?"

"I was just thinking, but it may not be any of my business, so please don't get angry if I'm overstepping."

Elizabeth turned her head toward Jessica and lowered her sunglasses trying to get her to get to the point.

"Okay, I get it…here it goes…have you thought about telling Brady about the baby?"

Elizabeth paused and chewed on her lower lip. She then sat up and readjusted her lounge chair and placed her head heavily on the back.

"You sound like Trina. I just talked to her again the other day. She asked me the same thing again."

"The friend from college who asked you to go to Florida, Trina?"

"Yeah, that's the one. She was telling me about her apartment, and asked me if I've talked to Brady yet, and if I haven't, would I be upset if she invited him to visit her?"

"What? Is she crazy?"

"No, she's not crazy, she's Trina. Anyway, what she said doesn't matter. But I have thought about calling him a few times this summer, but I don't know if I want to bother him with this. What if he's moved on and has a new girl, a new life? Do I want to force him to be a part of ours?"

"Elizabeth, you aren't forcing him to be a part of your life, but he does deserve to know he has a baby; that he's a father."

Elizabeth sighed. "I know. You're right. I will think about it some more but not right now. Please change the subject."

Jessica became thoughtful. "Okay, change of subject. So, are you gonna wear that cute, tiny blue and red summer dress you bought at the mall to Stacey's picnic later today? I think you should. It looks adorable on you, and sexy. Just tight enough to show off your cute momma figure and short enough so we can see those sexy golden legs of yours." Jessica wiggled her eyebrows at Elizabeth as she took a big swig of water.

"Really, like it matters. There's no one interested in this body anyway." Elizabeth waved her hands in front of her to show off her body and belly, laying her hands to rest on top of her pregnant pooch.

"See, that's where I know you're wrong. Jacob is only with that, well, you know." Jessica hesitated, unable to say the only word she could think of to describe Kristen.

"Hoe-bitch, is what you are wanting to say." Elizabeth interjected for her friend, glancing her way.

Jessica laughed at the name Elizabeth commonly called Kristen. "Yes, it is, thank you. Anyway, he is only with her to get under your skin. And she is eating up the attention."

"Maybe, but it doesn't matter. Remember, I'm the one who ended things and honestly, I shouldn't have even started anything. I just hope he's happy with his choice." Elizabeth looked down at the grass and watched some ants walking by, working on gathering food to take home to their tunnel.

Elizabeth laid her head back on her chair, closed her eyes and murmured. "I don't want to talk about Brady or Jacob anymore. Just make sure I don't burn, please."

"Here, just to keep the little one safe." Jessica placed a towel over Elizabeth's stomach. "I'll set my alarm for thirty minutes, then we'll have to go in to get ready. It starts at three." Elizabeth gave her friend the thumbs up sign and ended up dozing off to the sound of birds chirping, the feel of the sun on her skin, and the light breeze blowing through the trees.

It was almost four when the girls finally headed to Stacey and Jacob's backyard. Elizabeth took as long as she could to get ready. She was not excited about heading over there and wanted a good group of people there before her.

Jessica spotted some of their friends from their Sunday school class under the big weeping willow tree in the back corner of Stacey and Jacob's yard and headed in their direction. Elizabeth glanced around, was glad she did not see Jacob or Kristen, and followed behind Jessica when she was surprised from the back, caught in a bear hug, and swung around.

Laughing, and a little dizzy when her feet touched the ground again, she turned and saw it was Chad who accosted her. "Damn, Chad. Please don't scare me like that. Remember?" She patted her stomach while tilting her head and giving him a smirk and an irritated shake of her head.

Chad looked concerned and grabbed her arms. "Sorry." He bent down to talk to her belly. "Everyone good in there?" He stood up and gave her belly a soft pat. "He's all good, but maybe you shouldn't be using that kind of language in front of the little one. He can hear you, you know."

"She has you calling it a boy now, too, huh? Please let's just talk to it like it's a single baby. Not more than one. Yes, he or she is fine." Elizabeth giggled and linked her arm through Chad's, pulling him to the group under the tree.

Seeing Elizabeth approaching, some of the girls came to her and offered her a hug and a seat on the lawn chairs that were spread around. Elizabeth greeted everyone and graciously sat down. Chad found Jessica. Elizabeth smiled when she saw her best friend light up when Chad gave her a hug and returned his kiss. *She deserves to be happy*, thought Elizabeth.

The afternoon was warm and humid. Even under the tree, Elizabeth felt herself getting hot and sticky. She decided she needed a bottle of water and got up to get one from the cooler by the deck. Chad tried to intervene and offered to get her water, but she denied him.

Elizabeth walked across the yard to the side of the deck where the food was on tables and drinks were in coolers. She opened the one marked water and took a bottle of cold water from the cooler, closed the lid, stood up, and came in direct contact, again, with Jacob.

Jacob grabbed her arm before they collided, and took her in. His eyes traveled from her face, down her body, pausing for a beat at her baby belly, and slowly back up to her eyes. He gave her a small smile. "Hi, Elizabeth. You look nice. I like that dress on you."

Her mouth fell open in surprise and her eyes became wide at his reaction and words. Something inside her clicked and irritation shot through her at the thought that he could complement her like they were friends. "Hi, Jacob. Thanks. I appreciate it." She held his eyes, daring him to continue.

Taking her look as encouragement, he seemed to relax, and his smile became more genuine. "It's good to see you. I'm glad you decided to show up today. You really are looking good."

Elizabeth just stared at him amazed at how he was treating her. The guy who wouldn't give her the time of day in the grocery store, and treated her like a leper, then flaunted his girlfriend in the mall, was now complimenting her repeatedly like they were old friends and nothing ever happened between them. She shook her head at him in disgust as her irritation was itching to explode from inside her.

"Thanks, Jacob. It must be that pregnancy glow people are always talking about." Elizabeth turned to go, but stopped, pushed her shoulders back and lifted her head higher, ready to face him head on. "You know, Jacob, I don't understand you. You glance at my stomach, then look at me with hurt and disgust all over your face one day, but if I would have aborted the baby and I still had my skinny, tight, sexy stomach you loved instead of this small basketball growing, you would have still looked at me with disgust because of my actions. Now, today, you act like me being pregnant isn't a big deal and that we're friends. Well, I don't think we're friends, so I don't really know what you're up to."

His eyes clouded with confusion, and he tilted his head as if trying to comprehend what she said.

Elizabeth shook her head and smirked at his reaction. "Really? You don't know what I'm talking about?" She stared at him, watching his features. There was no change and still no recognition that he understood her at all. The irritation that had threatened to reveal itself spilled out. "Here, let me spell it out for you. Just a couple of days ago at the grocery store, do you remember how you treated me?"

His expression was still blank. Breathing out her frustration, she stomped a foot and rolled her eyes. Her words became cross. "I'll remind you; you treated me like a stranger. Like there was never anything between us. Look, I'm sorry I let things happen like they did and go as far as they did, but I can't, and won't say I'm sorry for this." She placed both her hands and the water bottle on her small baby bump. She spit out her next words while holding eye contact with those blue eyes she can get lost in.

"I won't be sorry for this. It has taken me a few months to be able to accept this as my new reality, but I am not sorry I'm pregnant. The actions which led to my pregnancy, maybe. But this is my life now." She rubbed her hands on her belly to emphasize the life inside her. "I made a decision and I'm gonna be a mother. If you can't look at me without that disgusted, hurt look on your face, then please, just stop looking at me!"

Jacob's expression changed to one of faked confidence and annoyance. A smirk grew across his lips. He looked at Elizabeth, really looked at her and took a step in her direction, closing the little bit of space there was between them. "You know, I would like to stop being annoyed and would like to be able to really move on. I don't know what happened to us, or why you walked away, but you make it hard for me to forget you when you're parading around here like nothing has ever happened between us. Dressed like you want all the attention."

Elizabeth took a step back as if he slapped her. Her mouth opened in surprise at the accusation that just came out of his mouth, and she raised her hand to stop any more comments coming from him.

"Really? You think that? How about you with that whore-bitch, hanging all over you like she won the grand prize at the county fair? I thought you were above her, but I guess not. One thing I have finally learned is that I really need to get to know the people I choose to sleep with. I need to stop choosing the low life." She held his gaze as she said this, daring him to continue.

He was so close to her that they could easily kiss. His eyes were hard and intense. They held hers, and searched hers, for a moment before he slowly glanced down at her lips and back up. Elizabeth's heart sped up and she felt the familiar heat build in her groin from his gaze, but she broke the spell between them by closing her eyes and giving her head a quick shake while backing up to put some space between them.

Regaining her composure, Elizabeth turned abruptly and stomped away with such force that she rammed right into the front of the whore-bitch she was just talking about. Her eyes blazed out of their sockets with both shock and rage. "Kristen, get the hell out of my way!" She said these words between gritted teeth. Even though she felt her blood pressure rising, Elizabeth tried her best to keep her composure. She tilted her head up high, as she pushed past Kristen and back to the surprised group who were watching the whole thing from under the weeping willow.

Elizabeth walked directly between Jessica and Chad. She looked at her friend and started taking deep breaths to calm herself before she fell apart.

Once Elizabeth calmed down, Jessica pulled her and held her at arm's length with admiration all over her face. "That was amazing! You are amazing! I don't know exactly what all you said, we couldn't hear everything, but you pissed off that, what do you call her again?"

Chad interjected for her, knowing she wouldn't say the words. "I think it's whore-bitch."

The way he said it made everyone under the tree start laughing. The laughter eased the stress Elizabeth felt. Chad found himself joining in. He didn't even feel bad when he turned around and saw his best friend arguing with the girl, he again made a bad choice to be with.

Chapter 34

Elizabeth did a good job of avoiding Jacob and Kristen the rest of the night. Getting tired, she wandered to the deck and took a seat on the outdoor couch with a couple girls from their young adult class at church, Desiree and Charity. Elizabeth met Charity and her husband Don that first night at Stacey and Jacob's dinner party. Charity, who is very pregnant, is expecting their first baby in October.

"How are you feeling, Charity? Can I get you anything, a water maybe?" Elizabeth asked before she got too comfortable on the couch.

Charity put her hands up to let her know she was good and shifted her position in her seat so she could look at Elizabeth easier. "I'm doing fine. The baby is very active tonight. Sometimes it gets a little uncomfortable."

The petite blonde put her hand on her stomach, then reached over, grabbed Elizabeth's hand, and laid it on the side of her pregnant belly. "Here, feel." Elizabeth did not have to wait long before she felt a thump against her hand followed quickly by a couple more thumps.

She looked at Charity with wonder and joy in her eyes. "Oh my gosh! Was that the baby?" Charity looked at Desiree and the two girls laughed at Elizabeth's reaction.

"It's pretty amazing, isn't it?" Desiree asked Elizabeth as she also laid her hand on her best friend's stomach. "I love feeling the little guy kick. I can't wait until he gets to meet his Auntie Des, and I get to spoil him rotten!"

"Move over Des. I need to feel my football star." Don, Charity's husband, pushed Desiree out of the way and sat down next to Charity with one arm around her shoulder and the other on her belly.

Elizabeth leaned out of the way to give them room. The baby kicked again. Charity's hand closed over Don's. They smiled and laughed together. Don leaned over and kissed his wife's belly. "Hey, little man. That's one heck of a kick you got there."

"You're not kidding." Replied Charity with a smile of exhaustion on her face. She looked at Elizabeth. "Just wait. Soon you'll be losing sleep because your little one will be kicking and punching you all night."

Elizabeth laughed and placed her hand on her bump. "I'm looking forward to it."

Don leaned in to give Charity a kiss. "I think I need to get you two home. It's been a long day." Don said, looking at his wife. Charity nodded her head in agreement.

Elizabeth stood up as the two departed, gave them hugs and watched them walk away with Don's arm around Charity, helping and leading her toward their car. Elizabeth smiled as she watched them. You could see how crazy the two of them were for each other.

Moving slightly to the left, Elizabeth froze as another couple got her attention over by a tree. Kristen and Jacob were enjoying a quiet moment with their lips locked together in a deep intense kiss. Elizabeth felt her stomach tied up in a knot, and her face grew hot, though, she knew it wasn't from the weather.

"Hey. I just love them together. Aren't they the sweetest?" Stacey interrupted Elizabeth's thoughts and caught her off guard.

Elizabeth broke her stare at Jacob and Kristen and turned to face Stacey. "Excuse Me?"

"Charity and Don. Don't you just love them? They were that cute in high school too. We all knew they would last forever."

Elizabeth, more relaxed now that she knew what couple Stacey was talking about, smiled and agreed with her. Turning away, she excused herself. She wanted to get away from Stacey. Though she did consider her a friend, with the ex-rated show going on over by the tree, standing with one of the actors' sisters just didn't sit well with her. She needed to find Chad and Jessica.

"Wait, Elizabeth. I'll go with you if you don't mind. I want to say something anyway." Stacey walked beside Elizabeth as they left the deck, and unfortunately had to pass the tree where Jacob and Kristen had still not come up for air. Trying her best to ignore the scene, she held her head high as she passed by.

"I'm sorry about that." Stacey acknowledged as she wrinkled her nose and curled her lip.

She continued when they were safely out of ear shot. "I don't know why he's made that decision again. They are not good for each other, but I don't know. I guess it's not my place to say. They're both adults, and so are you, but I think if you…"

Elizabeth put her hand up and shook her head, interrupting Stacey's words.

"Look, Stacey, if that's what Jacob wants, it's fine. I made the decision for us to stop seeing each other, not him. I didn't want Jacob to have to deal with me, and soon enough, a baby. If he keeps going back to her, maybe that is where he belongs."

Chad overheard this conversation and put in his two cents. "Bite your tongue woman! Kristen, though I don't feel she is quite the whore-bitch you call her, is a snake and is out to make only Kristen happy. She likes the game and the hunt. She'll hurt him again when she gets bored being in a relationship, and I will have to pick up the pieces of his broken heart. We've seen it so many times before."

The group around the tree nodded in agreement, some putting in comments about Kristen's behavior, or Jacob's choices.

Stacey, always the peacemaker and defender of the two, broke into the discussion. "Okay, everyone. Let's find something more positive to discuss. There must be more exciting drama to talk about other than my brother's bad choices in women." Stacey turned to Elizabeth, and placing her hand around her waist added, "present company not included." Elizabeth and the others laughed at that, and the conversation was changed.

Elizabeth, though she tried to tell herself she didn't care, noticed that Jacob and Kristen were no longer at the tree. Wondering where they went, she glanced stealthily around the yard, and stopped short when she saw them with their lips locked again in the doorway of the kitchen. They then entered the house and Elizabeth watched as Jacob leaned close to Kristen, making her laugh. They both entered the kitchen, and he closed the door behind him. Elizabeth's heart broke a little bit more.

It was late when Elizabeth finally said goodnight to her friends, left the party, and went back to her house. She let herself quietly into the kitchen and made herself a cup of green tea. While it steeped, she got comfortable settling into the corner of the couch in the sunroom with her tea in her hand. She bounced the tea bag in the hot water. She leaned her head back and sighed.

Jessica was going to spend the night with her, or at least that was the plan earlier in the day, but she ended up making a huge decision and decided to spend the night with Chad at his apartment instead. Remembering the conversation with Jessica made Elizabeth smile.

Jessica had come over to her, took her hand and pulled her away from the group. She told her that Chad asked her to spend the night with him. Jessica was apprehensive at first, not only because she was nervous about taking their relationship to the next level so soon, but she didn't want to leave Elizabeth hanging.

Just remembering her friend's concern for her made Elizabeth swell with pride and acceptance. She truly was thankful for Jessica, and even Chad. They really have become such close friends in such a short time. Thinking about her two friends together made Elizabeth smile even more. They were a cute couple and balanced each other out nicely. Elizabeth finished her tea and sighed.

"Well, little one, I guess we need to go to bed. I'm exhausted."

As if in answer, she felt for the first time what felt more like a kick than a flutter. It shocked her. She took in a quick breath with a smile and placed her hand on her stomach at the place where she felt the light thump.

"Oh, my goodness, little one. I guess you heard me."

Elizabeth's heart swelled with pride at the thought that even though she was feeling down and alone, she was given a reminder that she wasn't alone at all.

Feeling lighter and more content than she had all night, she made sure the door was locked, turned out the lights and headed upstairs to get them both to bed.

Chapter 35

Jacob leaned over Kristen and kissed her gently on her lips. She reached up and laced her arms around his neck, pulling him in for a longer, hotter, more seductive kiss.

She was ready to go again and wanted him to feel the same way. Jacob, still frustrated by his interaction with Elizabeth earlier, needed a break, so he cut the kiss off earlier than Kristen expected, irritating her.

Leaning up on her elbow, she watched him with rage in her eyes, as he got up and out of the bed. "What's up with you? You don't seem to be in this tonight? Didn't I make you feel good? And where are you going?"

"I'm good, Kristen. I just need to go grab a drink. Do you want me to bring you back anything?" Kristen huffed in an annoyed way, shook her head no, and flopped back down into the bed, not bothering to cover herself up. Jacob shrugged, slipped on his shorts that were on the floor where she took them off, and left his room, closing the door behind him.

As he got closer to the kitchen, he heard the familiar voices of his sister, Chad, and Jessica floating toward him. He was glad they were here. It gave him something to do instead of returning to Kristen right away. He entered the kitchen, saw the coolers on the floor, opened one, and took out a beer.

"Well, look who emerged from his cave. Are you allowed to be away from the leech you've been sucked onto all night?" Chad, only half-joking with his best friend, scooted his chair closer to Jessica and invited Jacob to sit down.

Jacob rolled his eyes, turned the extra chair around so the back touched the table, and straddled it while sitting down and leaning his elbows on the table. "Whatever, dude. Keep your thoughts to yourself, please. I'm not in the mood." Jacob took a long drink of his beer, then put the can down on the table. "What's keeping you two here so late anyway?" He asked, looking in Chad and Jessica's direction.

"Someone had to help your sister bring in the coolers and clean up a little. You were otherwise occupied, as I said earlier." Chad didn't make eye contact with Jacob. He kept his eyes straight ahead studying a picture on the wall.

Jessica looked between the two guys and turned to Stacey with a questioning lift of her eyebrows. Stacey shook her head, shrugged her shoulders, and asked her brother the question that was on everyone's mind. "What's going on, bro'?" She leaned over and gave Jacob's hand a squeeze. His hand closed over the tips of her fingers and gave her a squeeze back.

"Nothing. Just needed to get some air and space."

"Seriously, dude?" Interjected Chad. "You were quite happy ignoring everyone all night. Is that amazing girlfriend of yours not so amazing after all?" Jacob just turned to his friend with a blank stare as Chad continued. "You know what we all think about you and her as a couple. You really need to think twice before running back between her legs whenever things don't go right for you. Not only is it shallow for you, but it really isn't fair to her or your sister, as Stacey has to pick up the pieces of both of you when things go south."

Jacob's look turned dark and stormy. "You don't listen well, do ya, when you're told to keep your thoughts to yourself." Jacob turned up his beer can and emptied it in one big gulp, then stood up with enough force to shake the table, spilling Stacey and Jessica's wine in the process. Looking down at Chad, Jacob growled "Do you have anything else to say or are you going to leave?"

Chad pushed his chair out and squared up to Jacob, standing over his friend by a good four inches. "Really, dude, we're gonna do this? You're upset, I know that, and I also know why."

"And why is that?" Jacob stepped closer to his friend. He has never been intimidated by Chad's height or girth. Jessica placed her hand on Chad's arm and whispered his name. He nodded slightly, letting her know he had it under control. "Look, things with you and Elizabeth didn't turn out how you wanted them to. I know that, but using Kristen like you are, isn't fair to Kristen." Chad looked down in his friend's eyes. "It really isn't."

Jacob relaxed and backed away from Chad and slouched his shoulders and fell back down in his chair. The truth of his friend's words weighed heavily on him. "Chad, you're right. I was really hoping Elizabeth and I would work out. She really is amazing, and I'm having to deal with the fact she didn't want us together, but I'm happy with my choice. Being with Kristen. She is comfortable to me, and I enjoy being with her. It might not be where I thought I'd be, but it's good. It really is."

Jacob looked between Chad and Jessica, and his sister. He noticed Stacey's eye twitching to look behind him. He turned around to see Kristen leaning against the wall, looking confused and a little hurt.

Realizing she had probably heard what he just said, he got out of his chair and walked toward her. Reaching his hand out, he grasped her arm. As he touched her, she jerked back, like his touch burned her skin. "Kris, how much did you hear?" He walked toward her fast enough that she couldn't walk away, and he surrounded her in his arms.

"Enough to hear I'm your second choice." Jacob saw the anger and hurt well up in her eyes. He knew it wasn't sadness. He didn't really know if she was capable of that type of emotion, but he did know he had to squelch what he saw before it got out of hand and drama ensued.

"Kristen. You know that's not true." He closed his mouth over hers to keep her arguments at bay. He broke the kiss long enough to invite her to bed. "Come on and let me show you how not true it is. Let's go back to bed." He led her to his bedroom knowing she wouldn't deny him.

Jacob's bedroom door closed. Chad, Jessica, and Stacey looked at each other.

"Well, get ready for a storm when that hurricane makes landfall." Stacey made this comment, gathered their cans, and finished cleaning up the kitchen.

Chad tugged on Jessica's hand getting her to follow him to the door. It was late and time to go. They said their goodnights, and Chad and Jessica headed to his car and to his own bedroom.

Chapter 36

Elizabeth was caught in that state between dreaming and reality. Willing her eyes not to open, she tried her hardest to hold on to what little bit of her dream she had left. Like they usually do, the closer to awake she became, the more her dream seemed to float away. She couldn't remember the details of it anymore, just feelings. Feelings of love, peace, and acceptance filled her even though the details slowly left as consciousness took its place.

Finally, the scratchiness of her eyes being covered by her eyelids became too much of a bother. She reached over to feel for her phone when the sleepy dream-like state finally lost itself completely. She slowly opened her eyes to the very early morning light pouring in through the edges of her curtains.

Opening her eyes just a sliver, she glanced at her phone and noticed it was only five o'clock. A bit earlier than she would have liked, but she decided it was worth waking anyway. She stretched the sleepiness out of her body. First her legs, then her arms and back.

Standing up and walking to her dresser to put on a pair of shorts and a tank top, a thought quickly sliced through her. *I really should try and contact Brady. He needs to know about the baby.*

Confusion blasted through Elizabeth. "Where in the hell did that thought come from? It's so random!" She questioned the person looking back at her from the mirror.

A small bit of realization washed over her, like déjà vu. This was part of what she had been dreaming about before waking. Her dream had something to do with talking with a guy about a baby. She guessed the guy was Brady and the baby was theirs, but she couldn't be sure.

Looking at her reflection in the mirror, and covering her belly with her hands, she thought for a minute, then sighed deeply. "Okay, baby. Let's do this."

Before she lost her nerve, Elizabeth picked up her phone, scrolled through her contacts and found Brady's number was still there.

Elizabeth started a text. Didn't like it. Deleted it. Started over. She did this a few times before she talked herself into keeping it simple.

> Brady - this is so random - I was wondering if you would be able to meet. There's something we need to talk about. Elizabeth.

She quickly hit send and stared at her phone like it would instantly answer her. *It's five o'clock in the morning, Elizabeth. Get a life! Most sane people are still asleep!* Instead of waiting by her phone, she decided to go out for a morning walk and clear her head.

It was a beautiful morning for a walk. The humidity of the day had yet to show its hot and sticky face and Elizabeth felt better after a short walk around the block. She enjoyed watching the neighborhood come to life. Being as early in the morning as it was, it was still rather quiet. Most people were still enjoying their last little bit of sleep except for those who leave for work at the crack of dawn or need to let their dogs out to run in the yards.

Elizabeth waved to her neighbors. Some she has known for a long time, others she just knows their faces. A couple houses down, she said good morning to Mrs. Lynch, a retired schoolteacher. Elizabeth never had her but knew her. She was a sweet lady. She lost her husband a few years back and now it's just her and her dog, Muffy. Elizabeth stopped and gave Muffy a pet. She's a little

Corgi with adorable tiny legs. Elizabeth then smiled at Mrs. Lynch and told her good morning.

Rounding the corner, she was passing Jacob's house and came face to face with Jacob and Kristen as they said their goodbyes in the driveway, locked in a passionate kiss. They were getting ready to get into their own cars and head out to their jobs. Kristen, making eye contact with Elizabeth, pulled Jacob back in and gave him another long, sensual kiss for Elizabeth's benefit, she was sure.

Jacob climbed into his car and caught sight of Elizabeth as he pulled out of the driveway. They locked their eyes for a split second. Elizabeth had no clue what she saw there in his eyes, but it seemed like more than a casual glance. Finally, she was heading up the walk to the porch where her mother sat on the porch swing enjoying her morning cup of coffee.

Chapter 37

"Good morning, sunshine!" Her mother sang as her daughter came into sight. "You just missed your dad. He's hoping we can have dinner together tonight when he gets home. We both feel like we haven't seen you much lately."

Elizabeth sat down on the rocking chair across from her mom, leaned her head back and rocked a bit before she said anything.

"I would love that, Mom." She paused, staring off at nothing, then continued becoming thoughtful. "Mom, I've been thinking. I decided to contact the guy I think is the baby's father, Brady, so I sent him a text this morning."

She stopped rocking and looked at her mother. "I really felt I needed to do this. I don't expect anything from him. But I do think he deserves to know."

Her mother looked at her and smiled. "I think that is a good idea. He does deserve to know." Mrs. Parks leaned over to grab her daughter's hand. "I'm proud of you. I'm sure that wasn't an easy decision." She smiled a warm, pleased smile.

"Thanks, Mom. I'm hungry. I'm gonna go in and grab a bagel and a cup of coffee." Elizabeth got up and gave her mother a hug and a kiss on the cheek. She stopped suddenly when she felt a quick and soft kick on her side.

Turning around to look at her mother, she exclaimed with excitement. "Mom! The baby just kicked me!" Elizabeth sat down next to her mom on the swing, grabbed her hand, and placed it on the spot she just felt the kick. The two women looked off in the distance concentrating, with their hands on Elizabeth's belly waiting with anticipation.

Suddenly there was another little thump followed quickly by another. They both turned with huge smiles and their eyes wide with excitement. "Isn't that amazing, Mom! I felt it for the first-time last night when I was sitting in the sunroom having a cup of tea. Our baby is kicking me." Elizabeth's excitement bubbled over like a bottle of champagne exploding.

"That is the most amazing feeling. My baby's gonna have a baby and is making me a grandma." Still smiling, mother and daughter went inside to grab a bite to eat together.

Chapter 38

Elizabeth reached for the door of the boutique, but Jessica beat her to it and invited her into the store while bombarding her with accusations. "Elizabeth, what the heck! You've been ignoring my texts all morning. What's going on with you? Where have you been?"

Elizabeth glanced at her friend like she was crazy, walked to the backroom of the store to put her purse in the storage locker. Still ignoring Jessica's questioning, she tapped in her employee number to sign into her shift. "Good morning, Mrs. Stanzel." Elizabeth smiled at her boss. "Has she been this annoying all morning?" She looked at Jessica and blew her a loud kiss across the store.

"Well, she has been a bit impatient waiting for you to show up for work. Because of that, though, all the dusting and stocking is already completed. She's been quite busy." Mrs. Stanzel smiled at Jessica and gave Elizabeth a hug. "You are looking adorable today, Elizabeth. That's a cute dress on you."

"Thanks." She hugged her boss back and got busy organizing some of the earrings and necklace racks at the front counter.

"Well, girls, since you're both here, I'm gonna get some work done in the back and get out of here earlier than usual. Call me if you need me."

Jessica nodded at her boss while walking to the counter. She pulled up a stool to sit on and one for Elizabeth. It was an amazingly nice summer day, so she figured it would probably be a little slower than normal the rest of the afternoon. Why not enjoy the lull in customers and find out where her friend has been all morning.

Jessica sat down on the stool and situated herself facing Elizabeth, ready to hear all about why her friend has been ignoring her today.

Looking at Jessica, Elizabeth shook her head and chuckled. "You are being ridiculous! I spent my morning at the pregnancy center. We had a baby shower for one of the ladies who had her baby early. Then, I talked to someone I wasn't planning on talking to."

Jessica became curious about this. "Come on, who?"

Elizabeth ended up telling her about waking up this morning and the dream she had, or what she could remember about the dream. She ended her tale with the fact that she sent Brady a text telling him she wanted them to meet; she had something to talk with him about.

Surprised at this unexpected event, Jessica became filled with questions. "What made you do that? Have you heard from him yet?"

Looking off in the distance, Elizabeth answered her. "You and Trina badgering me for one, and you were both right. He needs to know about the baby. He won't have to be part of our lives unless he wants to. I'm not gonna force him into anything, but I feel he needs to have that choice."

She looked at Jessica with a thoughtful expression. "And to answer your question about if I've heard from him yet, yes, I have. He sent me a text while I was at the center, and I called him as soon as I got in my car." Elizabeth stopped and took a drink of water then walked to the sunglasses to straighten them.

"Really, are you serious!" Jessica stood with her hands on her hips looking at Elizabeth, wanting her to continue. "You can't say that and not tell me details. That can't be all there is to this story."

"Well, we decided we would meet in the city at the Farmer's Market on Saturday. It's about a forty-minute drive for both of us, so about the half-way mark between our houses. It's a public place, so it should be crowded enough not to be too uncomfortable, and it seemed a fair distance for both of us. I didn't tell him why, just that we needed to talk, and it was important, but something we needed to do in person."

Jessica sat back down on the stool and leaned her arm on the counter. "Wow! Okay! What time?"

"Saturday around six. I need your help, though, and maybe Chad's, too, if he wants to be involved."

Jessica's eyes danced with excitement.

"I would love for you two to come with me. Emotional support and all that. I may need it. Just thinking about facing him makes me a basket of nerves."

"I'm sure I can talk Chad into it. I'll have him meet us here at five when we close. He'll drive. Now what's this guy like? What can I expect?"

Elizabeth became thoughtful. "Well, he's about six feet, has brown hair that is wavy, almost curly. He wore it over his ears, always a little long. Dresses nice, works out, so he's got a nice body, and a really sexy, tight ass."

Jessica laughed at this. "Oh my gosh! You always talk about guys' butts!"

Elizabeth had a wide smile, which filled her face. "I know. The butt, known by most as the ass, is my favorite part to look at and Brady's is very easy to stare at, and amazing to hold and squeeze!" Elizabeth demonstrated ass squeezing with her hands and the two girls broke down laughing.

They were laughing so hard; they were almost crying. They had to pull themselves together when a group of older ladies walked into the store.

"Time to get back to work." Elizabeth walked away from Jessica and went to greet the women to see if she could help them find anything to purchase.

Chapter 39

Saturday came faster than Elizabeth expected and so did closing time at the boutique.

It was a good thing the store was busy today because now that it was time to close, Elizabeth's hands were shaking, and her heart was beating out of her chest.

"You ready?" Jessica wrapped her arm around Elizabeth to try and calm her.

Looking at her friend, Elizabeth smiled, placed her hand over Jessica's and nodded her head, breathing in deeply to calm her frayed nerves.

Chad was waiting out by his car when the girls stepped out of the store and locked the door behind them. "Look at these two beautiful ladies. How was your day?"

Chad slipped his arms around Jessica, dipped her, and crushed her lips with a kiss before standing her up again. Elizabeth laughed at their antics and couldn't help but notice how much Jessica's face lit up when she saw him.

The look of adoration for Chad was apparent when he stood her back up.

She knew they really liked each other, but being a part of this exchange made Elizabeth think that things between Jessica and Chad could be a bit more than they were letting on.

"Hello, am I interrupting here? Remember, you two are supporting me tonight. Will I just be in the way?" Elizabeth joked as she reached the passenger rear door, preparing to open it.

Jessica tore herself away from Chad and he turned and opened Elizabeth's door for her and ushered her into the car. Elizabeth smiled and nodded at him.

"M' Lady," he answered to her, closed the door behind her, then turned to Jessica and did the same to her, but added a "beautiful" before the lady and kissed her on her hand before he closed her door and ran around to the driver's side. Once they were all settled, and seat belts on, they headed down the road to the interstate toward the city.

The Farmer's Market was hopping when they reached the parking lot and searched for a spot. Elizabeth got out of the car after she checked her reflection in her compact mirror and reapplied some mascara and lipstick.

Jessica grabbed her hand and squeezed. "Come on, girl. You look beautiful."

Elizabeth returned her friend's squeeze and looked at Jessica. She took a deep breath, quietly thanking her for the support.

Smiling with encouragement, Jessica linked her arm through Elizabeth's and squeezed. "It's gonna work out perfectly. You got this and we're here for you if you need it."

"And if he ends up being a dick, I'll take him out. So, you're good." Chad, standing beside Jessica, reached around and gave Elizabeth a pat on the shoulder.

Laughing and shaking her head at the silliness that is Chad, she told them both thank you. She was so glad she had them here.

They started walking toward the outdoor cafe when Chad paused and turned toward the door leading to the inside restaurants. "Well, I'm gonna run inside really quick and grab a beer. Do either of you want anything?"

Elizabeth said she'd take a lemonade and Jessica wanted a beer also. Chad gave Jessica a quick peck on the cheek.

"I'll find y'all out back at the food court." He turned and walked away leaving the girls alone.

Jessica linked her arm through Elizabeth's, and they went to find an empty table.

The food court was bustling with activity. Elizabeth and Jessica enjoyed people watching and commenting on some of the things they saw. The area around them was a great place to be in the early fall. The weather was perfect and lots of families were taking advantage of the last bit of the long daylight hours.

As they were laughing at a group of little boys who were running around fighting with balloon swords, Elizabeth's phone buzzed. The text she read sent nerves running up her spine and all over her body.

Looking at Jessica, she picked up her phone, and showed her the text. "He's here."

She answered him, letting him know where they were sitting. About the same time, Chad came over with their drinks, sat down, and noticed the panicked look on Elizabeth's face.

"I'm guessing he's here." Jessica answered him with a nod.

"There he is." Jessica and Chad followed Elizabeth's gaze.

Jessica recognized him from the description Elizabeth gave her earlier. Her eyes became thoughtful and curious as she watched the handsome guy walk across the court.

It was obvious when he found Elizabeth in the crowd. His face lit up, and his step quickened toward them.

Brady looked hot as usual. His khaki shorts, untucked black button-up shirt, and loafers looked casual and comfortable. He walked with confidence and had a drink in his hand. He must have stopped inside, also for a beer, before looking for Elizabeth.

Elizabeth, watching him as he approached, felt that familiar quickening of her heart as their eyes met. She forgot she always had that reaction when she saw him. It caught her by surprise.

She smiled in response to his gaze and slightly tilted her head as she studied him. She was about to jump out of her seat to go meet him, but paused, remembered the extension of her belly, and sat back down slowly. Her confident expression was replaced with nerves.

Brady noticed the change and slowed a little, concern crossing his features. Elizabeth looked over at Chad and Jessica for support. Jessica gave her a slight nod and Chad told her she looked great, and she had this.

Brady approached the table. She liked what she saw. Graduation brought out the best in him. She could tell he spent a lot of time out in the sun, as his hair was sun-kissed with natural highlights, and his skin was dark.

He smiled at her, a wide amazing smile. This was the encouragement Elizabeth needed, and she stood up, with confidence. She knew she looked good and was glad she chose the yellow dress. It accented her hair and tanned skin.

She walked around the table and approached Brady. He was looking into her eyes and put his arms out toward her when he glanced down.

He paused slightly and took a small step back. He ran his hands through his hair, scrunching up his eyes in thought. The shock of seeing her belly was apparent. Elizabeth reached him and without pausing, pulled him into a hug. When they released each other, she quickly introduced Jessica and Chad, who stood up and greeted him, then quickly excused themselves to go for a walk.

Brady and Elizabeth were left alone. She invited him to sit down.

"Is this what you needed to talk to me about?" Brady gestured toward her.

Elizabeth nodded at him, her stomach fluttered with nerves, but she was determined to hold his gaze and not back down. "I'm due around Thanksgiving. Two more months."

Brady looked at her. He seemed to be studying her face while he was deep in thought, contemplating what she just said and what his eyes couldn't deny. They sat in silence for a bit, both sipping their drinks. Elizabeth watched him to see if she could read anything in his expression.

It was apparent that Brady wanted to say something but was holding back, so she broke the silence. "Look, Brady, I know this is awkward and I'm sure you have questions. Let me answer one now. My due date is around November 24th, that means this baby was conceived around February 17th. February was our month. You were the only one I was seeing and sleeping with."

She paused and made eye contact with him. "Do you remember? It was around the Valentine's Day Formal. We were being exclusive. Trying it out. I promise at that time it was only you. February, the entire month, was only you."

Brady became quiet and thoughtful. Elizabeth studied his eyes and could see him getting uncomfortable, so she continued before she lost him.

"Look, I wasn't going to tell you about this. I don't expect you to do anything, and I won't force you to. You're the father and I needed you to know."

Still no response just a blank stare. "That's it. I promise. You don't need to take responsibility. I don't want you to feel obligated. My parents and I will do everything. I'll never ask anything of you."

Brady looked up at her. His face became blank, and he pressed his thumb and middle finger against the bridge of his nose. He sat up straighter putting his other hand up, interrupting her.

"Wait a minute, Elizabeth. Just wait. Let me understand this. I'm still a little in shock and need to wrap my head around things. Give me a minute."

He spun around on his seat and stood up. He paced a few steps, stopped, came back, and sat down. He passed his eyes up and down her body and rested on her face.

His mouth opened to say something, but he shut it again and shook his head. "Can we walk? I need to walk."

"Sure." Elizabeth stood up slowly, picked up her watered-down lemonade and followed Brady out of the food court and onto the greenway.

They strolled in silence, both lost in thought. Elizabeth fidgeted with her cup as they walked, determined to give him as much quiet as he needed.

There were a lot of people in the green areas. A group of college-aged boys were throwing a frisbee. A man, probably a father, was playing catch with his young son. There was a woman sitting on a blanket with a baby in her arms watching the man and boy. Elizabeth figured they were a family. The woman seemed relaxed and peaceful watching them and was playing with the baby. Elizabeth tried not to think of what that would be like. This wasn't the time.

Finally, Brady broke the silence. He turned to look at her while he spoke. "Elizabeth, I want you to know I'm more shocked that you seem to think I wouldn't want to take care of my baby, than I'm shocked about you being pregnant. If it is mine…"

He stopped mid-sentence when he saw her eyes widen. "And I'm sure it is. I want to be a part of its life. Are you sure you got pregnant in February?"

She was trying to be understanding, so she just nodded her head yes, afraid that if she talked her irritation would be evident.

Seeing her reaction, Brady stepped off the trail and walked toward a tree. He stopped and leaned against it. She did the same. Elizabeth stared off at the scenery with the city in the background.

Brady was looking down at the ground, but finally reached out and took her hands. He rubbed his fingers over hers trying to get his thoughts together. "Elizabeth, I don't know what to say right now. Except, thank you."

Elizabeth froze and scrunched up her eyes. She had been running this moment through her head all week, and a thank you was not a scenario she imagined. She turned to look at him. He was a good head taller than she was, and she had to look up to make eye contact.

Even though it had only been a few months since they last saw each other, it looked like he had changed a lot. Matured a lot. She was sure she looked the same way because she had.

"Thank you?" It came out as a question.

He smiled his cute, crooked smile at her. "Yeah. Thank you." He squeezed her hands. "You didn't have to tell me anything about the baby. The chances of us ever seeing each other again were slim. You could have had the baby and never told me or anyone I was the father.

So, thank you. I don't know what that's gonna mean, but I appreciate it."

He moved his left hand up her arm rubbing it. A familiar, yet long forgotten flutter started in her belly.

She took in his facial features, his wavy brown hair, shorter than it was in college, his amazing body, still looking good, and his well-chiseled and handsome face. She used to know this face and this body like the back of her hand. Even though they never said they were boyfriend and girlfriend, never made it official, there was something unspoken about their relationship.

Brady slowly leaned in and lightly brushed his lips against hers. Elizabeth closed her eyes and returned the kiss. It was delicious. Slow at first, then longing filled Elizabeth as fireworks went off inside her. She pressed harder into his warm soft lips and found Brady eagerly answering her. She enjoyed the kiss as much now as she did a few short months ago.

It wasn't long before they broke apart. They stared into each other's eyes, neither one wanting to break the spell they felt between them. After a beat, they both found themselves grinning.

"Feels like we never stopped," whispered Brady, still watching her.

"Something like that," Elizabeth answered breathlessly.

Brady gave her one more amazing smile, kissed her again, quickly, softly, then tugged lightly, and they walked away hand in hand, both lost in the moment.

Elizabeth found herself watching a couple playing fetch with a dog, which wasn't quite listening to its owners. The antics of the dog were making Elizabeth chuckle. Brady broke into her quiet entertainment and handed her a dandelion.

"Here ya go. I know how you like these." Brady laughed at the look of amusement on Elizabeth's face.

"Thanks, how thoughtful." She glanced at him and let go of his hand picking at the weed he just gave her, smiling at the memory.

When they were in college, Elizabeth told Brady that her favorite color was yellow, and she liked yellow flowers the best. She meant roses, daffodils, daisies, and tulips. Brady, picking her up for a date, presented her with a bouquet of dandelions, a yellow flower, straight from the heart, and the lawn out in front of her dorm.

Brady broke into her memory. "So, do you know if the baby's a boy or girl?" He looked at her as they walked.

Focusing on the man walking beside her, she answered him the only way she could. She shook her head no.

"Honestly, I don't know if I want to. My mom and I went to the doctor when I was around sixteen weeks for a checkup and an ultrasound. They asked if I wanted to know the sex. I told them no, so they didn't tell me."

Elizabeth shrugged her shoulders. "Sometimes I wish I knew, but it won't matter either way. My friend Jessica, though, insists it's a boy."

"A boy. Would I prefer a son or daughter?" Brady looked up at the sky, becoming thoughtful. "I have a sister, and my dad said my brother and I together, even with all our rambunctious 'boyness,' were easier together than she was by herself. A daughter, especially if she looked anything like her mother, would make me have to stress over all the guys who would be chasing her. It would be a lot of work."

Elizabeth looked at him, nudging him a little. "I'm not quite sure how to take that. Is it supposed to be a compliment, or saying something else?"

"It's just that if she looks anything like you, I would be spending my time chasing the guys away. I'd probably be thrown in jail either because I shot someone or locked our daughter in her room."

Brady looked at Elizabeth and they both started laughing. "I'd be an overprotective dad and make her life miserable."

Shaking her head, Elizabeth changed the subject and asked him what he had been doing all summer. She found out that he went on a quick vacation to the beach with some of his fraternity brothers, then settled in working with his father at their family construction business. He told her a lot about the company and that his goal is to learn as much as he can so he can take it over when his dad gets ready to retire.

They talked about friends from college. Trina's moving to the beach, and Elizabeth told him about going back to the boutique to work for now. They walked and talked for a good hour. Filling each other in on family, friends, and summertime happenings.

The sun was beginning to set, and the night was turning cool, when Elizabeth's phone vibrated in her pocket. She took it out, read the text, and looked at Brady.

"It's Jessica. She wanted me to know that she and Chad are at the car, whenever I'm ready." She sent Jessica an answer letting her know she'll be there soon. "It is getting late."

Elizabeth took his hand, and she led him toward Chad's car. Jessica and Chad were leaning on it watching Elizabeth and Brady cross the lot.

Brady reached his hand out to shake Chad's and then Jessica's. "It was great meeting y'all. Thank you for supporting Elizabeth. I plan on coming to visit soon, we'll have to grab a bite to eat."

Chad agreed and Jessica leaned in and gave him a hug. "Thank you for being understanding. She was so nervous about telling you."

Elizabeth glared at her friend, heat creeping up her face.

Brady reached over to grab Elizabeth's hand looking her in the eyes. "She doesn't need to be nervous. I'll do what I can for our baby."

Brady said this in a reassuring way, and it made Elizabeth melt.

Seeing the reaction of her friend, Jessica glanced between the two, and was glad to see things seemed to work out. She and Chad, wanting to give them privacy, got into the car to wait.

Brady walked Elizabeth to the passenger door and opened it, but stopped her before she could get in. "Take care of yourself, and I was serious about wanting to come and see you. Let's plan a date soon."

Elizabeth nodded in agreement. "That sounds good. We will. Thank you for being so understanding about all this. I know it is a shock."

Brady looked down at her "Yes, it is, but don't thank me." He leaned in and gave her a quick sweet kiss. Elizabeth smiled up at him, ingraining his profile into her memory and got into the car. Brady closed the door, waved, turned, and walked away.

As they pulled out of the parking lot, Jessica turned in her seat to look at her friend. A smile beaming brightly on her face.

"So, that seemed to go really well."

She could tell by the glow on Elizabeth's face she agreed.

"Oh, and girl. You were right. He does have a nice ass." Jessica lifted her eyebrows to emphasize what she thought and quickly turned around.

Elizabeth laughed in shock at that word her friend just used, and the hurt look on Chad's face.

"Hey, Jess. Remember, I'm driving here." Chad tried to sound hurt.

Jessica reached her hand over and rubbed it on his thigh. "Don't worry. Yours is my number one ass."

"Okay, enough of the language already! That doesn't work for you. Look, Elizabeth, you've corrupted my girlfriend."

Elizabeth laughed in agreement with his statement. Then leaned her head back against the seat and placed her hands on her stomach and sighed with contentment. She was filled with happiness that the night worked out so well.

Chapter 40

Needing a little bit of exercise and fresh air, Elizabeth and her parents decided to go for a walk one night after dinner.

It was a perfect night, and the air was crisp and cool. There was a light breeze and the air smelled like fall, dry leaves on the ground, and fresh cut grass.

This family time brought back memories of when Mr. and Mrs. Parks would walk hand in hand and Elizabeth would lead them through the neighborhood on her bike.

Elizabeth always loved the way her parents loved each other. Even after thirty years together, nothing has changed. She knew she was lucky to have parents who were still married and crazy about each other. So many of her friends came from divorced households. Looking down at the swell that was unmistakable now, she was hopeful Brady would continue wanting to be a part of the baby's life, though how their roles would work, she wasn't sure.

"Mom and Dad." They both turned toward her. "Brady wants to come down this weekend and meet you both. We talked about him getting here around lunch. Do you think we could have sandwiches and you could get to know him? He really wants to be a part of the baby's life, so you'll need to meet him at some point."

Elizabeth was sure this wouldn't be a problem, but she was still a little apprehensive.

"I know it'll be awkward. We both like each other, but aren't serious, and I guess you know we've had a relationship. I sort of can't hide that." With this she placed her hands on her stomach and patted it. "What do you think? Will you meet him, and Dad, will you be nice?" She said this while scrunching up her face.

Mrs. Parks chuckled at her husband as he stopped walking and his mouth dropped open.

"She has a point, honey. You do sometimes get a little bit overprotective."

Mr. Parks looked at both his girls shaking his head with disbelief. "It hurts me that you two think that little of me, but of course I would love to meet him and make sure he's good enough for both my daughter and my grandchild."

"Thanks, Dad." Elizabeth grabbed his hand and gave it a squeeze. He returned the squeeze with a wink.

As they walked past Jacob's house, he pulled in the driveway and waved at them as he stepped out of his car. Mr. and Mrs. Parks waved back and greeted him with smiles and hellos. Elizabeth threw a quick nod in his direction and picked up her walking speed, ready to be back home. Her parents, not ones to miss much of anything, exchanged a look between them.

Early the next morning, Elizabeth woke up at dawn, her thoughts filled with Brady. They had been getting along so well and this made her heart flutter.

Even though she had known him for four years of college, there was something about him now that she didn't notice before. Maturity maybe, she wasn't sure, but she knew she liked it, and they were good together.

They learned a lot about each other through their phone conversations. He was focusing on helping his father with their family construction business. They had been working on a project and he had to be on the worksite most Saturday mornings, so it's been a couple weeks since that day in the park.

She hoped meeting her parents was a good idea. She didn't realize how nervous she was at the thought, so to help pass the time, she started to dust the furniture and vacuum the rugs.

Awake due to the excessive roar of a vacuum, Mr. and Mrs. Parks descended the stairs and found their daughter dressed and focused on cleaning. With sleep in her voice, Mrs. Parks interrupted Elizabeth, who jumped from fright.

"Geez, Mom! You scared me to death. Whatcha' do that for?" Elizabeth turned off the vacuum and held her hand over her heart, catching her breath.

"Are you nesting, honey?" Seeing the confused look in her daughter's eyes, she explained. "Nesting is when pregnant women have an uncontrollable desire to clean. It is said it's because the baby is coming soon. Well?"

Understanding dawned on Elizabeth's face. "No, Mom. I'm just getting ready for Brady. You know he's gonna be here soon."

"Umm, it's six a.m. He won't be here till noon. We have a little bit of time." Her mother left Elizabeth standing in the living room; she needed coffee and smelled some brewing.

The rest of the morning took forever in Elizabeth's eyes. As the hours slowly ticked on, she completed her cleaning, placed new towels in the powder room, and made chocolate chip cookies. Her dad, wanting to help, took it upon himself to run to the store to get deli meat, bread, and vegetables for sandwiches.

Elizabeth wandered onto the porch and sat in the swing. While she was waiting, she found herself thinking back to school and her relationship with Brady.

She knew they had both been attracted to each other. That was apparent in how they came together like magnets when they first met on the quad and later when they saw each other at the fraternity house.

They went on a couple dates together over the years and she was his unspoken date at all the formals his fraternity had. Most guys and girls thought they were an item. The few times she did see him with another girl, she became insanely jealous, and he admitted the same about her. That's why they decided to be exclusive for a while.

That lasted through the month of February and most of March. They never decided to stop seeing each other, it just mutually happened. Then the school year ended, and they left without discussing anything.

The one thing she was glad about was that she knew she got pregnant in February, the one month there is no question who would be the father. Brady knows that. It makes it a whole lot easier to accept.

Chapter 41

Finally, just after twelve, his truck pulled into the driveway.

Elizabeth stood up to welcome him and her stomach started fluttering. She could not deny that he was a good-looking guy, and she was attracted to him. He must have had his hair trimmed because it fell neater in waves. He looked good in his jeans, T-shirt, and boots. The smile he gave her when their eyes met made her stomach flutter even more.

"Hey, you." His typical greeting she always heard hadn't changed.

She answered him like she always did. "Hey, you, back."

That made him laugh, and he leaped up the four steps to her porch and wrapped his arms around her in a quick hug and kissed her cheek.

"I've missed you, but it's like we haven't been away from each other for four months."

Elizabeth smiled at him for saying that.

She took a deep breath, looked him in the eyes and grabbed his hand. "So, are you ready? I gotta admit, I'm a nervous wreck."

Brady squeezed her hand to reassure her. "No use being nervous when you have to face the truth. Let's do this."

She opened the door and led him into the house.

Her parents were sitting in the sunroom, and both stood up when they entered. Elizabeth could see them looking over Brady. She was sure her father was making a judgment and she hoped he judged well.

Brady stuck his hand out toward Elizabeth's dad. "Hi, Mr. Parks. I'm Brady Warren. It's nice to meet you."

Elizabeth's father just stared at the boy standing in front of him and nodded his head.

"Mrs. Parks. Nice to meet you also."

Mrs. Parks shot her husband a "be good" look and returned Brady's handshake smiling at him. "Brady, it's nice to meet you. Please take a seat." She pointed him to one of the single chairs sitting in front of the window. "Can I get you something to drink?"

"No, thank you. I'm fine for now." He took the seat she offered, with Elizabeth next to him. She looked over at Brady, smiling encouragingly even though her nerves were on fire.

A few seconds passed and the room was becoming uncomfortable, or maybe that was just Elizabeth.

Mr. Parks broke into the uncomfortable silence with questioning that would make a detective cringe. "So, Brady, tell me how you and Elizabeth met?"

Brady took a deep breath ready to do his best. "At school, on the quad during Freshman Roundup. Then she showed up later at my fraternity house when we had a rush party."

"Did you both date at school?"

"Well, on and off. We could never decide if we really wanted to be serious."

"You were serious enough to have sex with her. Or was it just a one-night stand?"

Elizabeth was shocked. "Dad!"

Mr. Parks didn't take his eyes off the boy sitting across from him. "Elizabeth, it's an important question. Well, Brady?"

Brady looked over at Elizabeth. Her eyes were wide with embarrassment and apology. Reaching out he grabbed her hand and gave her a reassuring smile, then turned to her father.

"Mr. Parks, I understand your questioning, and I'll be honest with you. I remember when I first saw Elizabeth. Like I said earlier, it was on the quad. She and I were put in the same group during Freshman Roundup. We didn't talk much then, but she caught my eye. She was unforgettable. Then later that night, she walked into the backyard of the fraternity house with some friends. I noticed her immediately, she looked amazing, and her smile took my breath away. Some of the guys I was standing with noticed the group of girls, and a couple commented on the pretty brunette. Since she was the only brunette in the group, I knew it was her they were talking about, so I made sure to make the first move. The girls got in line at the keg, and I walked over to them, and pulled them to the front of the line, filled Elizabeth's cup, handed it to her, and introduced myself."

Turning to Elizabeth, he finished. "The first thing I noticed was that she was even more breathtaking up close."

Elizabeth looked at him with shock, as she searched his face trying to figure out if he was serious, or just making it all up for her father's sake. She could feel herself blushing and gave him a shy smile. "I remember that night clearly, but never knew you thought that."

"Well, it's all true. We danced later and after that, it was an unwritten rule that Elizabeth and I were an item. We never talked about it, until this year, but that's how it was."

He tore his eyes slowly away from Elizabeth, turning back to her parents.

"Did we make some poor choices, Mr. and Mrs. Parks? Yes, you would probably say so. But it was never a one-night stand, and looking back, we should have made our relationship more serious than it was. I think we were both so focused on completing our degrees that a relationship was nothing either one of us thought about at the time. It was easier just being together when we could, and no one stressed if we couldn't. Maybe that's not what you wanted to hear, but it's the truth." Brady stopped talking and looked at Elizabeth's parents, hoping they noticed the sincerity in his words.

Not getting any response, he continued. "Honestly, sir, when I saw Elizabeth's text and we talked about meeting, I was excited and realized I missed seeing her. This…"

Brady reached over and placed his hand on Elizabeth's pregnant belly, rubbing it softly, "was a bit of a surprise I wasn't expecting, but…" Brady shrugged, again looking at her. "It is what it is, and I'm here now."

Elizabeth smiled at him and placed her hand over his.

Mr. Parks looked between the two young adults in front of him,

"Well, it is what it is. I guess we will see." He stood up with finality and Brady did the same. Mr. Parks reached his hand out; Brady grasped it.

"Brady, thank you for stepping up and being willing to do your part. Remember, she is my only child, so she's our favorite and our world. I want to make sure you understand that." Mr. Parks looked sternly into Brady's eyes.

"Of course, sir. She is an amazing person." Brady shook his hand back with assurance.

Mrs. Parks stood up and put her hands on both men. "Now that we have that worked out, let's eat. I'm starving."

The rest of the afternoon went well. The four of them talked and relaxed, getting to know each other. Mr. Parks wanted to know all about Brady's family's business and what his responsibilities were. He readily shared all the information they asked about and was excited to show them that he had a stable and well-paying job.

Elizabeth surveyed the people sitting around the table, trying to picture Brady as a permanent part of the family. She found that her feelings for him were the same as they seemed in college.

She enjoyed her time with him, liked their time together, was physically attracted to him, but didn't really see them as a couple. When thinking of who she would like to be with, Jacob still came to her mind. The way she felt when he looked at her, and the memory of their night together, still made her wish for a different outcome.

Realizing her thoughts kept drifting off, she shook her head and focused again on the discussion, put a smile on her face, and took a bite of her sandwich.

Chapter 42

Brady drove to the restaurant. He didn't miss the fact that Elizabeth had gotten quiet while they were eating with her parents, and this continued on their drive to meet Jessica and Chad.

Throwing quick glances her way, he found himself wondering what was going on inside her head. He reached across the seat and grabbed her hand to pull her a little closer. "Hey, you. Everything good? You've gotten quiet."

Elizabeth gave him a small smile and nodded.

Glancing at her quizzically, he decided to let it go. If she wanted to talk about things, she would. He turned back to concentrate on the road, and it didn't take long before they were turning into the parking lot.

Brady maneuvered his truck into a parking space, turned off the engine and quickly got out. Rushing around the truck, he opened Elizabeth's door and helped her out, grabbing her arm, and pulling her back toward him before she could get too far.

She turned to face him with questioning and impatience radiating in her eyes. "What's up? They're waiting for us."

Sighing with concern, Brady took her hands into his and looked at her.

"Elizabeth, I feel like there's something going on. You call me and tell me about the baby, and I feel like we have really been connecting, but today, I've been getting mixed messages from you. I need to know what's going through your head."

Elizabeth looked off in the distance, not really focusing on anything, but not sure how to put her thoughts and feelings into words.

She chewed on her bottom lip, thinking about the past few weeks. She was so glad Brady was here and interested in her and the baby, but she couldn't figure out why she wasn't happier. He wants a relationship, wants them together. She thought she'd be ecstatic about that. Instead, she found herself empty; her feelings muddled.

She turned back to look at him, really look at him. She took in all his features. Searched his eyes for answers, and raised her hand, brushing it along the side of his face. She combed her fingers into his soft wavy hair, down his back, over his arms, finally folding her fingers through his.

"Brady, I'm so glad you're here. I really am. I think I'm still getting used to it because honestly, I'm shocked. I didn't think you would stick around and want to be a part of this." As soon as these words left her lips, she saw the hurt which blazed in his eyes, and she cupped his face in her hands making him look at her; hoping he would understand.

"I know you want to be a part of us now, I'm just not sure how to proceed or what comes next. This frightens me. My plans this summer were to stay at home, save money, then head to Florida with Trina to start the next chapter of my life. This..." Letting go of him, she gestured toward her stomach. "... wasn't in the plans. This is more than I bargained for, and it's a little overwhelming."

He interrupted her thoughts by wrapping his arms around her waist and pulling her into him. Her arms answered him by intertwining around his neck. He pulled her toward him, so their mouths touched.

He kissed her gently but with purpose. Her hands tightened around his neck, and her fingers found their way into his soft curls. His hands went up her back to press her still closer to him. He deepened the kiss hoping to get a response.

Elizabeth found herself getting lost in this moment. She loved his kisses and found herself a little upset when he pulled away from her.

Brady looked at her and moved his hands to stroke the sides of her face. "It's more than I planned, too, but I've always liked you, Elizabeth. You're beautiful and fun. I love who I am when we're together. I thought of you so much over the summer and wondered if I should call you, and I'm not just saying that. I promise, and to be totally honest, I wish I would have called you first."

He hoped she believed him. He couldn't be sure. "I'm glad I'm here, and the way you return my kisses, it seems like you're glad I'm here, too."

Elizabeth smiled a small smile as she searched his brown eyes, the eyes she used to love gazing into, but wasn't sure what she was hoping to find.

I've been wanting a guy to feel this way about me, so why can't I just be good with this? He's everything I want. What's wrong with me now that I have him?

Instead, she said the only thing she could. "Thank you. I'm glad you're here, too."

She leaned in and kissed him, slow but deep, hoping he would believe her. "We should go inside. I'm sure Jessica and Chad are waiting on us."

Brady looked at her, grabbed her hand and brought her knuckles to his lips. "Then, let's get going." They walked into the restaurant together.

Chapter 43

"Hey, you two." Jessica waved across the restaurant to get Elizabeth's attention. Smiling in recognition and pulling Brady along, Elizabeth led him through the maze of tables to where Chad and Jessica were waiting.

Jessica and Chad stood up to welcome the new additions. Hugs and handshakes were shared, and Brady and Elizabeth took their seats at the table. Not one to beat around the bush, Jessica asked what she wanted to know.

"So how did things go?" She glanced back and forth impatiently between Elizabeth and Brady.

Full of confidence, Brady quickly answered her. "Honestly, I think it went well. Her dad didn't shoot me, so I'll take that as a positive sign."

Everyone laughed and Brady reached over and took Elizabeth's hand in his. The new couple filled the other two in on their morning. They all talked, laughed, ordered food, and continued a good solid conversation, enjoying each other's company.

Someone on the other side of the restaurant caught Chad's eye. He looked up, and without thinking made eye contact and waved the newcomer over.

"Hey, Jacob." Chad stood up to welcome his buddy, grasping his hand and pulling him in for a guy hug and hard pat on the back. Brady turned to greet everyone else and noticed the stranger at the table.

Elizabeth and Jessica glanced at each other when their new guest arrived, and Elizabeth gently pulled her hand out from Brady's grasp.

"Jacob, you should meet Brady. Brady, this is a friend of ours, Jacob." Chad introduced the two men.

As Brady and Jacob shook hands, Elizabeth became uncomfortable and hoped to become invisible. She tried to avoid the situation and sat back in her chair, but Brady grabbed her hand again, pulling her next to him.

Squirming uncomfortably, she slowly looked between the two men before her. Her feelings for them tore at her insides. She glanced quickly at Brady, then made eye contact with Jacob. Her eyes froze on his. It was then that she realized she still had feelings for Jacob. There was something between them. Even though she tried to ignore him, tried to forget about him, her feelings for him had not changed. She felt more for him in the short time she had known him, than for the father of her child who she'd known for four years.

Elizabeth searched Jacob's eyes trying to see if her feelings were reciprocated. She smiled, a warm and welcoming smile. "Hi, Jacob."

"Hi, Elizabeth. You look good." She just answered again with a smile and a nod. Jacob excused himself and went to sit with Stacey and her boyfriend, who just walked into the restaurant after him and were seated at a table. Elizabeth couldn't help but notice that Jacob was not with Kristen.

As her thoughts were lost in that last realization, she was brought back to the conversation and the others sitting with her when their food came, and they started to enjoy their meal. If Brady thought there was anything strange between Elizabeth and Jacob, he didn't mention it, but Elizabeth again found herself having a hard time staying focused on the conversation in front of her because her eyes kept wandering over to the view across the restaurant.

Elizabeth finished her meal and sat back to relax. She did not miss the fact that she had a perfect view of Jacob and noticed when he got up from the table with his phone in his hand.

Quickly, she excused herself to use the restroom, and watched as Jacob walked out the main door. She walked past the restroom and followed him out of the restaurant instead. He was on the phone when she exited but he hung up and looked at her as she walked toward him.

"Hi, Jacob."

Jacob looked up at her obviously confused and pocketed his cell phone. "Hi, Elizabeth."

He looked around, wondering what brought her outside. "Are you all leaving?"

Elizabeth shook her head no. "I just wanted to speak with you."

He looked at her with intensity. "So, is that the father?"

Elizabeth stopped briefly at this unexpected and direct question but answered him honestly. "Yes. Brady's the father. I contacted him. I thought he needed to know." She continued her approach.

Looking down at her, Jacob searched her face for an answer he wasn't sure he wanted to know. "He did need to know. It looks like he took it well. Is there something between you both now?"

She stepped even closer, closing the gap between them and looked into the blueness of his eyes. She was close enough to see the reflection of the parking lot lights in the light blue of those eyes.

"I'm not sure what's between us." She wasn't sure what man she was talking about when she said those words.

Jacob took her hands in his, more to stop her advance than hold her. "Elizabeth, what're you doing?"

Not pulling her eyes away from his, she answered him. "I'm not sure."

She stood on her tiptoes, pulled her hands from his, enclosed them around his neck, and closed her lips on Jacob's.

His lips were soft and warm, just as she remembered them. At first, he was reluctant, but she soon felt him give in and surrender to the kiss. She missed his lips and his kisses and showed him just how much. She deepened the kiss, and he answered her by folding her in his arms.

As quick as it heated up, it cooled off. Jacob broke their kiss and stepped away.

"Elizabeth, stop."

He separated himself from her and glanced quickly around the parking lot. "I really need to go. So do you." He looked at her as he said this, drinking in one last glance, and turned and walked away toward his car.

"Jacob? Why?" Elizabeth felt tears welling up in her eyes as she watched him continue to walk away.

He turned at her pleading words, but slowly walked backward, increasing the distance between him and the girl he once thought he might be falling in love with.

"Elizabeth, I have Kristen. You need Brady. You wanted this. I'm giving you what you asked for." He paused briefly holding onto her gaze for a little bit longer, then turned and quickly got into his car and drove out of the parking lot.

Standing there, watching him drive away, she couldn't stop the tears which fell down her face.

What have you done, Elizabeth?

She shook her head to clear her thoughts, wiped her face roughly, and turned to walk back to the restaurant.

Standing there when she entered the door was Brady. His eyes blazed with anger and jealousy. Elizabeth stopped in her tracks, speechless.

"I take it you and Jacob were a little more than friends."

"How much did you see?" Guilt filled her. She didn't want to hurt Brady and went and tried to comfort him.

He pulled away from her touch and put his hands in the air as if touching her would burn his skin. "I saw enough."

Knowing there was nothing she could say to explain her actions, she lowered her eyes and walked away from him back to the table.

Elizabeth and Brady did not talk on the drive back to her house. Pulling on her road, and into her driveway, she finally broke the silence. "I'm sorry, Brady. I should have told you about my relationship with Jacob. I broke things off with him soon after I found out about the baby."

Brady didn't answer until he put his truck in park and turned off the engine. With his hands on the wheel, and staring straight ahead, he asked her the question that was eating at him.

"So, do you still love him?"

Elizabeth looked at Brady. "It doesn't matter."

Brady's eyes went wide, and his brows were furrowed as he quickly snapped his head toward her. He searched her face hoping she would continue. When she didn't, he did. "It doesn't matter? Your feelings do matter, Elizabeth. They matter so much." He gestured with his hands back and forth between them. "This matters."

He turned away from her to hide the tears that filled his eyes. "You know what, Elizabeth, when you figure out what you want, please let me know."

He shook his head when she didn't fill the silence. "You should go."

Elizabeth sighed and reached for the truck handle. She opened the door and stepped out. "Brady…"

He didn't look at her but held up a hand to stop her from saying anything else. "Call me when you're over him, or when the baby's born."

Sighing, with desperation, she closed the door, but leaned in the window. "Brady, what can I say to fix things?"

"Seriously, Elizabeth?" He shook his head, his eyes wide in amazement. "I can't…I just can't… Again, when you figure things out, let me know. Now step away from the truck."

She did as he said and watched as the man, she has had feelings for and a relationship with for four years, pulled out of her driveway, back onto the road, and possibly out of her life forever.

Chapter 44

Elizabeth, once again, found herself lost in her thoughts, frustrated and angry. Brady really wanted to be involved in the pregnancy and birth. All the fears she had about him and the baby were unfounded.

He also seemed to have feelings for her. They could be a family and raise the baby together. So why was she making this so difficult? Why didn't she want to be with him? Why couldn't she just be happy?

But most of all, why couldn't she stop thinking of Jacob?

Dragging through her morning routine, Elizabeth found that she was having a hard time getting ready for work and her weekly doctor's appointment. She only had to work this week, then she was getting time off to prepare for the baby's birth.

"Good morning, Elizabeth. Is Brady meeting us at the doctor's today?" Mrs. Parks greeted her as Elizabeth entered the kitchen making her way toward the coffee pot. Elizabeth leaned on the counter waiting for the machine to brew her a cup of green tea, her new favorite morning drink.

"He won't be coming today, Mom. He's busy." Elizabeth was hoping to not have to talk about the fact that she hasn't talked to him since he dropped her off Saturday. She sent him some texts Sunday, and tried to call him, but all her attempts went unanswered.

"Oh, well, that stinks. I know you mentioned that he was wanting to see the ultrasound. Are you going to find out what the sex of the baby is? It would be great to know before he or she gets here."

Elizabeth shrugged her shoulders and felt herself getting irritated with this questioning. "I don't know. We'll see."

Mrs. Parks became concerned. "Elizabeth, honey, what's wrong?"

Elizabeth grabbed her freshly brewed tea, dropped heavily in the seat beside her mom, and grabbed a banana, peeling it slowly to waste time.

She contemplated just lying and not telling her mother anything, though, she knew she'd find out soon enough. Who knew if Brady would be coming around again anytime soon anyway. Her mom would eventually find out about the mess she made. No time like the present.

"Mom, I screwed up. Again." Elizabeth emphasized the 'again' as she took a big bite out of the banana. Her mother, always the patient one, waited for her to go on. Elizabeth chewed and thought over what to say.

Figuring the truth was the easiest, she told her mother about what happened Saturday night, how disjointed she was during the entire dinner, how she followed Jacob out to the parking lot, kissed him and that Brady saw the entire thing. She then told her mom about their drive home and the last words they spoke.

"Now he isn't answering my calls or texts." She paused, sighing heavily, and completed eating her banana, waiting for her mother's reaction.

Mrs. Parks thoughtfully looked at her. "I see. That does seem to be a mess."

Elizabeth dropped her empty banana peel on the counter and looked at her mom with a dumbfounded expression. "I see? That's all you can say? Really, Mom, I screwed up! One minute I'm so glad Brady is wanting to be with me and be a part of the baby's life. I am ecstatic! We are talking about plans, and things we can do. I like him, Mom. I do. I always have. But..." Elizabeth put her face in her hands. Breathing in very deeply, she wiped her hands down her face in frustration and continued. "But I can't get Jacob out of my mind."

Turning toward her mom, she pleaded, "Why can't I get Jacob out of my mind? Why can't I just be happy with Brady? When will I be good enough to have an amazing guy love me?"

Mrs. Parks placed her hand on Elizabeth's back. "Elizabeth, enough. You are an amazing person. Stop being so hard on yourself. Just take things one day at a time and relax. You'll figure things out and make the right decision, and you know Brady will come around when the baby's born. I'm sure he's hurt, but what will be, will be. Right now, though, we need to get to the doctor. You ready?"

Mrs. Parks got up from the counter, put their mugs in the sink and threw away the empty banana peel, ending the discussion.

Elizabeth, taking the cue, followed her mother out the door to the car.

The doctor's appointment went well, and everything was still going perfectly. At two centimeters dilated, her body was preparing for the birth, but it could still be weeks before the baby came.

When he asked if she wanted to know the baby's sex, Elizabeth couldn't get herself to say yes. Part of her was hoping Brady would have just shown up to support her, and when that didn't happen, she couldn't find out.

Not yet anyway. She wanted Brady to know the same time she did. So, she told the doctor no and he put the ultrasound picture in an envelope for her

Glancing at the envelope on the passenger seat next to her, Elizabeth wondered what the paper inside had written on it. The temptation to open it and peek was so strong, but she beat the temptation and stayed focused on the radio, singing away to the newest pop song blasting from her stereo speakers.

Before she got out of the car at the boutique, she took a picture of the envelope and sent Brady a text.

> Just want you to know that in this envelope is the sex of our baby. I didn't want to find out without you with me. Can we at least get together to open this, and see? No strings attached.

Elizabeth sat for a minute just staring at her phone screen. Not knowing why, she thought he would all of a sudden answer her, but a woman could hope, couldn't she?

Sighing deeply, she heaved herself out of her car, walked across the parking lot, and through the boutique doors, ready to start her last day of work for a while.

Chapter 45

Jessica ran up to the door to greet Elizabeth, grabbing her arm, and pulling her to the back of the store. "Hi, Elizabeth. How was the doctor? Is everything good? I'm sure it is."

Jessica's behavior had Elizabeth laughing and wondering what in the world was going on with her friend. She was getting ready to ask Jessica if she was on anything, when a loud, SURPRISE made Elizabeth jump and scream, covering her face with her hands.

When her heart went back to an almost regular rhythm, Elizabeth peeked between her fingers. Her eyes popped wide and her mouth opened in shock.

Looking into the back room, she saw streamers and balloons hanging everywhere in pink and blue. Tables were covered with tablecloths of the same colors. There were women from church, the pregnancy center, and the town smiling and clapping their hands at the surprise and fright that was apparent on Elizabeth's face.

Stacey came running over to her along with Desiree and a much skinnier Charity. Elizabeth found herself engulfed in a group hug surrounded by squealing women.

"What did y'all do?" Elizabeth asked, separating herself from the wall of friends.

"Are you surprised?" asked Jessica.

Looking around again, Elizabeth saw both her mother and Mrs. Stanzel smiling broadly at her. She then looked back at Jessica and the girls still surrounding her.

"Surprised? I'm more amazed. I had no idea!" Looking at Jessica, Elizabeth's smile filled her face. "I can't believe you kept this from me." She hugged her friends again, thanking them.

Elizabeth then walked over to her mother and wrapped her in a big hug, smacking a kiss on her cheek. "Is this why you were really pushing to find out whether the baby is a boy or girl?"

Her mom shrugged. "It would have meant a slight change in decorations. But everything looks beautiful anyway." She returned her daughter's hug.

Next, Elizabeth hugged her boss tightly, thanking her and strolled around the crowd, talking with everyone and thanking them for coming.

The afternoon was amazing. They played games, ate food, talked, and laughed. Elizabeth opened so many gifts, she was speechless. She had diapers, clothes, booties, bottles, pacifiers, stuffed animals, and lots more things she didn't even realize a baby needed but was sure she would be thankful she had when the time came.

Elizabeth was overwhelmed with the love that she was shown and made sure to thank everyone as the party died down and the ladies started to leave.

Jessica noticed the tears that started to fall down Elizabeth's cheeks and wrapped her friend in a hug. "Hey, it's supposed to be a fun day. You're not supposed to be crying."

Elizabeth laughed through the tears at her friend's whiny voice. "I know. It has been a fun day. It's been perfect. I'm just amazed at how awesome everything was, and everyone who cared so much. It's a bit overwhelming." Elizabeth hugged her friend back. "Thank you, so much. It really was a great time. I was so surprised." Elizabeth squeezed extra hard, before letting Jessica free from her grasp.

Jessica smiled wide. "I'm so glad. Mrs. Stanzel and your mom had tons of fun helping me plan it. Your doctor's appointment was a perfect time to keep you from getting here early. I just wish Brady would have been here with you. How's that going?" Elizabeth filled her in on the text she sent and her reasoning on not finding out the baby's sex.

Elizabeth shook her head in frustration. "I screwed up, and he must still be upset. I don't blame him at all. I really hurt him and have to deal with it, no matter how bad things get."

Jessica handed Elizabeth back her phone, after reading the last text she sent him. "I'm sorry things have become so crappy. But you know, in your final text you told him 'No strings attached.' That just might be the problem. He seems to want the strings and I think he also wants to be attached."

Elizabeth looked at Jessica thoughtfully and glanced down at the last text she sent. "You know, I didn't think of that. He told me not to contact him until I made a decision or the baby came. I guess 'no strings attached' isn't the decision he wants." Elizabeth shrugged her shoulders. "There's really nothing else I can promise him. I wish there was, and I don't know why there isn't."

"Well, there's nothing we can do about it right now. Let's help Mrs. Stanzel close and get these presents to your house. Maybe we can start decorating the nursery."

Jessica led Elizabeth out of the backroom, and they started going through the motions to close for the day. This was the simplest workday ever. Elizabeth just got paid to be the guest of honor at her own party. How awesome was that!?

Elizabeth carried some of the gifts from her car into the house.

"Hey there, Lilly Billy. Why are you carrying those things in here? Put them down. I'll empty your car." Her father took the few packages from her arms and placed them on the steps. "So, did you have fun?"

Elizabeth scrunched her eyes at her father. "I should have figured you were in on it. But yes, it was amazing. I'm a little hurt that you actually kept it a surprise from me, Dad."

Her dad just smiled and wiggled her eyebrows at Elizabeth. "What do you mean? I'm good at keeping surprises from you."

"Really, Dad? How about my sweet sixteen party? I think I remember you leaking something about that."

"Excuse me? Did I miss something about you telling our daughter about her sweet sixteen?" Mrs. Parks came into the foyer at this time, with her hands on her hips, interrupting the conversation.

"What? I don't know what Elizabeth's talking about." Mr. Parks smiled as he said this. The women laughed at the man they loved and surrounded him in a group hug.

It was then that Jessica came through the door with her arms loaded down with gifts. "Well, I guess I missed something. I'd love to be a part of the group hug, but my arms are full."

Elizabeth and her mom let Mr. Parks go. Mr. Parks took some of the gifts from Jessica and Mrs. Parks picked up the gifts left on the steps. "You know, girls, let's take these packages upstairs. There's something I need you to see, Elizabeth." Mr. Parks led the women upstairs into the nursery.

He opened the door and stepped aside to let Elizabeth go in first. She stopped suddenly as soon as she stepped past the threshold and her eyes got wide.

Just yesterday the room stood empty. Now it was filled with a crib, dressing table, dresser, bookshelf, and a glider rocker. Elizabeth walked through the room, dragging her hand over the smooth cherry wood of the dresser, and then the crib.

She stood over the crib which was placed right in front of the window which looked out over the backyard and its row of mature oak trees. She always loved this view. She stood in awe of what was all around her.

Her dad came up next to her and wrapped her in a side hug, as he also looked out the window. "How do you like it?"

"It's amazing, Dad. It's exactly what I was looking at online. It's perfect." She leaned over and hugged her father hard, squeezing him like she might lose him if she let go. "Thank you so much. I love it."

He returned the hug. "Good. I'm so glad. I want everything to be as perfect as possible for you and the little one. I know it's not going to be easy, but we are here to help you with anything you need. Your mom and I love you both so much."

He gave her an extra squeeze and dropped a kiss on top of her head. "Now let me go help your mom and Jessica unload all your gifts. You relax. It's been a long day." He separated himself from his daughter's hug and left the room to empty her car of gifts.

Elizabeth went to the glider rocker to sit and rest. She put her feet up on the ottoman, leaned her head back, closed her eyes, and rocked. It was a very comfortable chair, and she pictured herself rocking a little baby in her arms long into the night. She imagined a dark-haired baby with big brown eyes, just like his father, and realized she thought 'his' and remembered the envelope on her front seat, still sitting there.

Brady's face flashed through her mind, but then as if her brain didn't want her to get too comfortable with him, she then saw the sky-blue eyes she desired so much.

Jessica interrupted her thoughts. "This is the last of it. Your mom and dad are going to pick up some salad and pizza for dinner. What should we do first?"

Elizabeth looked around at all the gifts Jessica and her parents had brought up. She didn't remember them doing all that, so she must have taken a quick nap as she was rocking.

"Well, I guess we should open all the clothes, blankets, and sheets. We need to get those washed before we make the bed or put the clothes away."

Jessica nodded her head in agreement. "Sounds good. Let's get started." Jessica sat on the floor and passed Elizabeth some bags. Together they started opening packages and making piles to put in the washer.

Chapter 46

The next few days, Elizabeth occupied her time with organizing and decorating the nursery. Since she still did not know if she was having a boy or girl, she decorated the room with green and yellow pastels and teddy bears. She kept the walls the beige they always were. The dark cherry furniture, and accents of pale greens and yellows finished out the room and added just enough color. She loved the look she created.

Standing back admiring the now completed and ready bedroom, she smiled at what she saw. "So, baby, your room is finished. I know you'll love it here."

She picked her phone up from the bookshelf and snapped pictures standing in the doorway to get the full view. Without thinking twice, she sent all those pictures to Brady telling him she hoped he'd come by and see the nursery.

"Hi, hon. Are you finished?" Elizabeth turned and saw her mom coming down the hallway with a wash basket in her arms.

"Hey, Mom. Yeah. It looks really good. I love it." Elizabeth moved over so her mother could look in the baby's room.

She smiled and agreed. "You've been working hard. Why don't we go into town and grab a sandwich for lunch? We can stop by some stores quickly and pick up anything else you think you might need. It'll do you good to get out."

"That sounds great, Mom. I'll grab a jacket." Elizabeth left to grab her jacket from her room and run a brush through her hair and put her phone in her jacket pocket. As she walked down the steps, she heard a notification that she had a text. Ignoring it, she picked up her purse and followed her mom out the door.

They made it to the restaurant. Elizabeth planned on getting a salad but smelling the deli bread that always made her mouth water, she changed her mind and settled on a club sandwich with chips and water.

Not realizing how hungry she was until her meal was placed in front of her and she started eating, Elizabeth devoured her sandwich. Her mother was laughing at the speed in which her daughter shoved food into her mouth.

"Did you not eat today?"

Elizabeth swallowed and took a drink of water. "I honestly don't remember. I've been so focused on finishing the room. But mmm, this sandwich is always perfect."

She was interrupted by her phone ringing. Remembering the text she received at home, she pulled her phone out of her purse and froze when she saw who the call was from and turned the phone in her mom's direction.

"Brady? Elizabeth, aren't you going to answer it?"

An uneasy feeling, maybe more like panic, swept over her. She stared at the phone until it stopped ringing, then quickly heard a notification that she got a voicemail. Holding her mom's eyes, she tapped the voicemail notification and put it on speaker.

"Hi. I hope this is Elizabeth Parks."

Elizabeth looked with confusion at her mom and mouthed, "*It's not Brady*".

The message continued. *"I'm Christian, Brady's brother. I know he hasn't wanted to talk to you, but there's been an accident and Brady's in the hospital."*

Elizabeth froze at this news watching the phone like it was going to start talking on its own.

"He didn't want to tell you, but I really felt like you should know. He just had surgery on his leg. He should be awake soon. I know he really would like to see you, even if he won't admit it."

Christian went on to tell her the hospital name and Brady's room number. He added his phone number as a quick final thought if she wanted to talk to him directly.

The recording ended.

Elizabeth's mom reached across the table trying to get her daughter to make eye contact. "Do you want to go see him?"

Fear filled Elizabeth's eyes followed by tears. "Yes. I mean, no." Shaking her head she finally admitted. "I don't know, Mom. If he doesn't want to see me, why should I go?"

"Because you need him to know you care."

Elizabeth looked at her mom, speechless, lost in her thoughts. Tears rolled down her face. She thought of Brady and then Jacob ran into her mind. "I do, but I don't know how much. There's still Jacob."

Her mom stopped and took a deep breath while a flash of irritation crossed her face. "Really, Elizabeth? Think about it. You and Jacob might have had something, but it looks to me like he has moved on. I don't want to tell you what to feel, but I think you have moved on also. I feel that all that Jacob is, is your way of not having to face your real feelings. He is the easy way out. But you need to look at what's right here..." She held up Elizabeth's phone. "...in front of you, and possible." She held Elizabeth's gaze as Elizabeth looked at her mom, then glanced down at her phone.

"Come on, I'm going to take you to the hospital. You can decide if you want to see Brady when we get there." Mrs. Parks stood up, cleaned the sandwich papers and drinks from the table, and led her daughter out of the restaurant into the car.

Elizabeth's mind raced as she sat in the passenger seat. Feelings were flooding her insides. Worry, concern, fear, nervousness. They all churned together, making her scared she might throw up the sandwich and chips she just shoved in her mouth. She held her stomach, willing it to hold down the food, and also to feel close to the child whose father was injured.

When her mom pulled into the parking lot and searched for a spot to park, Elizabeth grabbed her phone and sent a text to Christian's number. It took a few seconds until she got an answer. During that time, her mom had found a spot, pulled in and turned off the car, waiting to see what her daughter was going to decide.

> It's Elizabeth. My mom and I are parking. Can I talk to you first before going in to see Brady?

> Sure. I'll meet you in the lobby at the main

> entrance. I'm wearing
> jeans, boots, and a red
> T-shirt.

"Christian's gonna meet us in the lobby. I want to talk to him first." Elizabeth let her mom know and got out of the car quickly before she lost her nerve.

When the two women made it to the entrance, Elizabeth's mother excused herself to call her dad, but she promised to meet up with Elizabeth inside.

Elizabeth stood outside the hospital, watching her mom walk away. She contemplated leaving and going back to the car, but that thought only took a second as she felt a kick in her stomach like the baby was letting her know he, or she, wanted to go inside.

"Okay, little one. We'll go." She took a deep calming breath and stepped through the large sliding doors which opened into the hospital lobby.

Chapter 47

Elizabeth would have recognized Christian without a description. He had the same brown wavy hair as Brady.

The two brothers looked so much alike Elizabeth did a quick double take trying to remember if Brady was a twin even though she knew that he wasn't.

Christian was a few years older, and Elizabeth thought she remembered Brady saying something about his nephews, Christian's sons.

He must have had a description of her also, because as soon as they made eye contact, he smiled and walked toward her.

When they got close, he put his hand out in greeting. "You must be Elizabeth."

Nodding her head yes, Elizabeth shook his hand.

"Well, you are just as pretty as Brady always said."

He looked down at her belly and his smile grew wider. "Wow. My brother is really gonna be a dad." Grasping both her hands and holding her gaze, he finished his sentence. "He's so excited. Really, he is. I also want you to know he talked about you all summer, even before you contacted him. His biggest regret was not keeping a relationship with you. He always talked about you as the 'one who got away.' He was so excited when you contacted him, and I have to admit, a little scared and shocked when you told him the news."

Elizabeth was overwhelmed at all she just heard. "He never said anything at school that he had real feelings for me. I thought we were just close friends. Anyway..." She waved her hand in front of them like she was trying to erase all that from memory. "What happened? How did he get here?"

"Well, that's a story he doesn't want you to know." Christian walked away and sat down on a couch in the waiting area. Elizabeth followed and took the seat across from him.

He looked at her as he continued. "He told me all about your talk at the park, the baby, how he felt. I can tell you, excited, isn't quite the word, but very happy? That might be good enough, anyway. He was happy that you both were talking, and he thought things were going well. To him, it was like you both picked right back up from where things were left at the end of school. He was nervous about becoming a dad, but never thought twice about standing up and taking responsibility. Our family is important to us." He looked at her, making sure she understood this.

"When he got back from your house the last time, he asked me if he could come over. He needed to talk to someone. Of course, I said yes. I could tell by the tone in his voice there was something wrong. He told me about how well things seemed to go with your parents and that he thought things were going well between you both. Then he told me about seeing you making out with that guy, Jacob, I think he said that was what his name was? In the parking lot."

Again, Christian stopped talking and made eye contact with her. "I've gotta tell you, he was hurt that you didn't deny your feelings for that guy. It was getting late. He decided to leave my house. I could tell he was upset, and I tried to get him to spend the night. Anyway, he insisted on driving home. At some point on the drive, he lost control, and hit a tree. He's lucky that he didn't get hurt worse than he did, or that he didn't hit anyone else."

Christian stood up and walked away before he turned and continued. "I should have forced him to stay at my place. He shouldn't have been driving. He was angry and frustrated." Christian covered his eyes with his hands.

Elizabeth could tell he was upset, and she didn't blame him for feeling that way at all. She slowly stood up and walked toward him cautiously. "How bad is he hurt? You said he had surgery."

Christian pushed his fingers on the bridge of his nose. "Like I told you on the phone, his surgery was on his leg. He needed to get a rod placed because the break was so serious, and he has a concussion. He'll be fine. He just needs time to heal." Elizabeth felt that there was a hidden message in those last words, and they hit her hard in her heart.

"Can I go see him?"

"Sure, but remember, he doesn't know you're here. I'll go in first and talk to him."

Elizabeth agreed and followed Christian into the elevator and down a hallway to another waiting room. He walked ahead to an older man and lady. He said something Elizabeth couldn't hear. The woman looked over at Elizabeth, nodded her head and walked toward her.

"Hi. You're Elizabeth?" Elizabeth nodded her head. "I'm Joanna Warren. Brady and Christian's mother. It's nice to finally meet you."

The pretty woman glanced down at Elizabeth's protruding belly and breathed in a quick, deep breath, covering her mouth with her hands. An older man came over to them and placed his arm around Joanna's waist.

"I'm sorry. I just can't believe it." She stopped herself in mid-sentence and her husband completed her thoughts.

"I think what she means is that we are both a little overwhelmed with the fact that we'll be grandparents very soon." He put his hand out to shake Elizabeth's. "I'm Tim."

Elizabeth returned his handshake, smiling at them both, but she was at a loss for words. "I'm so sorry. I promise, I really am."

Her phone made a noise, and she looked down and noticed a message from her mom. She was going to wait in the car. Elizabeth sent her back a text telling her she was upstairs outside Brady's room and just met his parents. She'd let her know when she was on her way.

At the same time, she tapped send, Christian came out of Brady's room and came over to her. Her heart sped up with anticipation.

"He's good with seeing you. You can go on in." He led Elizabeth to the door and gave her an encouraging smile. She opened the door and entered the room.

Brady was in bed, sitting up. He had his leg elevated on a few pillows, and an IV in his arm. He looked tired but gave her a weak smile when he saw her.

Elizabeth insecurely approached his bed. "Hi."

"Hey." He answered her back looking directly at her with eyes void of emotion.

"Can I sit down?" she asked, motioning to the chair. He nodded his head, so she pulled the chair closer to his bedside and took a seat.

Once she was comfortable, she glanced around at the machines. She also took in his appearance. He had a few scrapes on his face, and a fading greenish, yellowish bruise just above his left temple.

She looked at his cast, then dragged her eyes up to his face. "Does it hurt much?" She was sure that was a stupid question, but it was all she could think of saying.

Brady wiggled the tube going from the IV into his arm. "As long as I'm drinking this cocktail, I'm all good. I've been hurt worse." He smiled a little when he said this. His good spirits, even if they were fake, made her smile in return. And she didn't miss the hidden meaning in his words.

After a few seconds of silence, awkwardness, and just watching each other, Elizabeth finally spoke. "Brady, I'm so sorry this happened to you. I came as soon as I heard. I wish I knew before now."

Brady sat up as much as he could in his bed. "Elizabeth, stop. Please. My brother let me know he told you quite a bit. Look, it's simple. I was excited when I heard from you. I should have said some things before graduation, but I didn't. We were both so focused on ourselves. A little selfish. But Elizabeth..." He stopped what he was saying and took a big cleansing breath, looking directly at her. The look he gave her was so intense and serious. It gave Elizabeth a chill all the way down her spine. She could feel her stomach getting warm. She wanted to break his gaze but found she couldn't.

"Elizabeth, I'm sure this isn't the right time to say this, but I'm in love with you. I have been for a while. I don't want you to think this has to do with the baby. It doesn't. You are the sweetest person I know. I love spending time with you, dancing with you. I love the light in your eyes when you are talking about your latest passion. I enjoy just walking in the park and talking with you." The words he just spoke shocked her. She didn't know what to say or do. She dropped her eyes from his face and stared at the textures in the blanket he had around him.

Brady continued. "But look, I don't want you to feel obligated to feel the same way back. I don't expect anything from you but honesty." He paused, took a deep breath, caught her gaze, then continued. "That's why I need to ask you to leave. I was doing good before we talked. I was having a great summer and was enjoying learning the business with my dad. I need to be focused on that again and not be distracted with thoughts of you, thoughts of us."

Elizabeth shook her head in confusion and brought her eyes back up to his, tears threatening to spill over. "Brady, I don't understand. Why didn't you say anything at school about how you felt? You say you're in love with me, but at the same time you want me to leave you alone. That doesn't make sense. We have a baby coming soon."

She said this last part like she had to remind him she was pregnant. Like he could possibly forget.

He grasped her hands in his. "I know, Elizabeth. Trust me, I know. I will help you with the baby. I'm the father. I'll do my part. I just think it's best if we stay apart."

"But, Brady, I care about you. I thought we were gonna try to have something together. I thought that's what we wanted." Elizabeth found herself pleading with him, she squeezed her hands tighter around his, scared to let them go.

Brady chuckled at her words and rolled his eyes in frustration. "See. Elizabeth, that's exactly what I mean. We've known each other for four years already. We have had a relationship in the past. We already really know each other. We made a baby for God's sake. If it was meant to be, we wouldn't have to 'try' to have something, and by now, you would feel more than just 'caring' for me. You would already love me, like I love you." He stopped, clearly upset, frustrated, and tired.

Tired, not just from the accident, but from trying.

He massaged the side of his head. Elizabeth became concerned. She stood up quickly. "Brady, are you okay?"

He pulled his hand out of hers. "Just a headache. It happens with a concussion. I'm fine Elizabeth. I'll heal."

He looked up at her and held her gaze with determination. "You really need to go."

Elizabeth suddenly felt panic rising to the surface. She was scared to leave him here in this room, but she also couldn't tell him what he wanted to hear. She frantically searched her heart for the feelings she wanted to feel. The feelings she was surprised she couldn't find. Why couldn't she find them?

"Brady." Tears were again filling her eyes. She could find no more words to say. The blank and empty look on his face was all she could take. She leaned toward him to give him a kiss, but he turned his face slightly away from her and closed his eyes, so she kissed his cheek and quickly walked out of the room, past his family, down the hall to the elevator, and to her mother waiting in the car.

Chapter 48

Days flew by as Elizabeth counted down until she became a mother. She always had something to do, or an appointment to go to. The baby was still growing and seemed to be healthy. She kept Brady up to date with texts after her doctor's appointments, whenever she opened a new gift, or just that the baby was becoming more and more active. He never answered any of them.

"Hey, you." Jessica entered the kitchen sunroom where Elizabeth was sitting enjoying a cup of hot green tea lost in thought. "Whatcha' up to?" She plopped down next to Elizabeth and noticed she had a cup of tea in one hand, and an envelope in another. Elizabeth held the envelope up in the air.

Jessica saw it and took it from her friend's hand, turning it over and over. "What's this?"

Elizabeth looked at Jessica and shrugged her shoulders. "It's the ultrasound from a couple weeks ago. I've never opened it. I was hoping Brady would want to open it with me, but now he isn't interested and I'm really considering looking at it without him."

"You could facetime him. If he answers, you can open it with him on the phone. If he doesn't answer, open it anyway. Just do it."

Taking a deep breath, Elizabeth got up her courage. "You're right. I should just do it."

"Do what?" Mrs. Parks entered the room and involved herself in the conversation. Jessica filled her in. The excitement was evident in Mrs. Park's eyes. "I agree with Jessica. Just do it and see what happens."

Looking between her two favorite women gave Elizabeth the courage she needed. She picked up her phone, dialed Brady's number and waited to see if he would answer, even though she didn't expect him to.

The phone rang and rang.

She was getting ready to hang up when there was a click and Brady's face filled her screen.

Her heart leaped in her chest when she saw his image. A smile filled her face and her features lit up with the excitement of seeing him.

She couldn't mistake the fact that she missed him. He looked so good. His bruises were gone, and his scratches were healing.

She could tell that he was at a desk, and it looked like he was in a small room. It must have been his office.

"Hey, Elizabeth. Is everything alright?" He asked her.

"Yeah, it is. Are you at work? Am I bothering you?"

"Yeah, I came back to work yesterday. I'm on desk duty and just making phone calls and answering emails. I can't do much else. You caught me at a good time."

"How are you feeling? How's your leg?"

Brady faced his camera down. There was a cast on his leg, and he had it propped on a stool under the desk. "The cast is a bit bulky and very uncomfortable, but I'm able to move around, so I won't complain much anyway."

"I'm glad to hear that. You look good, Brady."

"Thanks. You're looking great yourself." He smiled at her. He paused and looked behind him saying something she couldn't understand.

"Sorry. My dad just came to the door. We have a meeting in a little bit. Anyway, what's up?"

She held the envelope in front of the camera. "I got this at the appointment I asked you to go to, quite a while back. You didn't show up and I didn't open it. I was wondering if you wanted to know if we are having a son or daughter." Brady was silent for a bit, and just stared into the camera. He finally found the words he needed. "Really, you've been waiting to open it with me?"

She nodded her head. He looked away from the camera, really seeming to think of the possibility. Then, turning back to face the camera, he nodded his head. "Yeah, let's do this."

Elizabeth shot a look of excitement over her phone at the two women who both smiled encouragingly at her.

She took a deep breath, "Here it goes."

She placed her phone against her mug of tea, and tore the envelope open, pulling out the picture inside. The picture was a black and white photo of a baby. On the bottom was typed *baby boy Parks*.

Elizabeth smiled a huge, excited grin and held it in front of the camera to focus only on the ultrasound photo. Brady was as quiet as she was, probably taking it all in.

"Brady, can you read it?" She asked this just to make sure he was still there.

"Yes, I can."

She turned the camera back to focus on her face, so she could see him. "It's a boy, Brady."

They made eye contact as much as you could through a phone screen.

Brady's smile reached his eyes. Elizabeth, feeling his excitement through the phone, met his smile with her own, laughing with excitement at their news.

"Elizabeth, thanks so much for sharing this with me. I really appreciate it, but I need to get back to work. Keep in touch, okay?"

"I will, I promise." She waved into the phone and hung up. Taking a deep breath, she sat there looking at the picture she still held. Her son, her boy. Joy filled her heart and her eyes. She snapped a picture of the ultrasound and sent it to Brady.

"Elizabeth?" She was jarred out of her thoughts and looked up at the two women who she forgot were in the room with her. Her mom came over and sat down next to her, putting out her hand for the ultrasound picture and she hugged her daughter. "He's beautiful already."

"Mom, he looks like an alien in that picture."

"It's okay, I know he's beautiful. I see his mother right here in front of me."

Elizabeth gave her momma a big hug, and Jessica came and joined in on the excitement.

Chapter 49

Elizabeth's due date came and went with no contractions and no baby. She sent Brady texts daily to keep him in the know. Sometimes he answered, sometimes he didn't, but Elizabeth tried hard not to worry too much about it. The nursery was ready, her suitcase was packed, and excitement and nerves filled every pain and bump she felt.

Finally, early on a Wednesday morning, a few days after her due date, stomach pain woke Elizabeth. She went into the bathroom thinking she just needed to go, but the pain didn't go away; it just increased. Walking surprisingly calmly down the hall, she knocked on her parents' door.

Less than an hour later she was at the hospital getting ready to deliver her baby. The contractions hurt, labor was harder and more painful than she thought, but once the epidural was in, things settled down, and just five hours after getting to the hospital, a warm, wet, and wrinkled bundle was placed in her arms.

Jackson Grant Parks-Warren was perfect. His little face was scrunched up in a wail that filled Elizabeth's heart with love. Her mother, who was in the delivery room with her, cried at the sight of her baby holding a baby.

Jessica, along with Elizabeth's parents, were at the hospital most of the first day. Brady, though he was invited, decided to wait until she went home to visit and meet his son. He and Elizabeth have only seen each other once since she sent him the text with the ultrasound. He stopped by her house and stayed for a bit, dropping off some gifts from his family.

Elizabeth was still unsure about her feelings for Brady. She wasn't sure that she could give him what he wanted, and she hoped they could at least stay friends for the baby's sake. She couldn't deny, though, that she missed him.

The next morning, Elizabeth was alone with her son. He was nursing; finally getting the hang of it. Elizabeth was amazed at the precious little bundle who needed her like no one ever had before. His fingers and toes were so little, and his skin was soft and new. Everything about him was perfect.

Glancing into her baby son's eyes, Elizabeth became overwhelmed with the thought that she no longer had to wonder if she would ever find true love and happiness. She had with this gift she held in her arms.

The peace and trust she saw there in those little, brown eyes filled her with awe. She caressed his soft chunky cheeks and leaned down to kiss his tiny nose.

"You are my little man. The one I have always prayed for. God knew I was meant to be your momma."

The amazement and peace that filled her took her breath away. She might not understand why, but she now realized she was where God meant for her to be and in those tiny, little, brown eyes is where she would find her peace and her forever love.

Chapter 50

Grant, as he was going to be called, was introduced to his home and bedroom on Friday morning.

Balloons and flowers from loving family and friends filled his room. Elizabeth relaxed in the glider, holding her son, and rocking him. She had a hard time putting him down and tearing herself away, so she just rocked and stared at his perfect little features. He was sleeping. She was content.

It had only been a couple days, but the feelings that went through Elizabeth were more intense than anything she thought possible. Her need to be loved changed. She now felt she only needed the love of her son, this beautiful boy. Becoming a mother made her stronger. Even though she wanted a relationship and a man to love her, she didn't need one. The unrelenting search she found herself in for years had come to a screeching halt the second this bundle of perfection was placed in her arms.

Yes, she still wanted more love, that of a man, but the love of this little person was enough for her, for now, unless...

There was a knock on the door, although the door stood wide open. Elizabeth, startled, looked up. She expected to see Jessica, but instead, it was Brady standing there.

Her eyes grew wide with surprise and her heartbeat sped up, but she quickly gained her composure and waved him in. He cautiously walked toward her with a look of nervousness on his face.

She smiled with pleasure and confidence when she saw him. Her heart skipped a beat when their eyes met. She saw so much of this man before her in their son. Grant's coloring was dark like Brady's and his dark curly hair was his father's.

"Hi." Elizabeth stood up carefully and walked over to Brady, smiling wide. "I'm glad you're here. Meet your son, Jackson Grant Parker-Warren." Brady looked down at the sleeping bundle in Elizabeth's arms, then up at her and gave her an amazed smile, his eyes wide.

"He's amazing. You gave him the name Warren?"

Elizabeth smiled at him. "Of course, you are his father."

Brady reached out, placing one hand on her arm, and the other hand touched the soft skin of the baby in her arms. His son.

Brady gently caressed the baby's little arms and tiny fingers. Looking up, he met Elizabeth's eyes and held her gaze. He smiled at her with amazement at the sight and feeling of their son. Elizabeth felt like she would melt in that look. Brady took her breath away. Her heartbeat faster as Brady reached up and brushed her cheek.

Reaching over she laid her hand over his and closed her eyes. "I'm so glad you're here, Brady. I was a little scared you wouldn't come."

She opened her eyes and held on to his gaze like her life depended on it; maybe it did. "I know I haven't dealt with all this well. Going through this pregnancy and thinking I lost you made me really look at things and focus on what is important. I had to learn to love myself, even like myself, before I could feel as if I was worthy of being loved and accepting love. I know I can do all this on my own, and I don't need you in our lives, but I really want you here, Brady. I need you here, in a different way. Not just because of Grant, but for me."

She hoped he understood her words, understood what she was trying to say. To make it easier, she moved in front of him so he could see her clearly. "At first, I thought I could do this on my own. Be a mother. Raise a child. I was confused about my feelings for you, and for Jacob, but I was wrong about all of it."

She stopped for a quick breath and seeing the encouragement in Brady's eyes, continued. "It took me way too long to realize my feelings for you. My feelings about us. We share a lot of memories and history. I care so much for you, Brady. I like us together. I want us together."

She stopped at this point and made sure she had his attention. She searched his eyes for any clues that he doubted what she said, but seeing nothing but encouragement, she smiled, breathed, and continued.

"I'm so sorry it took me so long to realize it, but I want us to be a family, you, me, and Grant. You make me a better person. I love you, Brady, I really do."

The joy on Brady's face shone. He searched her eyes to make sure what she said was true. Elizabeth could not hold back the tears any longer, they broke free, and started falling down her face. Brady wiped away one of the stray tears from her cheek and leaned in to give her a hug, with their son between them. He kissed her head.

He pulled away and held her face in his hands, searching her eyes. "I am so glad to hear you say that, Elizabeth. I love you, too."

Elizabeth thought her heart would beat out of her chest, and he finally leaned in and kissed her lips softly and gently. The kiss was filled with so much more than words could ever be said. She has kissed Brady so many times before, but it was never like this.

There was a whimper from the bundle between them. Separating themselves, they looked down at Grant and laughed at their son.

Elizabeth caught Brady's gaze. "Do you want to hold him?"

Brady looked back at her with uncertainty. She smiled reassuringly and passed their son into his arms.

Brady melted at the feel of the baby. Elizabeth cuddled next to them both, brushing her hands through Brady's hair.

"He's amazing." Brady had a hard time taking his eyes off the little person he was holding.

"I know. He's so handsome. Just like his daddy." Brady looked up at Elizabeth when she said these words. She leaned in, turning his face toward her and kissed him with a passion she didn't realize she felt. She didn't just love this man next to her, she needed him, but most of all, she wanted him.

Breaking her lips away from Brady's, she rested her head on his shoulder. She was happy. She was loved.

The baby made a cute little noise and scrunched up his little face.

They both looked at him and laughed together.

Acknowledgments

This book has been a life-long journey. Sometimes we don't believe in ourselves and put our passions off for a long time because we fear failing. We would rather never try and wonder if we could.

So, for everyone who stood by and always gave me encouraging words when I told you I was writing a book, I thank you.

My three best friends, Penny, Cherie, and Tonia–you all always stick by me with laughter and truth. You have faith in me even when I have none in myself. My life is better because I get to call you, my friends.

And of course, the ones on my dedication page. I am not me without all of you.

My three boys: Sean, Kyle, and Josh, you all said "Cool" when I told you I was writing my book. You may never read this because it's a romance, but I hope you try. If you don't, Sean, I know Sarah will, and Josh and Kyle, your future wives will. I love you guys- bunches!

My amazing husband, Sean. You hear a lot about marrying someone who makes you a better person. You do that for me. You put up with my self-doubt and you always encourage me. I finished this book because of you. Thank you so much. I love you.

And of course, my readers. Thank you for trying out a new book by a new author. I really hope you enjoyed it.

About the Author

Donna R. Madden is a mother of three and a wife of 28 years. She and her husband live in a small town north of Nashville. They share their house with their dog Lilly, and cat King Marcus Henry XXII, who they all affectionately call "Kitty Kitty."

She enjoys her job as a high school English teacher, where she tries her best to instill a love of literature and writing in her students.

Donna loves to tear through books any chance she can get. She loves romance and dystopian novels best, but she will read just about anything.

Outside of reading, she enjoys hanging out with her family and friends.

She also loves the great outdoors, the beach, and camping on their property in the hills of Kentucky.

More Than Enough is her debut novel.

Note to the Reader

Thank you for taking your time and reading *More Than Enough*. I hope you enjoyed reading it as much as I enjoyed writing it. If you enjoyed the story and characters, I would be so grateful to you if you would take the time and leave a review on Amazon for me. Keep your eyes open for the second in the series, *Forever More*, due out Summer 2023.

I would love to hear from my readers, so please connect with me, on Instagram and Facebook-- Donna R. Madden Writer

Or scan the QR code here to find links to my social media pages, my books, and to join my email list.

CPSIA information can be obtained
at www.ICGtesting.com
Printed in the USA
JSHW082206100323
38803JS00002B/7